A MAP OF EVERYTHING

A novel by:

Elizabeth Earley

JADED IBIS PRESS

sustainable literature by digital means™
an imprint of Jaded Ibis Productions

For Katy

Tragedy thrusts its reference onto every moment to follow

0. The End

There's a buried town in Italy where a thick layer of volcanic ash and stone fell in the first century, AD. Pompei was buried so quickly and hotly that, when excavated hundreds of years later, a single moment in time was found perfectly preserved. People with upturned heads, busy hands, embracing arms—vivid facial expressions, even—were preserved in situ. And so it is with me. When a seemingly senseless tragedy descends upon a family in an instant, that point in time becomes the preserving link that binds them together ever after, even in their scatterings. It leads to the establishment of unintended hurdles and blocks, false dead-ends from which it can be impossible to extract oneself. The tragedy thrusts its reference onto every moment to follow, colors everything, shapes everything. Through everything it becomes less a tragedy and more an event, one among many, its precedent allowing the materialization of great gifts. The event is an emblem, one that must be overcome, not through rash force but through transformative realization.

The emblem serves as a meditation, a kind of practice for believing it will all be—we will all be—it is, already, all—okay.

1. Hydrogen (Nonmetal; Primordial; Gas)

Her eyes still bulge. Twenty years later they bulge, as though the pressure from her swollen brain has pressed and pressed ceaselessly like time on a life, never letting up. They used to be blue—a big, watery blue that fixed on me and shimmered. Now they are gray and bulging like the sky pregnant with rain, gloomy and beautiful. I remember them being that bold, young blue, but that doesn't mean it's true. I was a child then, too young to see things for what they were.

She was a child too, but an older, more complicated kind: a teenager. We shared a bedroom and talked about everything. More accurately, she talked and I listened. June was always telling stories. She was gifted, exceptionally smart, an honor student, the model of responsibility and goodness. I knew her inner world, though, the one that concealed tall, brightly lit desires. I knew she thought of going all the way with her boyfriend, Travis. She explained what it felt like to let him kiss her, to let his hands press against her small breasts. She told me that when he pinched her nipples, it gave her a sick feeling in her stomach. When his hands tried to move below the region of her bellybutton, however, she drew the line. The boundary of her waistband was an impassable cliff. At least until she decided she was ready.

Then there was the time she confessed the big thing. We sat on her bed with our limbs folded and heads leaned in toward each other. She lowered her voice to a whisper and said, "I broke into a house last night." She smiled. Her chrome braces shone. My eyes shot open wide as they go and I chewed on my cuticles.

"It wasn't my idea. We had some beer and some wine coolers my friends snuck from their parents and we needed a place to drink them. I got drunk for the first time, I think. We ate some of their food like chips and stuff. I feel really bad," she said, but she didn't look like she felt bad. She looked pleased, exhilarated even. I just continued to stare at her and tear off bits of skin from around my fingernails with my teeth.

"Stop doing that," she said and pulled my hand away from my mouth. I held my hand out between us and regarded my raw, bleeding fingertips. She grimaced and sighed. I lowered my hand.

She dropped back onto her elbows. The lazy, easy way she moved suddenly seemed so sensual: sexy, even. There was a new sophistication creeping into her familiar face—it came along with the tan she was getting from more frequent trips to the tanning salon. Her hair was cropped at chin level in a wide, puffy cascade of blonde that swept out from the crown of her head like a bell. She looked older without her glasses.

"What happened? Did you get caught?" I asked.

"Of course we didn't get caught, silly. I wouldn't be sitting here if we did," she said. She rolled her eyes and looked away.

I couldn't believe it. My sister, a hardened criminal.

"What did it feel like to get drunk?" I asked, anticipating her answer with held breath.

"Nothing, really. I guess it didn't really work. I think I was too scared we'd get caught," she said and laughed. I laughed too. I had been drunk once when I was eight. I had stolen four beers from the refrigerator, ran out into the woods, and guzzled them all down, one after another. I remembered how the trees came alive then, every branch another hand to high five me. All was bright laughter and cheer. The world softened and turned golden, beckoning me in a new way. It was when I started feeling hungry all the time. Always hungry for more. I didn't tell June that. I knew that I would eventually. I had all the time in the world.

She flopped back on the bed. I chewed my fingers and considered the implications. More than anything, I was honored to be the keeper of her secrets. Nobody else in the family talked to me, at least not about anything important, so it carried serious weight. That day she talked about other things but all I could think of was her crime, its seductive naughtiness. I wanted her to talk more about it, but she sternly refused. She became the lesson-giver then, pointing a finger to my chest and demanding that I not get any crazy ideas. "It's wrong," she told me. This only made it more appealing.

At night when we slept, June would sometimes sleepwalk. Her eyes would be open and she would appear awake, but she would be different somehow, hollow and absent like a zombie. I often had nightmares about it. In the dreams she would pinch me and smile grotesquely, sometimes laugh, as though she were possessed. I would try to scream, "Wake up," but only a hoarse whisper would come out. Most of the time, we would be knee deep in water or mist almost as thick as water. I must have cried out during those nightmares because when I woke, there would be her face looming over me, shushing and soothing me. She had an enormous metal contraption that came from her mouth and wrapped around her head, some kind of industrial retainer that she was supposed to sleep in every night. That combined with the huge lenses of her glasses was a terrifying sight to wake up to in the dark, a terrifying sight that was there to comfort me.

A rearranging of bedrooms took place when June and her twin, my brother Jonas, turned sixteen. They received their own rooms while I moved in with my other brother, John, just down the hall. June took over our room. I still sat on her bed every night and listened to her stories. She started inserting French-speaking characters into them, as she was becoming fluent in her fourth year of honors French. She started speaking French in my dreams too, lispy words I didn't understand but that sounded beautiful. Most of the time, I fell asleep in her bed and would wake from my nightmare of her sleepwalking to her metallic breath and the warm closeness of her body. I would writhe around for a minute in panic, thinking I was still asleep and she was too, certain I felt the dampness of thick, pewter mist licking my ankles.

Four months after her sixteenth birthday, just days before my eleventh, less than a month before she was due to go to Paris with her French class, she took the car out on her own to pick up her paycheck from Horizons restaurant. It had been raining. The roads might have been slick with oil, she might have been looking somewhere else, reaching for something in the back seat, or just staring out her window at the sky. Nobody knows why she crossed left of center and crashed head-on into another car. She was not wearing her seatbelt. My mom was the only one to see her when they first brought her into the emergency room at Highland Hospital. She told me about the red and blue windbreaker, how they were cutting it from June's body with scissors. The worst was her teeth:

They had been ripped, root to tip from her gums, jutting from her mouth in a ragged arc, strung together and held in place by her braces.

9

2.   Helium (Noble Gas; Primordial; Gas)

We didn't know if she would live or die, but Mom knew that if she lived, she would want her teeth, so she called June's orthodontist. He came that day with his assistant. They went into the ICU where she was hooked up to life-giving machines by slender, plastic tubes like veins creeping out of her body. They worked on her teeth, fitting them back in place and twisting the wire from the braces around them in a tight, makeshift bracketing, planting them firmly in the gums where they would take root and heal. The awesome power of living flesh to grow, to patch up, would, combined with time, restore her mouth, whether she would need it again or not. When they left the ICU, the two men were glossy eyed and silent. I stood back and watched my mom take the hand of the orthodontist and squeeze it. His eyes were watery and red. His mouth opened then clamped shut again. A quick, nearly imperceptible nod was all he managed before walking away.

3.   Lithium (Alkaline Metal; Primordial; Solid)

We all spent the first several days at the hospital—my parents, my brothers, my other sister and me all draped over hard chairs and thinly padded couches in the ICU waiting room. Mom didn't leave once, not even to fetch things from home. People brought everything to her. The farthest she got from June was out on the sidewalk one floor below where she went to smoke cigarettes, a habit she had quit for a while but now shamelessly started again. Her eyes were swollen relics of nonstop weeping. Her hands shook ceaselessly. There was a darty, panicky edge to all her movements yet she was simultaneously slow. The weight of it all was in her eyes those first days and the slump of her body—half conscious, adrift.

I returned home to go back to school. I entered June's bedroom on that first night back and held my breath. I closed my eyes and felt her there, just next to me on her bed, smiling and whole. When I opened my eyes, everything was different somehow. It was all fake—a poorly constructed impression of her room like the set of a TV show. I looked at my feet and felt some important part of me fall out that way and stay trapped beneath the floor. I was hollow and cold. My fingertips throbbed. I stared out the window. The sky looked thick with low-hanging ghosts. I had something like a viewable prophesy then, a sense of the future filled with dulling solitude and strange dreams. Its damp certainty was real; I could smell it in the air. That pinching, smiling, phantom of her continued to haunt me, but I was wide awake. I was not sleeping.

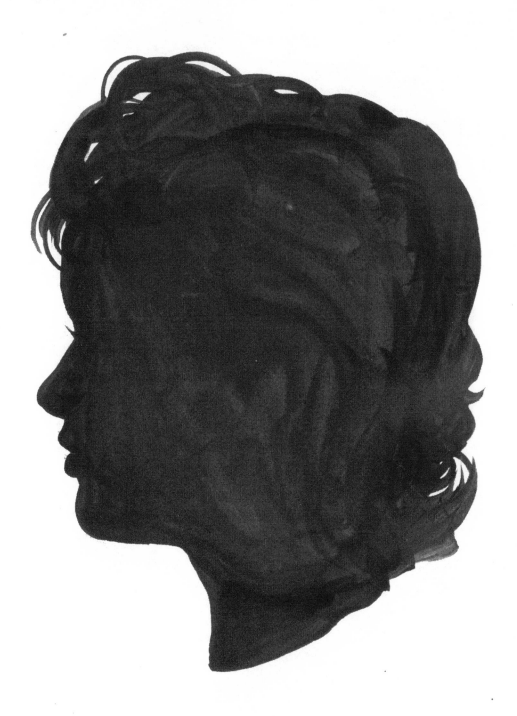

A barricade in the road,
a crowd of people beyond,
a fire truck, a big crane

4.   **Beryllium** (Primordial; Alkaline Earth Metal; Solid)

In the years following June's accident, stories about what we were doing during and in the weeks following the actual event were told within our family so often and with so much detail that they evolved into almost fabled tales that I could recount with confidence.

It happened like anything tragic happens—around a blind turn, then splat. It's in the debris of the aftermath where one might puzzle together a complete picture. A tableau of the day: the splintered beginnings of everything being different for everyone, forever.

5.   **Boron** (Metalloid; Primordial; Solid)

Jonas, second born

My brother Jonas (June's twin) and his girlfriend, Rachel, had spent the entire morning at the hospital. When Rachel miscarried, she didn't know she was pregnant. Without telling anyone but June, Jonas drove Rachel to the hospital. While she was behind a closed door being checked over, he slouched in the rigid waiting-room chair, blindly flipping through Tiger Beat, YM, Sassy, Bop; picking one up, fanning the pages, tossing it aside and grabbing another. Jonas bit his nails, crossed and uncrossed his ankles, felt a chilly film of sweat tickle the small of his back. His eyes darted around, scanning for anyone who might know him. What would he do? Hide, he thought, behind the pages of one of those shit magazines.

There was another guy about his age with black hair and a shimmering nose ring, a woman about the same age as our mom looking back at him with a frown. Jonas looked away, his eyes settling on a bowl of assorted condoms. He was fifteen when he started having sex with Rachel and they always made sure to use a condom, except for one time. Now, here they were.

Tiffany was singing, *I think we're alone now…* on the drive home. Rachel stared blankly out the window while Jonas drove her powder-blue Buick carefully toward home. He and June had just passed their driver's exams, and it was raining hard. He didn't have any experience driving in that kind of weather. He tapped his thumbs nervously on the steering wheel and turned off the radio. The drive was much longer on the way back, he thought. Eventually the rain died down and stopped. Rachel started crying softly. Jonas switched the radio back on, glancing over at her. She was letting the tears streak down her face with no attempt to wipe them away. They converged under her chin and dripped off, disappearing down the front of her shirt. When his eyes followed them to the swell of one breast, he looked back at the road and felt guilty for being turned on at a time like this. He was driving down Lake Avenue only a mile or two away from home when he saw a barricade in the road, a crowd of people beyond, a fire truck, a big crane. He squinted and thought he saw a flash of red and black bent metal. He stopped breathing, pulled the car over with a screech, and ran toward the scene.

A pink-haired woman was sitting in the back of one of the police cars, scowling and mumbling about her car, a pink Cadillac, parked off to the left in a driveway, the hood buckled and the fender bent.

When Jonas saw the Zephyr, he almost passed out. Black spots bled from nowhere and blurred before his eyes. His legs felt spongy. He leaned forward, hands on knees and closed his eyes. Rachel burst into tears and threw her arms around him. His whole body jerked at her touch. He pushed her back and stood up. She looked wounded but he didn't care; he couldn't. On the other side of the busted car, he saw his little brother, John, kneeling on the ground, arms outstretched over his head, face against the pavement, as if in a worshipful bow, bawling and shaking. A police officer crouched next to him with one hand on his shoulder.

"I'm so sorry, son, I think she's gone," the officer said. Jonas ran, shoved the officer away, and lifted John's skinny, limp body from the concrete, holding him tightly. Both boys shook with sobs while a crowd watched.

15

6. **Carbon** (Nonmetal; Primordial; Solid)

John, fourth born

John ran up Gorsline Avenue to Lake Avenue and headed east. He had been in his room listening to his new GN'R cassette when the sirens drowned out the whining high notes of Axl and the screeching guitar solos of Slash. He looked out the window at an entourage of ambulances and fire trucks blurring by. His heart galloped. He had never seen so many at once. There must be a house on fire or a car explosion. His mind shot to June, who had taken the car a short while before.

She had stopped in his room and dangled the keys in front of him, asked if he wanted to come along for the ride, but he had just unwrapped the clear wrapper and cracked open the cassette case for the first time. He had to hear every song on *Appetite for Destruction* before he went anywhere. His chest felt like it was caving in. He threw down the cassette case and took off. It couldn't be too far. She hadn't been gone long.

He ran hard, driving his long strides forward and pumping his arms. He had fought with June the night before. She found out he stole from the stash of alcohol she was saving for a party and confronted him. He denied it and dismissed her. She made fun of his hair, which was frizzy and long, short in the front, feathered on the sides, and long in the back. She told him his Adam's apple was too big and his ears stuck out. He shoved her and she fell back, hitting her spine on the hard edge of the open window. It knocked the wind out of her and she gasped for air. John had begged her to forgive him, admitted to taking some beers, and promised he would pay her back. She was making peace by inviting him along earlier. He put his head down and picked up speed, squares of concrete sliding, sounding off in beige tones beneath his feet.

He could still hear the sirens in the distance. He smelled his own sweat and it allayed his panicked pace to a steady trot. When he saw flashing lights in the distance, he broke into a full sprint. John shoved through a small crowd and leaped over yellow caution tape. He saw the car and stopped, panting. It was crumpled and torn apart, as if a great hand had bore it up, crushed it like a ball of tin foil, and thrown it down. Looming above was glinting crumpled metal clutched in the fork of a crane-like vehicle that carried the words "Jaws of Life" along its bright yellow body. Someone grabbed John's arm and tried to pull him back behind the line. He thought of Lee; had she gone with June after he turned her down? Had she been in that car too? Both Lee and June's faces flashed before him, smiling, shining. A weak, cracked "no," escaped him. His strength gone, he was dragged back, away from the car. A burst of energy came and he viciously ripped himself free, ran to the car, and collapsed on its ruined hood, his tears pooling in a metal dimple. The birds lined up on the telephone wire above like piano keys, their chirps like ominous questions buzzing in John's ears: "Lee, Lee, Lee?"

7. **Nitrogen** (Nonmetal; Primordial; Gas)

Lee, first born

Lee was changing into old sweats, getting ready to help Mom paint the living room, when the phone rang. She wondered if it was Craig calling again. She wouldn't take the call. She had visited him last weekend at Rochester Institute of Technology, had driven nearly an hour to get there and surprise him. Dressed in a red, lacy number under her clothes, a big smile on her face, she knocked on his dorm room door. It swung open and a cloud of white smoke tumbled out, a bare-chested, red-eyed Craig emerging like a ghost, some slut hanging on his back, topless.

"What the fuck?" Lee said, stepping back, waving a hand in front of her face then pulling her shirt over her nose and mouth to screen out the smoke.

"Lee?" Craig said stupidly, stepping toward her, his eyes growing wider with the delayed realization of being caught. Lee looked at his sculpted chest, lean stomach, the familiar trail of dark hair disappearing into the waistband of his blue-checkered boxer shorts. She looked up at the girl, her black eyes squinting.

The slut snaked her tongue in his ear. The dark tip of one white breast brushed against the back of his arm, peeking and bobbing out from behind him. Lee thought she might vomit. She turned and ran. Craig's voice boomed after her as she pounded open the emergency exit door at the end of the hall and tripped out into the parking lot. An alarm sounded. Lee scrambled to her feet and scurried to her car, choking back tears.

Craig came to our house drunk late the next night, and when she refused to see him, he stood in the front yard and screamed, "I'm sorry!" until my dad called the police. Since then, he'd called every day, and every day Lee refused to take the call.

She held still and turned her head toward her bedroom door, anticipating Mom calling her to the phone any second. What she heard instead was a strange kind of moan coming from downstairs, like the low, rumbled mew that Candy, our cat made while she was giving birth to a litter. Lee hurried down the stairs two at a time and landed in the living room just as Mom, with a blue splashed red bandana on her head, a blue-soaked paint brush in one hand, and a salt-white face, placed the phone gently in its cradle. Mom wavered and grabbed the plastic-covered chair beside her to stop herself from falling. She dropped the paintbrush on the floor. Lee ran to her side and slipped a steadying arm around her back.

"Mom, who was it? What happened?" Lee tried guiding her to the chair, but she resisted and broke free.

"It was the police. It's June. She had an accident--" Mom said, stumbling around looking for her car keys. "You should call your father and tell him to come to Highland Hospital. That's where they're taking her. Oh god, oh god, shit! Oh god--" Lee could see Mom's eyes blur with tears and instinctively they burned in hers too. "Keys!" Mom called out, stumbling out of the living room with its plastic-draped furniture pulled away from the walls, its half blue, half white trim.

"Where are my keys!" she screamed wildly, just as my dad handed them to her. My dad was silent and fuming. "Damn teenagers," he said before walking out the door. (John and I, the two youngest, have a different dad than Lee, June, and Jonas. Their dad left Mom when she was pregnant with June and Jonas, and Lee was just a toddler. She met our dad when

18

June and Jonas were infants and married him eight weeks later.)

Lee watched the maroon minivan pull out of the driveway. She picked up the phone and, with a shaky finger, dialed the numbers to call her dad. Her press-on nail hooked into the 9 hole and scraped along the circle all the way to the top. It felt like a long, slow-motion journey, the dial turning and clicking back into place after she let go, her mushroom-colored fingernail searching through a haze of fear for the three hole.

"Lee?" I said, appearing from the mouth of the stairs. "What's going on?" Lee held up a finger to me while she finished dialing.

8. Oxygen (Nonmetal; Primordial; Gas)

Anne, fifth born

I sat on the roof outside my bedroom window, smoking a cigarette from Mom's purse. It was difficult to navigate out the window with the sling on my arm, but I managed. Anyway, it didn't really hurt, although at times I lied so well, I convinced myself that it did. I had waited for it to stop raining. As soon as it did, the sun burst through different slits in the clouds, proud beams licking the neighborhood to a glistening sheen. I grabbed a towel to sit on and climbed out. I noticed the red and black Zephyr driving up Gorsline just as I lit up. There goes June again, I thought, the lucky one. Everyone got to do everything before I got to do a damn thing. John had a mini-bike; he got it when he turned twelve. Now, just four days away from my eleventh birthday, I figured I would be able to get one, too, the minute I turned twelve, so I marked it on my calendar to start the countdown. Only 370 days to go. When Mom told me that I would have to wait until I was fourteen, that John was a boy and that was a different story, I was so mad I could have punched John and Mom right in the face. Instead, I clenched my teeth, turned red, mumbled the F-word under my breath, and went to my room.

"What did you say?" Mom had asked.

"Nothing, god!" I snapped and ran up the stairs. Occasionally stealing cigarettes was the only way I could assert my private independence. That, and the intoxicating, almost erotic feeling of every so often stealing a beer from the refrigerator or from under Jonas's bed and drinking it back in the woods where nobody would see me and where I could bury the evidence.

I was thinking about the day that June and Jonas got that car, how we all took a drive in it. John and I were in the huge back seat: June, Lee, and Jonas all up front. John had punched my shoulder teasingly, and it took a moment before I remembered that it was supposed to hurt.

"Ow!"

"Leave her alone," Lee said, turning around, slapping John across the top of his head.

"She's faking!" John said and punched me again. I bared my teeth at him and he made to slap my face. I winced away and he laughed. My arm looked so fragile in the sling, so tender. I had always been intrigued with slings and splints and bandages, and took any opportunity to be able to wear one, even if I had to fake an injury. One time, Lee broke her arm and I stared longingly at the full-length cast holding her elevated limb in traction, bent at the elbow.

I lay back on the sloped roof and closed my eyes, hands behind my head. I thought about the dream I had the night before where I was a boy making out with an older girl, kissing open-mouthed, the petal soft swell of a bare breast against my palm. I heard sirens close by, sat up, and looked, but they had already passed. I didn't notice John running up the street moments later in that direction. When I heard Mom screaming for her keys as if she were on fire, I climbed back in my room, secured the screen in place, situated my arm in its sling, and went downstairs.

9. Fluorine (Halogen; Primordial; Gas)

Mom

Mom was thinking of ice, had it fixed in her mind like a photograph pinned to corkboard, static and crisp. She was standing on a ladder in the living room painting the wood trim a lake shade of blue, watching the lateral motion of her arm, the smooth horizontal strokes of the brush.

"I'm gonna go to Horizons and pick up my paycheck." June said.

"No, don't go just now." Mom looked out the window at the blurry sheets of rain drenching the crippled mulberry tree and beyond that, sweeping along the pavement. "It's raining too hard."

June moped out of the room. Our parents had decided to get the twins a car after their driver's exam. They thought it would be useful to have them run errands, pick up and drop off John and me, run to the store, do any variety of chores perpetually needed in our family of seven. Before long, June appeared again, keys in hand.

"It stopped raining," she said, nodding toward the window. Mom looked outside at the glistening pavement, sunlit blacktop, slicked tar strips patching the cracks.

"Ok, you can go now," Mom said. "Don't forget your seatbelt," she added, but too late. She heard the back door slam and saw the big, square Zephyr pull out of the driveway and glide down the street.

10. Neon (Noble Gas; Primordial; Gas)

June, third born

June pulled her red and blue windbreaker over her t-shirt while coasting down Gorsline Avenue then switched on the heat. She flipped on her turn signal and made a full stop at the stop sign, even though no cars were coming. Pulling out onto Lake Avenue, she felt a wave of exhilaration. She was driving now, had a car of her own—well, almost her own. Jonas's appointment with Rachel was today, she thought, and wondered how that was going. She knew that her twin brother was having sex even before he told her. She sensed the change in him. He never kept anything from her too long, so her suspicion was rapidly confirmed. June had been dating Travis for almost six months but wasn't ready for that.

"Maybe when I'm seventeen," she said to herself, picturing Travis's face, the strong angle of his jaw, his brown eyes boring into hers. She kept her eyes open when they kissed because she liked the view she had of the side of his face, how it curved into his neck, wrapped by the blue and white sky beyond. They usually met at Seneca Park to talk and make out. A few times they had gone pretty far, and June had to grab Travis's hand as it worked at unbuttoning her jeans.

"Stop that," she would say. "I'm not ready for that." He always apologized sheepishly, mumbling how he'd gotten carried away. The fact that Jonas was doing it almost made her want to try it, too, until he got himself in trouble. Then she knew she was right. Mom had asked her if she ever thought about it, but she turned red and said, "No way!" She laughed out loud at that thought, shaking her head. She had too much to lose: an upcoming trip to Paris with her Honors French class (she had become fluent), a shot at class president, and if she held her ranking for two more years, she would be valedictorian in 1990. She noticed the sunbeams over the lake to her left, how they exploded the sky and lit up the choppy water in patches like shards of glass. Her head turned from the road to the sky to the road, then back to the sky. The thrashing blue-green of the lake against the gray, burst through with fire orange. June indulged in a long look when an open area offered an unobstructed view. It was so beautiful that she didn't realize she was holding her breath. When the car started drifting left of center, she didn't realize that either.

11. **Sodium** (Alkaline Metal; Primordial; Solid)

The smell of casseroles was nauseating. Also, my arm itched. The longer I scratched, the worse the green gray pit of sick in my gut felt. The green bean casserole looked like what I imagined sick would look like, if it were food. The buttery, creamy smell clashed against this image and made me want to vomit. The brownish tuna casserole and the one that looked like Hamburger Helper in a glass pan smelled like frogs. The ones that hopped from the creek that John and I used to catch tadpoles and crayfish in. It seemed like years before, but had only been weeks. Already, I could barely remember what it felt like to be a kid and do kid things.

Maybe it was a crayfish casserole. John used to pull off their pinchers and lay them on the ground where they would open and close, open and close—tiny, disembodied appendages with a mind all their own. Like how a decapitated head's eyes still look around after it comes off, watching the body from a wrong angle like beneath the feet, seeing its own thick toes curl and arch. At least that's what I'd seen in horror movies. I'd never seen an actual dead body with its head cut off, but thinking about it made me think of June, her head slamming into glass.

Smelling the casseroles and daydreaming about dismembered crayfish, I thought about when I walked into the ICU on that first night, holding Lee's hand. There was a smell like medicine and plastic and dirty diapers. It was dizzying, the smell and the beeping and the hushed voices in the dark. Only the nurse's station was illuminated; most of the curtained-off beds were dark caves with figures hunched over broken bodies. The ICU was a dark egg with a white and silver nurse's station as its yolk. We walked a half moon around the yolk before we found June, presided over by my mom and a stern-looking nurse. I approached her, holding my breath, feeling my guts ball up in my throat. Her face was not her face. The pale, bloated, bulgy-eyed, cut-and-stitched object floating there against the pillow was monstrous. A tube disappeared into her neck like a power cord with jaws. Suddenly I felt fine, convinced I was playing a part in a horror movie and this thing in the bed would reel up and bear bloody fangs at any moment. Behind it all was the camera crew and the makeup artists and the guy who says, "Scene two, take four," then clacks his board.

Lee took June's hand on the other side of the bed from me and cried.

"We're here. June. We're here. Anne and me, we're here. We love you," she said, her voice low, clogged with tamped-down sobs. Serious laughter threatened to erupt from me and before I could stop it, a little wail escaped, which everyone took for a desperate kind of crying. I felt a hand on my shoulder.

Lee rubbed June's arm with one hand and held her hand with the other. I mimicked her on my side of the bed, mechanically did what she did, said what she said. June's hand felt cold and chunky. I squeezed it. I rubbed her arm. "We're here, we're here, we're here..." The cold hand turned my hand cold and the monster face inflated. Her eyeballs were moving behind veils of pale lid. I leaned in closer to watch them. The delicate circuitry of veins in the domed eyelids seemed to slide around in translucent oil like shoals of tadpoles beneath the creek's slick surface. "We're here, we're here, we're here..."

Her head slamming into glass, her neck breaking. Snap. Frog and crayfish casseroles. I scratched harder, digging my fingernails in deeper until I felt pain and looked down to see a red, raw spot on my arm. I stopped itching.

"Anne, come in here and eat something, honey, you need to eat," Dee said. She was my mom's best friend, our godmother and neighbor. She came over after the accident happened and cleaned and cried and cooked. People from church brought more food and flowers and cried.

"Come eat," she said.

Shatter. Snap.

"I'm not hungry," I said.

Sliding veins, slipping, bulging. Crack.

"I know, honey, but you have to eat. Now get in here." She ladled the green gray slop onto a plate and the itch came back. The house had never been cleaner.

"We're here, we're here…"

"What did you say, honey? Come eat."

Snap. Slip.

"We're here."

The skin was red and raw like a burn. My fingers were cold. I'd never seen so many casseroles, so much food. Cold, heavy hands. Thick chunks for fingers. Crack.

"What did you do to your arm?" She said, suddenly right in front of me, the bulk of her nearly on top of me. She grabbed my hand and rubbed my arm. I felt my face get wet and tasted vomit in my mouth. I slapped my hand over my mouth to keep from puking and realized I was crying.

"Oh honey," she moaned and smashed me against her, a warm, soft mass.

"We're here."

Slip.

"I'm here," she said.

I shook against her, swallowing sour saliva, snot and tears between my cheek and her bosom. On the wall beside us, there was a shelf lined with five silver saucers, our baby cups. June's was small and coppery and smooth like a shot glass or an egg cup, identical to Jonas's, distinguished only by the engraved names. It was two down from mine, which had a small handle and a lip around the top. The pewter surface reflected a far-away, distorted image of my wet, red face jammed against Dee's sand-colored blouse, her glasses warped into one huge lens framing a melting brown eye.

She was surrounded by teeth
— molars and incisors and canines —
all whole and unbroken
and bone-white

12. **Magnesium** (Alkaline Earth Metal; Primordial; Solid)

Paris, day one

After several hours that felt like several days sitting nearly motionless on the plane, we arrived in Paris—June, Lee, Mom, and me. The European morning was the crest of our midnight, witnessing us bleary-eyed, unloading June's traveling wheelchair from the back of a taxi then guiding it over cobbled roads, sloshing through small blue pools of foam and rainwater. Mom had secured a hotel for us, but it was too early yet to check in. We dropped our luggage off in the lobby and set out to find a café where we could breakfast with the heft and the weight of it all. *It all* being what got us there, finally, after twenty years. June would finally see the *Mona Lisa*, and I would be the one to show it to her. I admit, I half expected, albeit half rejected, that she would experience some kind of profound shift upon seeing the long-awaited painting. It was apt that a simple, dark-haired woman with the wisp of a smile trailing on her mouth (as though she had just finished smiling and was now resting her face from the effort) would be the thing to blast a new pathway in June's brain, igniting old synapses, blowing the dust off whole sets of stagnant cut-off data, kindling an electrical storm of activity in those dark, warm chambers so long sleeping like a dormant volcano.

June had a gallon-sized baggie of disposable cameras and took pictures of everything. Perched sanguinely in the chair, she snapped away at the facades of buildings, the street ahead, down alleyways we passed by, and most famously, at the two asses of whichever of us was walking ahead. Several times during that walk, I looked at my sister smiling against the backdrop of an old cobbled road and thought it symbolic of something important. Streets in a very old town, how they snake every which way, laying spontaneous passageways for walking—they mirrored the trajectory of our convergent paths over the prior two decades, which had been anything but the neat grids I thought they'd be. And they had led us here.

This was it. The apogee of the aftermath of a brain being damaged, of bones being smashed, of a neck being snapped—the brain and bones and neck of a sixteen-year-old girl in a family like ours.

We sat down at a café, encountering the first of many problems we'd have: the size of the place. All the tables were so close together you could barely wedge two bodies in apposing chairs much less park a wheelchair. But the waiter scurried to accommodate us, pushing one square, chrome table to the side and whisking away a chair from the neighboring table, then standing back with offering hands for us to maneuver her in. "*Merci, merci,*" June said several times. Lee said, "Thank you."

The waiter took the French menus and replaced them with English ones, which we studied in silence. "What time is it at home?" June asked. I opened my mouth to tell her, having quickly calculated, but then caught Mom's warning glance and short shake of the head.

"Let's rearrange our sense of time to get acclimated," Mom said, winking at me. "It's about 6:30 in the morning here, so we're having breakfast. When we get into our hotel room, we'll take a nap to catch up then go hit the town. We'll be nice and tired by evening and by tomorrow, our bodies will be on Paris time," she said.

She was right. Telling June what time it was at home was likely to panic her and cause her to lay her head down on the table right then and there to fall asleep. She was, post-accident, very much a creature of routine. Eating and sleeping at certain times and intervals were non-negotiables for her.

Most items on the menu involved egg, which was undesirable for everyone. Although Mom ended up ordering an omelet, the rest of us got fruit and croissants. June got some *fromage.* She kept surprising us by recalling her French. She spoke it with everyone we encountered and for the most part, people understood her. "She was fluent before the accident," Mom said proudly. "It's coming back to her now."

Despite her exhaustion, June was possessed by joy. She even looked different. Her skin looked suppler, smoother. The acne looked less severe and she always had the hint of a smile around her mouth. When the waiter returned to check on us, I watched June's mouth slowly sounding out slippery French syllables: "*Puis-je avoir un petit jus d'orange s'il vous plaît?*"

The waiter nodded and hurried off. We all stared at her, dumbfounded.

"I asked him for orange juice," she said.

Mom laughed and beamed. I nearly cried.

The wondrous plasticity of the brain—how it forges new pathways to dig up old, buried information. I wondered then how much of learning is actually some kind of remembering something long forgotten, yet known.

If the Parisians we encountered had trouble understanding June, it wasn't for her lack of accuracy with the language, but the slow and strained sound of her voice. When they spoke it back to her, the rapidity tripped over her head like a flat rock skimming water. She had to ask the person to repeat themselves several times and still lost most of what was said. She got much more than the rest of us did though. It's fascinating, really. The same letters, arranged differently, forming new, unfamiliar sounds with corresponding meanings we struggled to puzzle out. What's even more fascinating was having June as our primary interpreter of that meaning when at home, it was often the other way around. Right away, it filled her with a sense of importance and purpose that made her visibly buoyant.

13. Aluminum (Poor Metal; Primordial; Solid)

A few days after the accident, I waited at the end of our street for the school bus holding my book bag like it was a cat, cradling it in my arms with the strap spilling over like a tail. I felt the street stretch back and up behind me. If the bus hadn't come, I might have tumbled forward into the road and been crushed under it.

The double doors opened and Mrs. Kitter looked down at me from her seat. Her eyes were red-rimmed and she forced a smile. She had been our bus driver forever, all of us. She drove the elementary school bus and I was the only one left. She started with Lee in kindergarten, drove Jonas and June all through their primary school years, then John and me, all the way to just me. It was the end of my fifth-grade year. John was already in seventh grade. Next year, I would join him at Rogers, and Mrs. Kitter would be done with our family.

I climbed onto the bus, avoiding eye contact. The way anyone outside my family looked at me since the accident was unbearable—a cross between fear and incomprehensible pity. The narrow aisle between the bench seats was black and corrugated. I stared down at it and made my way toward the back without looking at anyone, but the awareness of their eyes on me and the sound of my name and June's name in their whispering turned me red and sweaty. I hadn't eaten a thing in days and the acid in my stomach burned for something, anything to digest. I swung into a seat, scooted all the way to the window, and plopped my book bag next to me so nobody would try sitting there. The kids in the seat in front of me instantly got up on their knees and turned around. They leaned over the back of the seat with crossed arms and peered at me.

James, a known troublemaker, was by the window looking at me with blithe eyes beside Lacey, a curly-haired, chubby girl who lived in a big house on the lake not far from us. She was an only child and her parents were weird—her dad was too old and wore adult diapers while her mom was too beautiful and had lots of affairs, the details of which she discussed with Lacey before she even had pubic hair. I knew because she told me, uninvited. They once invited me to the country club where they were members to swim. In the locker room after we were done, Lacey stripped off her wet bathing suit, sat cross-legged on the bench and plucked at some baby black hairs that had started to sprout between her legs. "I'm starting to get pubic hairs on my vagina," she had said, stating it proudly.

It's what came to mind every time I saw her on the bus in the morning. She had always been jealous of my big family and would try to compensate by showing off her expensive gifts. Once, when I got a scooter for my birthday, the basic model from Odd Lots, Lacey showed up later that day with a name brand, shiny purple and silver scooter with gold tassels on the handlebars.

31

That morning, I might have traded my life for hers if given the choice. "What happened to your sister?" she asked with a tinge of satisfaction in her tone, even though her expression was one of genuine concern.

I didn't answer, just looked away and stared out the window, scowling. James instantly lost interest and turned back around to face forward, mumbling something as he went.

"What'd you say, James?" Lacey asked with a little giggle.

"I said her sister's a slut," he called out loud enough for everyone to hear. My whole body instantly turned hot and without thinking, I shot up out of my seat, reached over, grabbed a fistful of his hair, and slammed his head hard against the side of the bus. The sound of his skull against the metal wall of the bus was a clean crack followed by a groan emitted from his throat. I thought he might have started crying then, but I couldn't be sure because I dropped into my seat just as quickly as I'd leapt up and went back to staring out the window, feeling the heat in my face, shaking a little from the slowly subsiding adrenaline. Slamming his head like that felt good but I easily could have killed him. Everyone gasped when it happened and Mrs. Kitter pulled the bus over.

"What's going on back here?" she demanded in her brusque voice, stomping back toward us.

"She pulled my hair and slammed my head into the wall," James said, whining. I felt Mrs. Kitter look at me but I didn't budge, just sat with my arms crossed and stared unwaveringly out the window, my eyes fixed on a fire hydrant.

"He called her sister a bad name," another kid said from somewhere behind me. I looked up then at Mrs. Kitter. Her lips clamped together and she glared at James.

"Don't you say anything about her sister again," she said to him, stabbing her index finger in his direction for emphasis. The corners of her mouth trembled. She didn't look at me again, just turned around and walked back to the front of the bus. There was complete silence and stillness in the aftermath; the great hull of swaying bodies starting again to move down the road—the engine's wheeze and the hiss of the gears—was the only sound.

14. Silicon (Metalloid; Primordial; Solid)

When the bus reached the school, I let all the kids get off before I moved. Only when I was sure that everyone was gone, I hoisted my book bag over my shoulder and moved slowly, not wanting to walk into the building, face my classroom. Mrs. Kitter was standing outside the door of the bus waiting for me. Her face was a cascade of anguish, all the features pulled down as if by a doubling up of gravity. I stepped off the bus and she grabbed me roughly, pulled me against her and cried. I stood there limply, letting her cling to me, letting her get it out.

"June's so beautiful and so smart. I'm so sorry, so sorry! I just love all you kids. Oh dear god," she said, just wailing now, howling and yelping in the parking lot outside the school. I stayed in her clenched embrace and didn't move. Being witness to someone turned animal by grief has a paralyzing effect. I had once watched a mob movie where a person was being tortured, fingers cut off one by one with wire cutters, and the reaction was like this—deep, guttural cries between gasps for air. I wriggled my arms free from where they were pinned between us and wrapped them around her, pressing close. Her pain bled into my own and pooled in the pit of my gut. It burned as though a ripe jalapeno had just sprouted in my stomach and burst, its fiery seeds spreading bits of flame.

15. Phosphorus (Nonmetal; Primordial; Solid)

It took a few minutes for her to calm down. I stepped away, keeping one hand on her arm. I had never paid much attention to Mrs. Kitter. We'd never talked, never touched one another before. She merely watched me step onto the school bus every day for years just like all the other kids. It was shocking to discover that she cared so deeply about my sister and me, to hear her say she loved us, to watch her fall apart in front of me. Still, I took no comfort from her display. Instead, I felt I should comfort her.

She patted my hand resting on her arm and moved it off. "Get to class now, you'll be late," she said. She walked away and onto the bus. I walked into the school building as the engine rumbled up behind me. I was late. The halls were empty and the bell had rung.

Entering my fifth grade classroom was the same as getting on the bus, all the heads turned and the talking dimmed to whispers. Before I could sit down, my teacher, Mrs. Sheets, called me to the front. I approached her slack-mouthed, sapped empty from the morning so far. She pulled a chair from behind her desk and situated it in the center of the room facing the class.

"Sit, please," she said. I obeyed, feeling anxiety rise and clamor in my ears so that I almost didn't hear what she said next.

"Tell the class what happened to your sister. We should all hear about this unfortunate teenaged driving accident. Was she wearing her seatbelt?"

All the faces in the classroom were a chorus of shock and anticipation. My arms lay limp, with my hands like bricks. I opened my mouth to speak and said a few words, something about the ICU and her face, tadpoles and frogs. I felt the hotness of the tears on my face before I realized I was crying and my words abruptly ceased. The faces before me contorted and my thoughts congested, piled up. I burst from the chair and ran for the door, knocking desks askew in my wake. Out in the hall, I fell against the wall and gasped for air, like I'd been held under water and just emerged.

Mrs. Sheets appeared standing in front of me. She glared down at me with an unreadable expression. She lifted a hand toward me and I flinched. She let it fall. I looked to the double doors at the end of the hall. She grabbed me and held me against her. She smelled chemical, like acetone and rubbing alcohol. She was saying something I couldn't make out. The sound in my ears was getting loud, like a sustained cymbal clash.

I shoved her away and ran down the hall, slamming through the double doors, back out into the parking lot.

16. Sulfur (Nonmetal; Primordial; Solid)

I half expected to see the bus still there and if it had been, I would have asked Mrs. Kitter for a ride to Highland Hospital. I ran toward home, cutting down side streets and through back yards, through gardens and up sidewalks. I got tired and stopped in front of a green plastic mailbox at the end of someone's driveway. It was a big house in a nice neighborhood. Everything about its façade and the surrounding landscape looked flawless. The windows revealed nothing of the interior; only the whites of closed blinds stared back at me. I pictured a fireplace inside with a plush throw rug in front of it, a family with kids in their pajamas and one of the parents reading to them there in a circle. I looked up the street and saw it all the way up, bounties of bowed heads with warm hearths and peaceful hearts. I opened the mailbox and removed the contents—envelopes looking official. I tore them to pieces and threw the pieces on the perfect green lawn. Behind me, I heard a noise. I turned to see my own furious red face reflected in the tinted glass of a parked car, the mutilated mail-strewn grass stretching behind.

I half walked, half ran the rest of the way home. Nobody was there and the doors were locked. I got my bike out of the garage and started on my way. The wind on Lake Avenue was whipping me wobbly. My hair, ripped loose of its perpetual ponytail, flew into my eyes. After a couple of blocks, it started to rain. At first, just a few drops, then downpour. I rode harder, leaning into it. The sky was attacking me with fat, speeding water pellets snapping and stinging cold against my face.

17. **Chlorine** (Halogen; Primordial; Gas)

There was a routine each day at the hospital: arrive through the west parking garage after school, pass by the gift shop and cafeteria (look in through the glass to the mirror behind the counter to catch my own face and lock eyes with my eyes just briefly as I go; this is to remind myself of my existence), stick my head into the red chapel and check for people praying (I liked to watch them and imagine them reaching something with their silent conjuration), press the elevator button that protrudes from the wall like a spigot, wait too long for the doors to slide open from the center outward, ride up to the fourth floor step-down ICU (keeping my eyes on my feet to avoid my face in the elevator mirror, which is much too close in there), go to my sister's room, sixth door on the left, and walk in.

Mom would be there next to June's bed and sometimes my dad. If my dad was there, he would be seated on the padded chair against the wall watching the news on the wall-mounted television. He would be fidgeting, shuffling his feet, petting his beard, biting his lower lip, twisting a piece of his coarse, black hair into a tight coil, releasing, combing it through with his fingers, then starting over with a new piece. Mom would be thoroughly engaged with my sister, who lay comatose in her hospital bed with a large, metal halo brace on, held in place by four metal screws embedded in her skull, the skin around each screw scabbed and leaking red.

Mom might be washing June's hair with the dry shampoo, a process that involved shaking a powder onto her hair and brushing it through with a bristled hairbrush for a solid ten minutes. Or, she might be clipping the lifeless fingernails at the end of June's dead weight hands. This always gave me pause. I would worry that (much like the hazards of chewing with a swollen, numb mouth after having fillings at the dentist) Mom might clip off a piece of the puffy pink skin.

June's fingers were plump and soft for months after her accident, almost plush around the cuticle and nail like fleshy little doughs with chips of opaque glass pressed flat into them. If she wasn't clipping her fingernails or dry washing her hair, Mom might be putting ice chips on

36

June's cracked, dry lips or bending her legs and arms one at a time to stimulate circulation. No matter what Mom was doing to June every day when I arrived after school, she was always, always talking. If she wasn't telling June a blow-by-blow of her day or of her plans for the next day, she was reading to her from a magazine or a book.

"It doesn't matter what you talk about or read, as long as a familiar sounding voice is going at all times," Mom would always say. Even though June's doctor insisted that she could not hear or be aware of anything (for this, we nicknamed him Doctor Doom), my mom had read (in a book called *Children With Disabilities*) that after a traumatic brain injury, especially a closed, diffuse axonal injury like June's (nerve fibers throughout the brain have been damaged or torn, usually by violent motion such as that which occurs in a car crash), emergence from coma does not occur suddenly or smoothly, but rather follows a wave-like motion, a rising and falling of levels of consciousness over time, the first signs of which were often a heightened response to external stimuli, especially the voices of family members. Mom urged us to keep the content light when we spoke to June: nothing negative or frightening.

"If you need to cry or be angry or complain about something, you should quietly leave," she would say. Mom practiced this herself rather habitually, always politely excusing herself to June with full command of her emotions before retreating down the hall or into the restroom to fall apart completely.

After making my initial appearance in June's room, I would go down to the room full of vending machines where I would always find my brother, John. He would be down on his hands and knees with the side of his face pressed against the floor, peering into the dark space beneath the soda and candy machines for any lost change. A shocking amount of change could be found there, having rolled under into oblivion after being dropped by a grieving family member or hustling employee too busy to attempt retrieving it. I would immediately drop to the floor near him and join in on the hunt. Sometimes, our hands would knock into each other when we both reached for the same coin. In situations like this, he would invariably win. In the end, however, we always tallied up the money and split it evenly between us.

At around seven o' clock, everyone would meet in the hospital cafeteria for dinner. Sometimes, when I was sick of the same old food selections down there or just not hungry, I would skip this family get-together and keep June company instead. These were somewhat spooky visits, because the lights would be low and the Doors would be playing, her favorite band before the accident.

You know the day destroys the night

Night divides the day

Tried to run

Tried to hide

Break on through to the other side...

I would sit on a stool beside her bed, stare at her bloated, pink and white face, and align my breathing with the rhythm of the song. Leaving the music on was another idea my mom picked up from reading a book about music therapy and neurological rehabilitation. She found a study that showed how patients in a persistent vegetative state brought on by a traumatic brain injury would respond consciously to familiar music and rhythm. June may not have responded consciously during her dimly lit dinner-hour serenade, but when I was present for it, I responded unconsciously.

With breathing and relaxation, the songs teleported me back in time and across space to where I was sitting in June's room listening along with her while she painted her toenails. I heard her wispy voice singing along. I saw the cotton balls between her toes; I even felt the bedspread beneath me where I lounged beside her.

Simultaneously, I could feel myself still in her hospital room, watching her comatose features and searching for a response. It was as though I straddled time: one figurative foot in the hospital room with my sister broken and indefinitely sleeping, and the other back in her room at home where she was awake and alive. One of these times, something went wrong. Instead of straddling time, I found myself trapped in a nightmare version of the past.

I stood up and walked to the mirror. My legs were heavy and slow, preventing me from moving with the urgency I felt. My face in the mirror looked wavery, my hair stood on end, floating. I smiled and saw that my teeth were very loose and coming out. I caught them in my hand, then inspected the tender, red gum, naked and gaping, inflamed around the tooth holes. I watched as the holes closed up and smoothed over and when I looked back at June on her bed, she was surrounded by teeth, molars and incisors and canines, all whole and unbroken and bone white, all with their roots. She picked them up one at a time and fastened them together at the roots with metal twine, a long tooth necklace, a growing string of teeth that wrapped around and around her.

I wanted to help her, to string together more teeth, even my own, to fasten them tightly around her, an enameled armor to protect her, but I could not move or breathe or make a sound.

People are strange, when you're a stranger

Faces look ugly when you're alone

Women seem wicked, when you're unwanted

Streets are uneven, when you're down

When you're strange—faces come out of the rain (rain, rain)...

Slowly, with panic expanding my lungs to nearly bursting, I made my way to the windowsill where I climbed out onto the roof. The night sky glittered and danced, the air could not be felt, but it was different. I went from slow-swaying seaweed to thick, shifting sand, wave-battered and revealed. I stood at the edge of the roof, preparing to jump, and took one last look over my shoulder. She was there on her bed, swollen and sleeping, the halo brace and the tubes and the hospital gown weighing her down, holding her down. The music stopped and jarred me awake. I was there in her hospital room, the lights had come on, and I was standing on the stool at its precarious edge, looking down into the confused face of my mother.

"What are you doing?" she asked in a clipped whisper, glancing nervously toward June. I climbed down from the stool and sat. I touched my teeth, pulled on them, and bit the pads of my fingertips.

"What were you doing?" she asked again. I looked at my sister with my skin still between my teeth. I felt weedy, too tired to explain.

18. Argon (Noble Gas; Primordial; Gas)

To tribes in Indonesia, the volcano capital of the world, volcanoes do not spew things out without reason. They bring justice and vengeance. When an eruption is violent, the tribespeople ask shamans and priests why it happened and what they should do next. The answer to the latter question is always some ritual, some offering to the volcano to appease it. While they want its lava to mix with the soil and keep their crops vital, they ask that it not visit its destruction upon their village again.

After a particularly violent eruption of the Merapi volcano in central Java, at a nearby village, survivors lit incense and placed rice and fruit and blood in small, makeshift boats, then sent the miniature flotilla down a river toward the volcano. The blood was from the youngest surviving member of the village, cut just below the eye—a gesture to gain favor.

19. Potassium (Alkaline Metal; Primordial; Solid)

I was in the sixth grade when I beat myself up. It had been eight or nine months since the accident and June was still deep in a coma. It was common practice for my brother and me to go to the hospital for a few hours every day after school. On one such day, I was sitting in the school bathroom feeling dread. I didn't want to go. There was nothing for me to say and nobody ever said anything. I was in the middle of biting my fingers to a bloody pulp when I had a fantasy of walking into the hospital with a puffy black eye. Mom would turn from June's bedside and gasp, then rush to me and hold my face in her hands. She would probably cry or at least be very upset. She would ask me what had happened but

I would just shrug and act all tough like it didn't matter, like I was fine. She would wrap up some ice in a cloth, sit in the padded chair against the wall, and pull me onto her lap. She would place the ice gently against my black eye, look at me with sadness and love the way she looked at June, and run her fingers through my hair the way she did with June's.

I made a fist as tight as I could get it, looked at it for a minute while I worked up the courage, then punched myself in the eye with the hard part of my knuckle. It hurt and my eye started to water, but it wasn't enough. I tried it again and again, maybe six times, but my arm would invariably hesitate and lose power just before my fist connected. It was as though my body contained a built-in mechanism to prevent me from delivering the full power of my punch on my own eye. I looked around in the toilet stall, considered getting on my knees and knocking my face against the porcelain, but that would have been less precise. My eyes rested on the metal toilet paper holder. I touched its sharp corner. In slow motion, I lowered my face to it, practicing my aim, lining up the bone just under my right eye with the hard corner. I flattened my palms against the side of the stall on either side of the metal box, took a few practice bows, and hurled myself down face first against the box. Unspeakable pain exploded through my head and for a moment, everything went black.

I nearly fell but caught myself on the toilet. I held half of my face and steadied myself with the other hand against the wall. It wasn't until I noticed the blood on the metal box that I realized my hand was wet. It was covered in blood. I stood up on shaky legs and walked out of the stall cautiously, grateful that the bathroom was empty. I washed my hands and face and looked in the mirror. My eye had already begun to swell and darken. A small but deep triangular cut oozed in the center of the wounded area. It hurt so much I thought I might cry, but the reflection in the mirror was smiling.

By the time I arrived at the hospital, I had the story worked out in my head: Some crazy kid beat the hell out of me with brass knuckles. I imagined this kid would have manhandled me a bit before wailing on my face, grabbed me by the collar and threw me around, perhaps, so I tugged at the neck of my tee shirt until it tore a little bit. I walked into June's hospital room to the familiar smells of dry shampoo powder, disinfectant, and urine. I stood in the doorway to the dimly lit cave of a room and saw my mom from that distance, perched on a stool, bent forward, a bit hunched but with the hard, squared shoulders that came with her steel determination to take care of things. Fix things.

The exhaustion sat in the dark crescent pockets beneath her eyes, in the new slackness of her features, as though her skull and bones had shrunk a bit inside her skin. There was also my sister, who resembled a dead person in a hospital bed, all gray and shell-like. I watched and waited for my mom to look up from the magazine article she was reading aloud to June. When she finally did, she squinted at me and said, "Oh my god, honey, what happened?" Her voice was hushed, quieter than her reading voice had been, as though June might hear and become upset by it. I shrugged and stood tough, just like I imagined.

But the rest of it didn't go as planned. My mom looked over my shoulder to one of the nurses who was coming in behind me and nodded toward me. "Would you look at her face," she said in the same hushed voice. The nurse turned me around and lowered her face to mine. She lifted my chin and studied my eye. Behind me in the room, I heard my mom's voice reading again, nice and loud.

20. Calcium (Alkaline Earth Metal; Primordial; Solid)

"Come on, honey, we'll clean this up," the nurse said. She took me to the nurse's station where she soaked a cotton ball in something brown and made to dab it on my cut. I pulled my face back and asked what it was. "Iodine," she said.

"Isn't that one of the elements in the periodic table?" I asked, confused.

She chuckled and nodded. "It is, yes, as is oxygen, which we're breathing right now. And we have calcium in our bones and iron in our blood. Everything is made of elements."

I thought about that and had an image in my mind of the Big Bang happening, spraying clouds of gas and debris out from nothing at unfathomable speeds, hurling all these elements that would create worlds, create life. It all started with a huge, violent explosion.

"Why iodine?"

"It kills the bad bacteria. It's an antiseptic. I could use alcohol if you'd prefer, but iodine stings less."

I relaxed and let her dab it against my cut. I clamped my teeth together and took the sting like the tough guy I wanted to be. The nurse gave me an amused smile, her pretty mouth curled up and down simultaneously like she was stifling another chuckle. Her eyes were soft and brown and a little curious. I could tell she wanted to know what happened but was waiting for me to offer the story. I decided to remain mysterious.

"Have you seen worse?" I asked her.

"Oh yes, much worse," she said and laughed, utterly dismissing all my hard work. I stayed quiet then and let her finish cleaning it. She put a white gauze pad delicately against it then taped it in place.

When she was done, she patted me on the top of the head and told me to go in and see my sister.

Mom was still reading, but not quite as loudly. It was just the three of us in the room; my brother hadn't arrived yet, or if he had, he was down in the cafeteria getting dinner. I sat in the padded chair against the wall and listened to her voice reading. It was only a few more sentences before she finished the article, folded the magazine closed, and put it down. She rubbed her eyes and looked up.

"Will you come sit with her while I go get something to eat? I'm starving," she said, getting to her feet warily. I brushed passed her as I went to take her seat and she patted my shoulder.

"Thanks, honey," she said and walked out, not even noticing my bandage. I sat beside June's bed and held her cold hand. She was propped up on pillows with her head, neck, and back ramrod straight, held in traction

43

by the body and neck brace. In addition to the closed head injury, which was the worst, she had broken her ankle, both her knees, her pelvis in seven places, and her neck. I leaned forward and put my face close to hers, smelling the plastic smell of the thick tube that disappeared into her neck just beneath her Adam's apple, and something else I could never identify but that was always present on her skin. It was like the smell of a leather jacket that had been hanging in a musty closet for too long. I kissed her between the eyes and brushed my bandage against the cool skin of her cheek.

"Hi June," I said and watched her face. Sometimes, her eyeballs moved beneath the lids but just then they were still. I tried to think of a story to tell her, one she told me, or one that I made up on my own, but nothing would come. There had been no stories since the accident.

They were what I missed the most. "Would you like to hear a story?" I asked. It was what she used to ask me late at night when it was dark and we were each in our beds and I couldn't sleep. From my pillow I could see the moon above the trees outside the window, how it laid down soft, white light on the windowsill where shadows of branches tangled in the wind. Her voice would rise from that moonlight, high and sweet, draw it into the room, steal its light, make it her own. In the story, there was a neighbor boy who had a sand box and a poor girl with rags for clothes who wanted to play but he would not. She was too ugly. Something happened. Her family gained wealth, she returned transformed, and the boy was happy to play. The girl, still the same person as before, revealed her true identity and the boy learned a profound lesson. My sister made stories like tiny architectures with people, parks, trees, roads, houses, rooms, objects, clothes. She made whole worlds, rich and vivid, and invited me into them.

That day in her hospital bed, her face was pale and moonlike. Looking at it, I could hear her voice in my head. I told her the story the way she told it to me, as much as I remembered of it. I wondered if she heard me, certain that somehow, somewhere, she did.

21. **Scandium** (Transition Metal; Primordial; Solid)

Paris, day 1

Meanwhile, while June had the new time accepted in her brain and was fine, the rest of us were increasingly fatigued and grumpy. It didn't help that Paris greeted us on our first day with low, gray crowds and fits of pissy rain. Having finished some food, all I wanted was warmth and sleep. I stared out the window at the rain starting again, watched it collect on the glass and converge into droplets. As the droplets plumped, their weight couldn't hold, so they collapsed into a rivulet, taking down other droplets as it went, leaving room for a new droplet to form and follow in its path. As the rain picked up, the rivulets multiplied and criss-crossed on the glass, surging into little rivers like arteries of water and hundreds of smaller creeks like veins.

"We should get umbrellas," I said.

"Or ponchos," Lee said, "I think I saw some at a place we passed."

"No. Ponchos won't keep us dry. We need umbrellas," I said, raising my voice. People at a nearby table looked over.

"How do you hold an umbrella and push June at the same time," Lee snapped back, rolling her eyes like it was the dumbest idea she's ever heard.

"Are you serious? Are you overwhelmed at the thought, Lee? Are you one of those people who can't chew gum and walk simultaneously?" I said. Lee opened her mouth to speak and Mom cut in. "Girls," she said. That was all. Lee glared at me and I smiled and winked, diffusing the nasty. She smiled back then slumped in her chair and closed her eyes.

When we finally checked into our hotel room, it was five in the morning at home and we were wrecked. The room was on a high floor, offering an amazing panoramic view of Paris, including the Eiffel Tower, which was within walking distance.

"Mom, wow. This is a great room," Lee said, throwing her bag down on a cot to claim it. It was a fairly large space, too, with two rooms separated by a hallway and a sizeable bathroom. Mom offered to sleep in the bedroom with June where they would share a queen-sized bed. Lee and I slept on two cots in the room with the TV and the huge window. Almost immediately, we all lay down to nap. Even from the other room with the door closed down the hall, I could hear June snoring. What a saint Mom was. I fell asleep to the rhythm of those muffled snores that must have sounded like thunder lying right beside her.

22. **Titanium** (Transition Metal; Primordial; Solid)

I might have been eleven or twelve when I took June to the shower myself. My mom usually took her or sometimes a nurse and I was often in attendance, assisting in some way, but never had I done it on my own. June's floor in the hospital was particularly busy that day and the nurses were short staffed, so when it came time for her shower, I volunteered, assuming that my mom or one of the nurses would be along any time to take over.

The Glasgow Coma Scale gives a range of numbers to represent the different stages of coma based on response to external stimuli. By that scale, June was at a level nine when I took her to the shower, meaning she responded to her name being called by looking at me, she was able to sometimes focus her eyes on me, and if I made a face at her, she would mimic and make the same face back, much like a baby.

She sat robed and glassy-eyed in her wheelchair, which I pushed up close to the shower stall, one among a row of several identical stalls divided with metal partitions. Inside the shower was a waterproof chair, squat and sturdy with holes in the seat to drain the water falling off the body, with a back and two arms to pen in the unsteady, unbalanced weight it supported. My first task, and the hardest, was to maneuver her into the shower chair. I had observed this being done countless times and felt somewhat confident that I could do it, but I was hesitant and afraid. I let her sit there with her robe on for several minutes while I looked toward the door, wondering if I should get a nurse, or wait for my mom. June stared at the wall, her eyes unfocused, her lips pursed a little as if she were waiting for a kiss.

Unable to resist, I bent down and kissed her, put my mouth to hers. There was a sensation of nourishment in it, like I was a baby bird feeding from the open mouth of my mother, bitter tasting and unpleasant, but necessary and automatic. I helped her out of her robe, bending her forward and pulling free her arms, then letting it collapse open around her, cascading over the sides of the chair, revealing her.

I looked her over, noticing everything. My eyes stuck to the deep red scar on her throat where the tracheal tube had been; it was sunken in and shadowed. It appeared so tender and raw in the context of her pale naked body, the fair skin stretching out all around it made nearly pastel in comparison. Scars were everywhere: squat ankle scars, long knee scars, nearly indistinct, smaller scars around her pelvis and on her arms. The untouched places, her thighs and breasts, looked sculpted from soft, pink and white clay. I tried to keep my eyes there; it seemed to tame the fiery grief burning my ribs.

I leaned down and hooked my arms underneath hers, my hands clasped behind her back, hugging her. I stood still there, cheek-to-cheek with her in that gentle and awkward embrace. Then I counted to three, whispered the numbers in her ear like I had seen my mom do to prepare her for the lift. I waited a few beats after three just to see if she would respond at all, some part of her go tense with effort to stand, but nothing happened. I pulled her body up on unsteady legs and she fell forward against me.

I held her tightly to my chest, pushed my hips in against hers to brace her weight. I was nearly as tall as her and strong enough to hold her up, but too uneasy to try moving right away. We stood there like that, me holding her naked body in my arms, pressed together like petals, breathing. I nearly cried at the weight and the helplessness of her. I breathed deeply and squeezed the tears back in. I held her tighter, was... ; to collapse into her and meld and disappear. The heat of our two bodies became overwhelming and I started to sweat. The pivot, swing, and lower maneuver to get her positioned safely in the shower chair was the trickiest part. I tried to see it in my mind before attempting anything, but I only saw myself dropping her, letting her go, crumpling under her, failing. I considered lowering her right back down into her wheelchair and giving up, going back and waiting for my mom, but I needed to succeed. My mom needed to know that I was capable of this, that I was strong enough. I needed to know.

With renewed courage, I stepped back with one leg, leaned forward just slightly, flexed my arms and back into a rigid framework, turned us both from the hips like a dancer, and lowered her as gracefully as possible to her seat. I pulled away from her slowly, carefully, almost regretfully. Something had happened. I knew it even then. What was so tragic and meaningless for so long, what up until then had been nothing but hollow, agonizing misery for us all, somehow magically, although briefly, filled with dense purpose.

If there were such things as souls that existed before and beyond and in spite of our bodies, they would have wanted that moment to occur; they would have set up the conditions for it, and in its happening, would have been pleased. To have my big sister lean on me like that, naked, dependent in my arms, thick with complicated history and implications of an even more complicated future, covered in scars. It was a sad and colossal gift.

23. Vanadium (Transition Metal; Primordial; Solid)

My mom was pregnant with the twins when her first husband left her for another woman. He announced that he was in love and was gone by the time she found out there would be two babies. When he came back to gather some of his things, she sat him down to tell him the good news. His head fell into his hands in a gesture of such despair and disappointment. She thought she might have told him he would soon die.

"I guess this means I have to come back," he said.

"No," she said, shaking her head in amazement. "You're not coming back."

Lee was two, so after he'd gone, she couldn't sit down to cry. She had a toddler to tend to. Before long, Mom was bigger than she'd ever been in her life and divorced. The doctor's appointments were humiliating episodes. In those days, no one hid their distain for an unmarried pregnant woman, not even other women. Being divorced was worse yet, because ultimately it meant that she'd failed at being a wife. And now she would have three children to raise alone.

The twins were raucous inside her. The weight of her depression expanded faster than her girth, its heft foreshadowing the plight of their joined lives. She moved like a great hull, tending to Lee with the mustered slowness of an elderly person. The last month of pregnancy was a cold, dark January. When the time came, the car was snowed in. She called 911, but they warned her it might take some time and prepped her for handling the birth on her own. There was nothing she could do but try to sanitize scissors and towels between the contractions.

They were born on the bathroom floor. Lee watched helplessly from the doorway, closing her eyes when it was too much. Jonas came first, tumbling onto the towel between her legs. June came a full minute later, falling over Jonas and onto the floor where dog hair and dirt stuck to her. Their slick pink bodies wailed. My mom scooped them up onto her belly and cleaned them off with one of the towels. She wished she'd cleaned the floor in time.

24. Chromium (Transition Metal; Primordial; Solid)

All five of us shared a bedroom when I was little, younger than five, which would have made John seven; June and Jonas, ten; and Lee, twelve. John and I shared a bunk bed against one wall, Jonas and June shared a bunk bed against the opposite wall, and Lee had her own bed along the windowsill. We were crowded together in that front bedroom, the same one that June and I would later share until the time when June would have it to herself. The heap of us made the room much smaller then, but we were happy there. I looked forward to bedtime and felt safe in the warm dark, smiling in a loose pile with my siblings.

Most nights, it would be hours before any of us got to sleep because we couldn't stop talking and laughing and playing games. If it got too loud, we would hear heavy footfalls ascending the stairs. It would be Mom or Dad noisily and slowly coming to tell us to go to sleep, to be quiet. By the time they reached the room, though, we would all be feigning sleep, stiff and still with our heads turned toward the walls or buried under the covers, choking down giggles only to have them erupt when the shadow from the hall retreated and the footfalls slipped away, back down the stairs. There was something so satisfying about letting it out after holding it in.

Lee would be the one to tire of the antics first and just want to go to sleep. At first, she would try to be stern and authoritative, but the boys would just mock her and repeat everything she said in the most annoying fashion. Then, she'd switch tactics and make a game of it. Once, she said, "Hey, I have an idea, let's play a new game. We'll be as quiet as we can for as long as we can. The first person to talk loses."

Everyone fell immediately silent; not even a rustle of sheets could be heard. Cricket chirps filled the room and the wind blew softly through the open window, licking the curtains. Farther off, the sounds of the occasional car passing on Lake Avenue like soft shoring waves. June giggled, which set off a cascade of giggling from Jonas to John to me.

"Shhhh!" Lee said. A moment went by before she said, "Time

out, no laughing or making any sound of any kind including talking or you lose. Time in." A few more moments of chirping silence slid by before Jonas said, "Time out. I just wanted to say 'time out' so I could talk. Time in."

June and John and I stifled giggles.

"Time out," John said. "If Jonas can talk, I can talk and still win the game. Time in."

June's voice followed by saying "Time out," laughing hard and loud then saying "Time in," which made everybody laugh except Lee.

"Time out, no more time outs! Time in," Lee said.

I remember waiting in anticipation for another small voice to rise up out of the chirping, but nobody wanted to lose. Without the voices, I felt scared and alone, so I got up out of my bed like I did most nights and went to Jonas and June's bunk. They took turns getting the top bunk (in my bunk, John always got the top) and I wasn't sure who was on the bottom that night. I stood beside it peering toward the head on the pillow, trying to see who it was in the shadows. The cover turned down and Jonas propped up on one elbow. He squinted at me then rolled his eyes and patted the mattress beside him. I crawled in and snuggled my back against him. I was asleep in minutes.

The sky's beneath us

25. Manganese (Transition Metal; Primordial; Solid)

Lee, first born

Lee stared at herself in the mirror in the school bathroom, then looked down at her purse. Her makeup needed touching up but she didn't have the energy to reach for it. The door swung open and a trio of giggling girls walked in. They fell silent when they saw Lee, bumping into one another like a halted chain gang. They looked her up and down in unison. Lee looked down at herself. She was dressed in sweatpants and flip-flops, a worn, oversized wrestling T-shirt of Craig's, and had her hair pulled back into a messy bun with no earrings and barely any makeup. *I look like shit*, she thought. The girls were dressed in skirts and accessorized appropriately. Their hair was poofed and flared in all the right places and their eyeshadow colors matched their nail polish shades.

They lined up in front of the mirror beside Lee and began primping. Cans of Aqua Net, eyelash curlers, lipsticks, and compacts were produced from purses and eagerly employed. Lee watched them like a dumbfounded child watching underwater sea creatures in a walk-up aquarium at the zoo. Their motions were synchronized and automatic, effortless, inherent to a female, teenaged culture with which Lee no longer felt familiar.

How could anyone bother with such frivolity? How could anyone, anywhere, go on with life as usual?

She stared at her own face in the mirror. There was a distinct change in it. She noticed it then, in the context of the primping girls and their unaffected faces, their superficial chatter. She couldn't say specifically what it was, nor could she say that she disliked it or that it was at all a negative change. But it was unmistakable. No amount of makeup would mask it. No number of trips to the tanning salon would remove it.

The girls grew louder and more animated by the moment. Their high-pitched voices sounded shrill when amplified by the bathroom. What was worse, their bodies began to thrash, bent double then rapidly righted to flip the hair, which was sprayed amply in the process. Lee found herself in a thickening aerosol haze. She covered her mouth and coughed, grabbed her purse, and walked out.

She walked slowly to her locker, feeling the gravity of her face, its features being pulled down wearily. She opened her locker to find some of June's school books inside. They had shared lockers, all three of them—Lee, June, and Jonas. Lee picked up June's French workbook and fanned the pages, letting them rest open on a spread filled with neat cursive. Solemn and indecipherable, the words mocked the weightiness of the handwriting—loops and lines of ink like vivid blue ghosts screaming at her that they are never to be replicated. They will be a part of a history that will get increasingly hard to reconcile with its trajectory. A few fat, quick tears splat on the page, spreading whole words into wet blue blotches.

26. Iron (Transition Metal; Primordial; Solid)

Jonas, second born

He showed up at the Golden Jade for work feeling half alive. He didn't want to be there, but he didn't want to be home or at the hospital, either. His head hurt and he could swear his neck and pelvis were aching with sympathy pains. Twin pains. As twins, the two of them had always been in sync. When they were eight, June was home while Jonas was out riding bikes with friends. June began crying and complaining that her knee hurt, seemingly for no reason. Mom inspected it, saw no injury, and was trying to calm her down enough to find out what happened when Jonas came walking in with a bleeding knee. He had fallen from his bike several streets away.

It was a few days after the accident, and Jonas had a cooking shift at the Jade. He walked in through the back kitchen door and was assaulted by the smell of fried meat and soy sauce. Adam was working, washing dishes just a few feet away when Jonas punched in and grabbed his apron. Jonas hated Adam with his long, black hair and his Metallica

T-shirts, his stupid bullshit comments and idiotic laugh. On a regular day, Jonas wanted to tape Adam's balls together then rip off the tape.

"Hey, you sure you want to be here?" Jonas's boss, Zan asked. "You can take as much time as you need, you know?" He spoke with the slightest hint of a Chinese accent. His long black hair was pulled back in a ponytail and packed into a hair net, making him look girlish. Beads of sweat glistened from his upper lip. He dried his hands on a towel and stepped toward Jonas.

"No, it's fine," Jonas said, stepping away and tying his apron, not wanting anyone anywhere near him.

"How is she?" Zan asked, stopping his advance and leaning on the stainless steel counter, smeared with duck blood. Beside him were lines of whole, decapitated, freshly plucked ducks, braised pig's feet, and Chinese yams.

"She's bad," Jonas said and paused, choking back the urge to vomit, whether produced by the food awaiting preparation or the feelings that question produced, or both. "The car was mangled."

"Fucking sardine can, huh, man?" Adam said and laughed his dumb-fuck laugh. Jonas's rage flared so hot and fast he was almost dizzy from it. In one instant, he drove his fist so hard into Adam's face, his nose split apart like a bashed pomegranate and he was down. Jonas was on top of him delivering blow after blow to the kid's wildly bloody face until three guys, his boss included, finally pulled him off, lifting him into the air with red fists still flying.

"Jonas, what the fuck, man?" Zan screamed, pinning him back against the wall next to the time clock. Jonas stopped and froze, staring at the moaning, writhing kid on the floor, his hair matted with blood. He looked at the frightened faces of his coworkers, the stunned, wide eyes of Zan. He felt nothing. Jonas ripped off his apron, causing everyone to jump back from him. He punched the time clock so hard it shattered, and walked out with bleeding, aching knuckles.

27. Cobalt (Transition Metal; Primordial; Solid)

June, third born

June is in excruciating pain. But mostly, she's thirsty. Never in her life has she ever wanted anything more than a refreshing drink. It isn't good to want things so much. It's how she got herself into this trouble to begin with. She'd been on the bus to school when a boy sat next to her and promised to quench her parched throat with a tall, cold glass of water if she would first have sex with him. She agreed. She had no other choice. She was that thirsty.

Only he never delivered on that glass of water, and now she's even more parched as well as throbbing in pain from between her legs. She had given birth to five babies, each one ripping out from her body more painfully than the one before it. Each one had been pressed so hard inside her that their collective pressure shattered her bones. She's only sixteen and she doesn't know how to take care of babies so she left them in the woods. She's worried that they will starve to death or die of exposure or be eaten by a large animal.

The gray, wrinkled cerebral tissue afloat inside her skull is bruised, riddled with damaged zones. Tender, folded flesh, electrical flesh with vital impulses that once resembled a lightning storm or the Northern Lights now is docile and dark. Quiet. No longer capable of making the same connections and complex calculations it once had on a moment-by-moment basis, like how to lift your arm and arrange your fingers around an object to then handle it, perform some task with it.

But a new, deeper place is colored now, charged with synapses creating whole other worlds—ones where gods and space debris mingle. This is where June meets Zeek, crouched in a cave peering out at her with yellow eyes. She approaches and he emerges. A womanish man-beast, Zeek has long blonde hair in perfect coils, pinkish hairless cheeks, and a cherubian mouth, yet he is, from the neck down, a muscular torso attached to the body of a mule with four hoofed limbs beneath him and two outstretched arms before him, reaching for her.

Somehow, June isn't afraid of the womanish man-beast. She knows he will help her, get her a drink. She walks, stumbling into his embrace and winces at the pain in her body. She crumbles on the ground at his hoofs. He lifts her onto his back and gallops away.

28. Nickel (Transition Metal; Primordial; Solid)

John, fourth born

John didn't care anymore if he passed or failed seventh grade. It was too late in the year to do shit about it, anyway. Every year since fourth grade, he'd gone to summer school. What did it matter if he went again?

Before home room, he found his friend, Jesse, where he knew he'd be—grinding the curbs on his skateboard in the school's side parking lot. Jesse saw him and stopped.

"Dude. You look like shit. Your dog die?" Jesse started to smile but then frowned when John's creased, clenched expression didn't change. "Seriously. What?"

"You got your bong?" John asked. Jesse shook his head.

"No way, not at school," he said.

John didn't move. Didn't blink.

"It's in the fort, though," Jesse said. The fort was a treehouse that the boys had built in the woods behind Jesse's house with real plywood and drywall that they stole from the construction sites at new housing developments. It was spacious and sturdy and stocked with plenty of weed and Swisher Sweet cigars. Sometimes, it had a partial bottle of whiskey that Jesse stole from his dad's liquor cabinet.

"Let's go," John said, and turned to go without waiting for an answer.

"Whoa, dude, and skip school?" Jesse said, snatching up his board and trotting to keep up.

"Yeah," John said. His frizzy mullet hair stood up in the wind and his ears turned pepper red. Not only did they stick out, but they turned various shades of maroon whenever he had a feeling of any kind.

Jesse didn't ask any other questions until they got to the fort and the bong was packed tight. When John lit up and took the first hit, long and deep, Jesse asked again. John stared back at him, holding the smoke in hard. Jesse took the bong, brought it to his lips, lit, and inhaled just as a small cloud of smoke exploded out of John's mouth.

"My sister, June. She had a car accident. She might not make it," John said. The last few words pitched up to a near squeak and gave way to racking sobs complete with little screams and gasps. Jesse stopped smoking and looked down at his lap. He said nothing nor did he move a single inch. Just sat there stiffly, holding his breath while John wailed and toppled sideways in the small space. John felt snot drip out of his nose and drool spill from his lips with his head pressed to the plywood floor of the treehouse. He drew in another ragged breath and tasted sawdust, dirt, ash.

29. Copper (Transition Metal; Primordial; Solid)

Mom

All she did was sit beside June, eat beside June, sleep beside June. After quitting for months, she started smoking again because it just didn't matter anymore. So what if smoking killed her a few years early? Here it was—a variation of the proverbial I-could-get-hit-by-a-bus-tomorrow excuse so often used to justify the life-threatening risks of smoking—it had happened! To her own daughter! Who had never smoked! Had she even had her first kiss? The question alone made Mom's stomach feel like a twisted, wrung washcloth. She bent double and nearly vomited right there on the floor next to June's hospital bed.

This was her baby: this pale, comatose body being kept alive by electricity running through machines that breathed for her, fed her, hydrated her. Suddenly, Mom was terrified there would be some mass power outage. The rhythmic suck and sigh of the mechanical lungs and the persistent beeping of the machine heartbeat would cease. This was her baby! Mom collapsed then, laid her whole torso across June's bed, stroked June's cheek with gentle desperation, and sobbed and sobbed.

30. Zinc (Transition Metal; Primordial; Solid)

Anne, fifth born

I was shocked to discover how suddenly and utterly alone I was in the world. No one was there to watch my comings and goings. No one to wonder whether I had eaten or if I were hungry or if I would know what to feed myself. No one to wait for me to come home or make me go to bed. At first it felt strange and lonely, but I quickly grew to appreciate the freedom. And the loneliness didn't last long.

I was visiting one of my favorite trees when I met him. It was an apple tree along the perimeter of the field with a split trunk and many thick climbing branches. I was making my way up the tricky part—walking up the inner thighs, if you will, of the dual trunk, my own legs opening wider as the tree's legs did, until I had to be close to doing the splits where I could reach and grab hold of a branch to hoist myself up an into the abundant higher branches. He was already up there, hanging upside down among the branches like a pear, with a face equally as naïve. He was blonde and blue eyed with an upside-down smile that turned his face redder with the blood rush. I nearly fell out of the tree when I saw him there, waving and smiling.

"How are you doing that?" I asked.

"It's easy," he said, "just fold your legs over a branch and hook your feet under the branch next to it. Then, let go and dangle like this." He let his arms fall groundward, wiggling his fingers toward the grass below. It looked far to fall, especially on your head. It scared me, but I wanted to try it anyway. As though reading my thoughts, he said, "Don't be scared, try it. I won't let you fall."

I tried it. Just like he said on a branch next to him, so that when I let go, I faced him and we giggled. My head filled and felt full, pressurized. I opened my mouth wide as it would go and stuck out my tongue, giving it a release, but my ears felt tight and taut as drums. The world stretched out behind him—the ground a ceiling and the sky a bottomless floor. Everything was toppled and wayward and this made me feel more comfortable in my body.

"The sky's beneath us," I said. His hair stood on end and his face was nearly purple.

With one swift motion, he swung up, grasped the branch between his knees with both hands, unhooked his legs and fell upright, dangling for a moment from his hands before falling gracefully to the ground with a soft thump. I followed his lead and repeated the maneuver, only I fell less gracefully and stumbled when I hit, scraping both my knees. I would have fallen on my hands and face too if he hadn't caught me. I stood up and looked at him. Somehow, he was familiar.

"I'm Andy," he said.

"Do I know you?" I asked.

"Of course," he said and smiled. Instantly, I remembered where I'd seen him before: in our kitchen. When I was very little, maybe four or five, I had a bad dream. In the middle of the night, I got out of bed to go down to my parents' room and get my mom. Passing through the kitchen on the way, I was halted by a little boy, about my age, with one hand on the corner of the kitchen table and one hand on the basement doorknob, knees up, swinging to and fro on his arms, smiling this same way. It had taken me a moment to go from curious surprise to terror when I realized he was translucent—I could see the dining-room windowsill behind him through his chest. I'd screamed then and ran back up to my bed.

Standing there before him at age eleven, I recognized him as that little ghost boy, only he was older now and no longer transparent.

"Are you a ghost?" I asked and reached out to grab his arm, a firm bicep in my hand. He laughed.

"No, not exactly, but something like it," he said.

61

J'avais envie de dire bonjour

31. Gallium (Poor Metal; Primordial; Solid)

Paris, logistics

Le Louvre is, June used to say, more than 800 years old, though it's only been a museum for about 200 years. She said it started out as an elaborate palace. She couldn't wait to walk among its halls, imagining the kings and courts of yore. This was before the accident, of course, when she was anticipating her class trip to Paris. I remember feeling jealous but also excited for her.

Assuming I would one day get to go, too, and wanting to get prepared, I asked her to teach me French. She was sitting at her dressing table doing her hair and makeup one morning before school. I stood behind her in a stained blue sweatshirt, sporting the feathered mullet I had at the time. She was applying eye shadow with her lids lowered and her mouth pulled down into a small *o* and her face very close to the mirror like she was about to kiss her reflection. Without knowing it, I was imitating her face; when she lowered her hand and leaned back to look at me, she laughed.

"What are you doing?" she chortled. I caught a glimpse of my ridiculous expression over her shoulder before it fell off with awareness. I blushed.

"Are you wearing that?" she asked snottily and wrinkled her nose as if I smelled bad.

"Teach me," I whined. She smiled and dropped her eye shadow, fingering different lipsticks in her collection.

"Ok, ok," she said. "Here's a song you can remember, ready?"

I nodded. She sang out, "Je m' baladais sur l' avenue, Le coeur ouvert à l' inconnu, J'avais envie de dire bonjour... Aux Champs-Elysées, Aux Champs-Elysées..."

"What's it mean?" I asked. She told me. It's about a famous avenue in Paris, the Champs-Elysées.

"That's silly," I said.

"It's French," she said and winked.

With the song in my head, I went about my day and soon felt annoyed with its stickiness. Even now, all these years later, that song floats through my head whenever I'm reminded of anything French.

As a result, though, two of the places on our list to visit during our trip to Paris were Le Louvre and the Champs-Elysées. And, of course, the Eiffel Tower, but we could only plan one major tourist attraction per day. June and company in Paris were not exactly a well-oiled machine.

First, we had to avoid the main mode of transportation, the Métro. It's an underground subway that's hectic and fast and just doesn't lend itself well to slow movers and wheelchairs. Only certain stops even have elevators. As an alternative mode of transport, we purchased city tour bus tickets with unlimited on and off access at all the major attractions. With a bus of this sort, we could fold up and carry June's wheelchair on board while she used the hand railing to make her way up and into a seat. The tour bus drivers were patient with this time-consuming process, a benefit we would have never gotten from a city bus. We planned to do this for two days and visit Le Louvre and Notre-Dame one day, then Champs-Elysées and whatever else another day.

Second, we had a strict feeding and medicating schedule to keep with June. She had to eat at regular intervals and her meds, of course, which were crucial, had to be taken with food. Allowing plenty of time to sit down somewhere for a meal at least three times in the day as well as time for snacks between was a challenge.

Third, there was the bathroom issue. What this meant, basically, is that if we were ever more than three to five minutes away from one at any given time, there would be an accident and the day's plan would potentially derail. As insurance, June wore an extra absorbent "pad," (an adult diaper she sometimes wears for events such as these) and carried an extra in her purse. The emergency happened daily, though, and often more than once in the day. Each pad was, after all, good for only one incident, following which we had to get in the general vicinity of a bathroom rather quickly, lest it happen again before she had a chance to change.

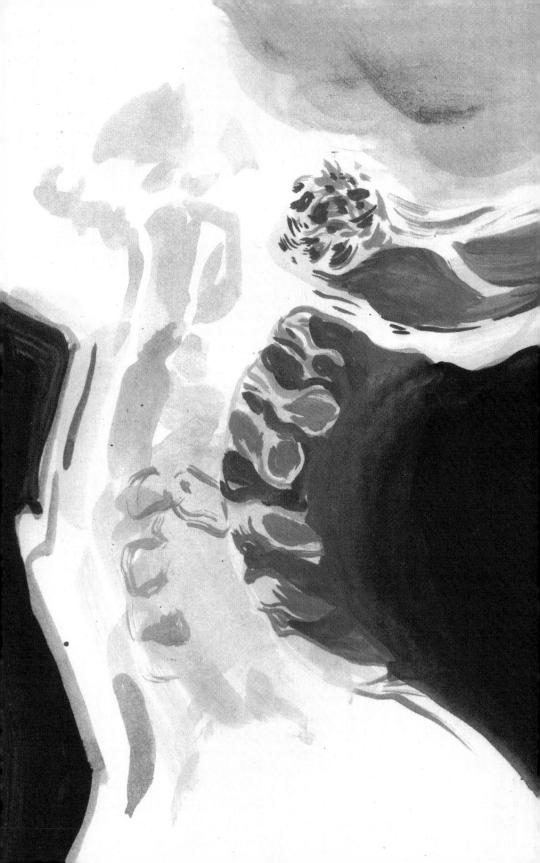

You are that inscrutable brightness

32. **Germanium** (Metalloid; Primordial; Solid)

In Hawaii, volcano eruptions are beneficial acts of creation. Hawaiians see their lives mirrored in the volcanic activity. There, lava often gushes slowly from a long crack in the earth. The hot, viscous material creates a smooth, skin-like texture along the fissure. Because this resembles a huge vagina, natives see it as the menstruation of the goddess Pele, with the red lava always flowing toward the sea, the same path women took in ancient times to cleanse themselves.

33. **Arsenic** (Metalloid; Primordial; Solid)

Andy started showing up after the tree-climbing encounter whenever I was alone, which was most of the time. Sometimes, if I was home and John or Jonas or Lee was there, I would leave to be alone. I would run across the field behind our house and into the woods where there was a grove of wild grape vines. The grapes were deep purple orbs with tight, tart skins. I liked to tear the skin off with my two front teeth, eat that, then inspect the translucent center, its texture like mucus but firmer. I likened them to eyeballs. Sometimes, I would hold one or two skinned grapes in my bare palm and close my eyes. While chewing the bitter skins, I would imagine that I was handling disembodied eyeballs. If I pretended that the eyeballs were an animal's, I would feel so sad that actual tears would come out. If I pretended they were human eyeballs, I felt okay about it. I preferred the former fantasy, because it was the only time that I could get myself to cry. Since the accident happened (around then it had been days or weeks), I hadn't cried hardly at all. I heard Lee crying all the time. Sometimes Jonas and John, too. But I couldn't do it on my own. I needed a sad sound or a sad thought, like the rain hitting the cat food plate on the back porch or the thought of cat eyeballs in my palm. Or, leopard eyeballs or dog eyeballs. Or, sometimes, even fish eyeballs. But a big fish, like a whale. If they were whale eyeballs, I would sob.

Andy came when I was crying with my eyes closed. I knew he was standing there even before I opened my eyes. He never asked why I was crying. He rarely asked anything. He told me things. He said that I was not to take this life too seriously. That, like numbers—how the number nine can be expressed in various ways, perhaps infinite ways, such as with nine bananas or nine pieces of cake or the character for the number nine or nine lines drawn in a pattern or a pile of nine shirts—I was just an expression of the idea of me. All the expressions of the number nine are both created and destroyed. They are thought up and put into form, then taken out of form. But the idea of the number nine exists independently of these expressions and can't be created nor have its origin traced, if there is such an origin. After explaining this to me, searching my face for comprehension, and finding it there, whole, he was excited. Giddy, even.

"You are not this," he said, grabbing and squeezing my hand. "You are, all of you are," he said, circling his index finger in the air, "unique expressions of *the is*."

He lost me there. Recognizing this, he took another approach.

"You, this body," he said, "from head top to toe tip, is nothing more than thought, itself."

This (as well as many things he told me) confused me. Even if I were a unique idea of the is, whatever that was, how could it have no beginning and no end? He told me to think of it as a circle. He called it the infinite round. That was me. Just like the number nine. A circle of sorts, expressed as a girl with teeth and skin and long, tangled hair.

Once, I was sitting in the lap of an oversized tree in the woods with a cigarette I had stolen from my mom's purse. I had forgotten a lighter. Andy appeared and was able to light it for me, just by looking at it. This was how I knew he was real, that I wasn't only imaging him. Whatever he was, no one else could see or hear him, but he sometimes touched the physical world through me, like when he lit my cigarette or told me about these ideas that no eleven-year-old could have thought up. I remember, once, telling John one of the ideas. It was the idea about time.

"It's not really linear," I said.

"What?" He said. He was sitting on the floor in his room building a bong out of an empty plastic two-liter bottle.

"Time. We think time proceeds forward because we have memories of the past. We think there is a future because we think about tomorrow or next week. But we think that way because we measure it that way. It's a way to orient us in space. Really, it's all right here, right now," I said. He turned around to face me and wrinkled his forehead.

"Have you been smoking?" He asked, in an accusatory tone like I'd stolen some of his weed.

"Only cigarettes sometimes," I said. I suddenly felt nervous, like I'd been caught but I didn't know with what. John had a way of always knowing when I was hiding something or lying, even if I didn't know yet.

"What have you been reading?" He asked, still facing me, still bunching his forehead.

"Nothing much," I said.

He turned around and went back to his bong, saying, "Well, stop. You're freaking me out."

I walked out then, reflecting on what I'd said and how I knew about it. An invisible boy told me. Visible only to me. Was I crazy? I knew that I probably was. I knew not to tell anyone about Andy. But I did tell one person. It was the guidance counselor at school, Mrs. Frame. She didn't come into my life until I started middle school, about three months after the accident.

I had spent the summer in the woods with Andy. It was difficult to suddenly be around so many other kids. In so many ways, I was different from the year before. I had started menstruating that summer. It felt like a hot weight in my pelvis, rooting me inside my body. I had put on weight that summer, too. In charge of my own diet, I ate mostly sugar, but also, sometimes, potato chips. I didn't notice that I'd become chubby until a boy at school called me thunder thighs. It upset me very much and I tried not to eat so I would lose the extra weight, but I couldn't stop eating. Andy told me not to worry about it, that it didn't matter what I looked like just then. He told me that he was my mirror and promised to remind me of my impossible beauty whenever I couldn't see it. I didn't understand.

"Look at that light," he said and pointed to the sun. I squinted at it.

"I can't," I said.

"Exactly," he said.

"I don't get it," I said.

"You are that inscrutable brightness hidden behind a mask, filtered through a mask. Behind the mask, you play a role and you get lost in that role. Whether the role be banal or magical, whether the mask be ugly or beautiful, whether either be perceived or not, the fact of the brightness remains." While he spoke, his eyes grew white and radiant, like moons. I didn't register the meaning of his words intellectually. I was eleven. Their impact, however, was felt. Something inside ached in immediate and spontaneous recognition.

34. Selenium (Nonmetal; Primordial; Solid)

"The left half of the human brain is associated with speech. The right half is associated with human emotion." It's Zeek speaking. June hears only a voice but sees nothing. The pain is gone. The air is neither hot nor cold. There is no sensation of weight nor of gravity. No support, nothing to be supported. No light.

"Where are we?" she asks.

"Open your seeing apparatus," he says. She searches for a way to do this, but there is no sense of eyes, closed or open.

"Tell me how," she says.

"Why do you think magic is an inevitable part of every human childhood?" he asks. June has no answer.

71

"Within the early phases of a human life there are devices inherent to its condition that allow it to transform the ordinary world into something magical. A twig becomes a wand. A leaf becomes its spontaneous creation. An inanimate rock speaks and is suddenly a witch. While the child enters into this world as playful, the characters referenced by the objects quickly seize the child and are real. Visceral fear takes shape in the gut of the child in response to the rock witch. The wand waves, stirring the air with the power of belief.

"The belief is a game. Indeed, the whole of life is an elaborate game. A festival of passing forms. The devices are from Truth. Play is from Truth. Everything that makes up the human life is from play. Language is derived from playing with sounds. All scientific data collected and analyzed for formulations of Truth are derived from curiosity—play."

As June listens, white shapes form like castles from sand. The shapes fill with color and dimension until she finds herself there: in a white room with no windows or doors, standing next to Zeek dressed all in white, facing a framed painting suspended mid-air before her. The painting is of herself, lying in a hospital bed attached to many strings, which are attached to something bigger beyond the frame. Her body is translucent, revealing bones and beating organs. The strings affix to many swollen structures inside her body, red and inflamed, from the top of her head to her ankles. The structures, she sees, are her pain. The strings are feeding the pain; they are conduits for pain.

"You are a chosen one," says Zeek. "We've given you this highest of roads. Your suffering will be powerful as you will be powerful, drastically transforming the lives of everyone who loves you—your constellation of peoples."

"You will play the game of belief in imagining the conspiracy of this constellation against you, but it will, in reality, be the helplessness and limitations of your physical self against you. You will play the game of belief in imagining that you are getting better and better over time, but you will, in reality, be getting ever worse. Your body will be your prison."

June stares at the painting and her puppet, pain-riddled form in it. "How will I do it?" she asks, unable to fathom existing for one mere minute in that form.

"Just as a baby chick knows instinctively to run for cover when a hawk passes over, your every reaction, moment by moment, will arise from the innate structures of your soul. You will simply find yourself motivated to respond appropriately from your condition to your situation. Without knowing why, you will be compelled to participate in the festival of passing forms. It will be as automatic as breathing."

"What about my family? My sisters, brothers, mom, dad?" June asks.

"Your constellation," Zeek says. Just then, the painting changes: the translucent puppet dissolves into light and falls away, farther out, bringing into view a scattering of other points of light around it, each connected to the other end of a string.

"My constellation," June repeats.

"It's the natural environment to which your constellation will innately come to terms. You are the key that will unlock their deepest inner resources, all. Just as a human baby is utterly helpless during the first years of its existence in the world, and its character is subject to the pressures and imprints of its constellation, so are you returning to your human life in a similarly helpless state, where instead, the individual characters of your constellation will be subject to the pressures and imprints of you."

June looks down to find her body and immediately buckles from the pain, held upright only by the strings. She opens her mouth to shout the word but her voice is gone. Her throat is parched, as though filled with dust motes, its surface like hard, cracked, earthen rock. Mom had taught us all sign language as babies, so she lifts one puppet arm to speak through its hand. *Scissors*, she signs.

Dear June

35. **Bromine** (Halogen, Primordial; Liquid)

Dear June,

I was sitting next to you on the plane on the way to Paris, watching you watching the TV monitor in the seatback, your pupils darting after the moving images, your face and hands twitching, and I felt so close to you. The usual vague fear and discomfort I feel in your presence yielded to an enigmatic, great tenderness toward you and nothing but. It reminded me of another time.

The memory of you in the hospital, still in a coma. You were in the halo brace to hold your broken neck in traction. It was a big, heavy, steel contraption comprised of a harness around your torso that connected to a metal ring around your head, affixed by four screws around your crown, through the skin, anchored in bone. Sometimes, movement and irritation would cause the screw holes to bleed a little and tiny lines of blood trickled down from your temples, making you resemble Frankenstein's Monster. There were arches shaved into your hairline where dark stubble grew and dried blood attached.

You were restless in your coma during the halo days. To avoid strapping you to a regular bed, the hospital gave you a bed like a padded cubicle, where you could move around and only hit the padded walls of the bed. Long, skinny tubes extended from your arms and abdomen, a thicker tube for breathing in your trachea, and attached to hanging pouches of varicolored liquids, like a matrix of web attached to filled egg sacs.

There was a long, slow, gradual awakening over the nine months that the doctors deemed you officially comatose. In the later months of that period, you started to communicate with sign language. You held up a shaky hand and made the sign for *scissors,* the two first fingers closed and open, closed and open, mimicking cutting. Your desire, I presumed, was to cut all the tubes and break free. Then, you began to fingerspell slowly, continually, so that I had to write down the letters your hand made and piece together what you were trying to tell me: T-Y-T-H-I-R-S-T-Y-T-H-I-R-S...

Thirsty. Of course you were. There had not been a single drop of liquid passed over your tongue in the better part of a year. You were not dehydrated. Your body received its nutrients, electrolytes and fluids through the tubes, but your mouth must have been cotton. The doctors were reluctant to try swallowing until the tracheal tube was out, which they decided not to remove until you were more aware, more communicative. Mom was able to talk them into letting her give you small amounts of ice chips. The pleasure on your face when she placed those bits of frozen water on your tongue was ecstatic. Then, the nurses brought us packages of little pink, mint-flavored sponges on a stick like lollipops, which we would dunk into cool, fresh water then swab around the inside of your mouth, cleaning out the collected mouth paste.

This time is the last I can remember feeling as close to you as I did on the plane. Back then, I would lie down beside you, wrap awkward arms around you with the halo brace and the tubes in the way, and sometimes, quietly, I would whisper back to you the same stories you had made up for me. There were many, many times like that during which I was never uncomfortable, never afraid.

On the plane, not wanting to let the moment pass, I leaned over and hugged you fiercely. I pushed my face into your neck and mumbled that I loved you. For a moment, I felt you resist and pull away. But soon, within a few seconds, your arms reached around me and you rested your face against my head. You made a sound. In it, I heard your old voice. The one before the accident. The drone of the airplane blared, drowning it out. I wanted to go back. I wanted to sit and patiently sponge your mouth and feed you bits of ice chips, play music and talk to you.

The drone of the airplane blared, drowning it out.

I don't know why I wrote this. More for myself than for you. Even though I will never let you read it, I believe there is some transmission of this sentiment happening on some higher energetic level between us, just by writing it. So I want to apologize for wishing you back into a coma, thirsty and begging for scissors. And I want to thank you for allowing that sudden embrace to happen.

Gratefully,

Your sister

This is a fertile and eruptive world

36. Krypton (Noble Gas; Primordial; Gas)

Paris, day two

Despite the slow pace, our second day in Paris had a lengthy agenda. As a prelude to the Eiffel Tower and a River Seine tour, we included a trip to Notre-Dame Cathedral. Approaching the place from across a wide courtyard, it appeared to grow in mass and complexity. Ornate spires reaching dramatically into the sky, flying buttresses in all their gothic glory, ogee arches adorned with figures too varied to discern from that distance. June's neck craned back farther the closer Lee rolled her. Mom gasped and Lee stopped every few feet to snap photos.

June's eyes were trained on something in particular, high on the building's façade. I followed her gaze to the spire that had a procession of figures either ascending or descending—perhaps saints. But above them was a figure even more striking, clinging to one of the spires—a half man, half beast, horned creature. I wasn't sure whether it disturbed or comforted me.

"June, what're you looking at?" I asked. Her response was mumbled and quiet. She didn't take her eyes off the spot that held her stare. I bent down to put my ear close to her mouth, but all I caught was, "…a piece of wing, the feathers soaking in the wailing… Zeek…"

"June, did you say Zeek?" She looked at me but didn't answer. Mom and Lee stopped and honed their attention, too. Zeek was a name she mentioned often when she was insane, unmedicated. It was a psych ward name, and we didn't like to hear it.

"What?" She asked, looking briefly puzzled before staring again at the cathedral, eyes roaming all over it this time. I shrugged at Mom and Lee and they shrugged back. We kept moving toward the entrance. There was a bit of a line spillage out into the courtyard, but it moved fast. Walking in was more like emerging out from somewhere than entering. It was somehow more spacious than the open sky. Sweet chamber chorus music pulled us deeper in among pillars larger than redwood trees; vaulted cathedral ceilings; glowing banks of lit candles; antique chandeliers; huge, well-worn tiles; and pale, lavender-colored stained-glass windows along the sides. Above the elaborate altar was a bright stained-glass window with angels and saints painted in blues, yellows, and reds designed into them. The walls were chunks of concrete like large, asymmetrical castle stone.

There were alcoves along the sides of the building with huge, tiered candleholders carrying a number of lit candles. There was a stand of unlit votives inviting us to take and light one for the spiritual benefit of someone in exchange for two Euros. June, to my surprise, took this very seriously.

"I want to light a candle for Jonas," she said. The simple and unexpected desire, and the altruism of it, touched me. Jonas was having surgery on his back for some chronic arthritic condition. It was unusual that she would think of him (or anyone else) at a time and place like this, and I wondered if it was twin telepathy, or the smallest moment of warmth. She was uncharacteristically deft with the candle—taking it, placing it, lighting it with another. I wondered about that other candle—for whose benefit it had been lit, and what would be made of that person's warmth touching Jonas's?

We walked on slowly. Under the chamber music, I swore I heard the flutter of wings—perhaps a pigeon stuck inside somewhere. I had a sense similar to nostalgia but not. Neither was it déjà-vu. It was like this place remembered me. Not in some ethereal sense of just any alleged holy space feeling welcoming, either. I mean those very same worn, stone walls, those mammoth plinths remembered me. They had seen me before, perhaps in some other form, and they were pleased at my return. The place forced its magnificence on me and gave me the feeling that I'd lost something. The rose stained glass took up my discomfort and made a sound like the fluttering of wings. June smiled

Outside, we walked in the direction of the Left Bank. There were performers on the bridge, dancers and jugglers, even human statues. But what took our collective attention over all these was an old man covered in pigeons. The birds perched everywhere, on his arms, in his lap, atop his balding head. He held his arms out with palms skyward, cupping birdseed. I rolled June closer and he began speaking to her in French.

June held out her arms and leaned forward. The old man turned her palms up, then pressed their centers to make her cup them. He poured birdseed from a glass jar into them and, at once, the birds came to gather along her arms and eat directly from her hands. Lee looked away and grimaced but June was elated. I took pictures from every angle, including one from the ground facing up with the cathedral in the background. In this last one, later, I spotted the man-beast on the spire high above June's head in the photo. It appeared to be watching her among all the people. And only her.

37. Rubidium (Alkaline Metal; Primordial; Solid)

Mrs. Frame called me into her office from homeroom one day with a note. I went to see her. She said she knew about June and wanted to support me, if I wanted and needed any. If she'd been anyone else, I would have walked out, maybe after spitting on her floor just to look mean and tough. But there was something about her. The attention she gave simultaneously quelled me and ignited a hunger for more of it. I wanted to tell her things I'd never told anyone. I told her that I drank and smoked. I told her about Andy.

"Shock affects people differently," she said. I was sitting on the overstuffed chair in her office, studying her reaction. But she had no reaction. She didn't shame me or tell me that I was crazy or bad. She just listened to everything I told her and gave me reasons why it was okay, why I was okay.

I spent that sixth-grade year as the worst kind of outcast. Kids teased me and made fun of me, and it wasn't long before even the nerdy kids wouldn't be my friends. The cafeteria was a dreaded place after the first few weeks of school because I kept getting kicked off tables. The tables were clearly organized in groups of kids by level of popularity. There were the most popular tables along the left, the mid-level popularity tables along the right, and a spattering of unpopular kids arranged around tables down the middle. I started out the year on the right, moving down a table every couple days when I was either told that I wasn't welcome, or when all the empty seats would be "saved" with articles of clothing or book bags and there was suddenly no room for me. I sat among some of the middle tables for a few days, but felt like kids from my former tables were laughing at me. I started eating my lunch in Mrs. Frame's office after that. Or, on days she wasn't around, I ate my lunch in the hall by my locker.

During these lunches in the hall, Andy would write me letters. It would be my hand doing the work, holding the pen, but his voice in my head and his words on the page. The handwriting even looked different. Sometimes, he drew pictures, little diagrams to illustrate how the world worked, who I was, who he was, where we all belonged.

"If you took away judgments and labels, what would be left? Only what is. The physical world is just an expression of the unseen forces behind it. This is a fertile and eruptive world. Just like you learned in your Earth Science class, for two billion years, the Earth spewed molten rock that woke the world in to being, into expression. Volcanoes vented the gasses that formed the atmosphere and the oceans. Your body could not exist without them. If not for the fire under the surface, the Earth would be a barren geoid. Volcanoes build mountains and create new land. They recycle life-giving minerals. Most atoms in your body were once inside the earth. Volcanoes brought them to the surface."

When I asked him what he meant, he said, "Don't you see it? Destruction and creation are the same energy. They are one infinite round."

I wondered about that. What was creation if it was also destruction? Was that what people mean when they said 'God?'

"Is God real?" I asked him, sitting in the hall, writing in the notebook we used. I poised the pen beneath those words to write his answer, but resisted what he wanted to write. Finally, I gave in.

"Yes."

"Well what the hell is it?" I wrote, feeling angry and not understanding why.

"What you think of as God, what people call God is not something that can be articulated, but it can be approximated by calling it everything, the organizing principle of everything, and the intelligence that presides over that organization."

"What are you?" I asked next.

He told me he had lived a life like mine, only he had been a boy who died of heart disease. He had had a little sister in that life, and he said I reminded him of her. He said several times that he would protect me and not let anything hurt me. I asked him why he didn't do that for June. He told me June had her own attendants and that her accident was probably carved in. I didn't know what that meant, so he explained.

38. Strontium (Alkaline Earth Metal; Primordial; Solid)

He said that as time progresses, it unfolds before us like a roll of carpet, and folds up behind us like the same carpet rolling up. In this sense, all of time, all that a life contains is all right here, right now. He then drew a picture of a stick person standing on a scroll-like structure— the scroll on its left, he marked "past," the scroll on its right, he marked "future," and the whole thing he marked, "now."

As it unfolds, he said, we decorate it beneath our feet. We decorate it with our choices and those can be anything. There are no good or bad choices, only patterns and images that emerge, whether pleasing or not. Sometimes, though, there are images already there—pictures already built into the life unfolding. These were the things commonly referred to as fated, only he didn't agree with that concept completely. Because, he explained, the images could be altered, whether built-in or not. To think of something unpleasant (or, pleasant, for that matter) as fated is to think of a situation as hopeless or fixed. Nothing, Andy asserted, is fixed. The built-in parts are, in a sense, planned, but also malleable, and always useful.

Not knowing what to make of most of what Andy said caused me to grow bored and annoyed with his words. As the school year bore on, I wanted normal friends. Toward this end, I sought to befriend the only other outcast in the sixth grade that year: Becca. She was a fighter, a troublemaker. She was feared and therefore respected. There was probably no lunch table she couldn't sit at. I began intercepting her in the parking lot before school where she would be smoking cigarettes. One such day, I learned that she hated home economics class. One of the required supplies was a pincushion, which I had brought with me. "How the fuck they gonna teach me to sew? Me! Pin cushion, my ass." I gave her mine, telling her I would simply steal another one. To that, she snickered and flashed me a look that I swore held something like admiration.

During my hallway lunch hour that day, instead of letter-writing from Andy, I went into the darkened home economics classroom. The bins were along one wall of the classroom and they contained personal property of students. Namely, supplies required for home economics. Quietly, I crossed over to them and rummaged through the various student bins until I found a pincushion to steal. While doing so, I kept looking over my shoulder with the sensation of being watched. Assuming Andy was there and imagining some sense of disapproval from him, I told him in my thoughts to fuck off and leave me alone.

I can't leave you alone. I'm always with you. But I'm not saying anything. You have a conscious and I'm not it. I have no opinion, pro or con, about your actions right now.

The words came as thoughts and I began to feel schizophrenic as well as miserable and friendless. Somehow, his unconditionally approving presence was irritating. I thought: Oh yeah? No opinion? Really? And as a sort of test, I produced a lighter from my back pocket and held the flame to one of the plastic covers over one of the sewing machines. It melted away on contact, dissolving into a curled black and releasing a terrible chemical burn smell. I continued burning plastic covers throughout the room until all the sewing machines were exposed. Then, strictly for oomph, I knocked some books off shelves, letting them lay fanned and bent on the floor. Andy said nothing.

I walked out, turning at the doorway to survey my damage. There was a single, heavily used book among the floor-strewn batch whose spine had snapped. It was twisted at the break so that one half faced down and the other, guts up. The small black words on the dented page jittered and jumped like fleas.

39. Yttrium (Transition Metal; Primordial; Solid)

I bend down to loosen the laces on my boot, relieve a blister on my ankle when "You Can't Hide Your Lying Eyes" comes on by the Eagles. My mind leaps, not to the time its tune distinguishes for me, long ago when an invisible sort of blister took form on my body, but to a night two or three years after that.

You were fifteen years old, maybe sixteen, sitting on the couch, very high, attempting to watch television and eat pretzels. The picture would periodically freeze and rise, the whole of your vision stilled suddenly like a snapshot that tugged free and floated, shrinking as it lifted, like a slowly deflating balloon. Behind and around it, everything progressed as usual: the moving, flashing pictures on the screen, the flickering light bulb in the lamp to the left, the dog licking herself on the floor in June's lap. The strobe quality to the light and the dog licking without the apparent notice of June, her eyes locked on the television screen, hunched, slack-mouthed. All of it advancing unbroken as the snapshot of just moments before kept rising up to the top left corner of your periphery before dissolving with a fizzling, hissing sound. Almost immediately after it disappeared, another snapshot, then the shrinking and rising again. As for the pretzels, they were turning to sand between your teeth. Your tongue felt swollen and dry, filmy inside your parched mouth, like clammy cotton. The sensation of taste was altogether missing, leaving a terrible numbness. Earlier that evening, you had smoked weed with Jason. Only later you realized he had laced the joint with LSD. You had smoked weed several times before then, but never with such dramatic results. You were sitting in his living room in the dark watching Disney's *Fantasia*. "This is amazing when you're stoned," he said, pulling the joint suddenly from behind his ear, as though it had grown there beneath his fuzzy black hair, magically produced by the oils of his scalp. Had you not been slightly drunk, you might never have put the foul little thing to your lips, but as you were, you wanted to see what more would happen to the swirling, dancing colors and contorted funhouse figures through the murky lens of marijuana. You watched him light it and inhale deeply. He squinted, puffed out his cheeks, and with his rather bulbous nose, suddenly resembled a grotesque clown face. He passed it to you and you welcomed the sweet smolder into your lungs. You looked at Jason. He was smiling at you, his face changed again, glowing somehow with perfect, shimmering skin. Without warning and before your eyes, his faced altered—it morphed from his familiar, average self into a gorgeous man with sea-blue eyes. You gaped as this new stranger pulled with perfect lips on the joint and passed it back to you. You inhaled, held the smoke, and watched as the face changed again, seamlessly shaping itself this time into a beautiful woman with a pink, plush mouth, smiling slightly to reveal beckoning, gleaming teeth. The glow from the TV screen danced on her flawless face in soft, red tones like bonfire light. She was irresistible. You fit your mouth against hers and kissed her deeply, tasting his tangy, slightly rotten flavor, which took you back (for the first time since) to the night you had heard that song.

Thirteen years old—Jason, his friend, and you playing Super Mario Brothers in the basement of his friend's house, The Eagles on the stereo. Once you remembered it as 12, but the drinks you had that night are fewer now, ten or nine glasses of Absolut with Kool-Aid. You passed out in the middle of climbing the stairs on your way to the bathroom. There are scraps of what you remember after that. You remember your shirt being pulled off as you fell back on the floor, Jason's tangy, spoiled taste in your mouth, something solid pressing into you while someone was standing on your hands, as though to make certain your body lie where it was. Not floating or rising or going home. They took turns and you left your body anyway, watching from above a little lifeless girl on the floor get fucked and fucked and fucked.

When you woke the next morning, your ring was smashed so flat it turned your finger blue and your body ached everywhere. Your mind clamped down then, closed like a vice pinching the previous night off from existence. But instead of disappearing like it was supposed to, it grew new skin, filled full, trapping that memory and that music inside like pus, where they would burn and bulge and not escape. You spent those next two or three years around Jason as if nothing ever happened, until that night when an acid-induced hallucination led to a kiss whose taste triggered the heretofore sealed off memory, rubbed against it like the tough leather edge of a boot, broke it open, numbed your mouth like a scald.

The cold music presses the air like a face to glass and I loosen my laces, push down my sock to reveal smooth, unmarred skin. The phantom blister throbs. I stand up and walk out, switching off the music.

I am beaming the knowledge
into you.
I am beaming you
all of my knowledge

40. Zirconium (Transition Metal; Primordial; Solid)

Paris, day two

We went next to the Eiffel Tower. The line was long and we didn't have time, but it was what June wanted. As we approached the end of the line, a worker from the entrance gate waved us forward and let us in through a side opening in the gate, allowing us to bypass the others. He smiled at June and said, "Bonjour!" then rattled off a bunch more words in French none of us understood. Mom asked how much the tickets were, trying it in French with the help of her phrasebook, but the short, curly-haired Eiffel Tower man shook his head in response and took us directly to the elevator. I felt a little guilty cutting in front of everyone, but not enough to refuse.

We took the elevator to the lowermost level and wheeled June around the perimeter. In the souvenir shop, I watched the clerk watch June check the prices on each item she picked up then set back down. As soon as we left the store, he followed and handed June a free Eiffel Tower keychain, which she loved. Although their actions were beneficial, it sometimes upset June that they paid attention to her at all, but this depended on her mood. She wanted to blend in, but what she didn't know is that she'd also grown used to the extra attention. She craved that attention sometimes even more than she felt shame about her disability, so she graciously accepted it in whatever form it appeared.

June wanted to look over the edge, so I helped her out of her chair. Mom and Lee hung back, afraid of heights. June took a few wobbly steps to the precipice and looked down. I did the same beside her. The first level was much higher than it appeared from the ground. Looking down, the people looked like a colony of insects gathered around a few grains of sugar. I told June that and she laughed. Her hair was blowing across her face and into her mouth. I reached out and tucked it behind her ear only for it to blow straight across again. I put my arm around her and we huddled against the wind. Distant sounds of Paris reached us like breath, like the city exhaling in the gloaming. Frayed clouds lit pink from the setting sun took on predatory shapes.

"Don't the clouds look like raptors and pterodactyls?" I asked her. She didn't answer or react in any way. Maybe she didn't hear me—perhaps I was on her deaf side.

"June," I said, and squeezed her in the loop of my arm.

"Mmm?" She said.

"I have to ask you something about earlier," I said. The din behind us and the throaty voice of the city's noises crowded into the silence that followed. We looked at one another. With our faces so close, I noticed something stuck in her teeth. She had the attention of a child waiting to hear something exciting.

"Remember at the cathedral when you said something about Zeek?" I asked, loudly enough that she would hear me but not so loud that Lee or Mom would hear from where they were, about twenty feet away, seated on a bench.

"Yeah," she said, which surprised me. I hadn't expected that she'd been aware she was even saying it at the time.

"What about him? What were you saying?" I asked.

"I just remembered something," she said and looked over the railing again at the insect people.

"What's that?" I asked. She didn't answer. Her mouth was turned down, twitching slightly, her hair across her eyes.

"June."

She looked at me.

"What did you remember about Zeek?" Something fluttered in my gut. I glanced back at Mom and Lee. I wasn't supposed to encourage talk of Zeek. We were supposed to reinforce, if ever she spoke the name, that he wasn't real, that he was from a dream she had while in a coma. Maybe it was this proximity—the closeness of our faces and the distance from the world below—that allowed me to step boldly over the assumed boundary. Something about the negative space stalled and interrupted my caution, even with clear memories of the psych-ward nonversations of yore; between us in that moment, there was a geometry prying dark things wide, a provisional contiguous fuse where anything goes.

"The more I cried, the more his wings got wet with the tears," she said. "I was on his back and by the time we got there, his wings were soaking, dripping tears." Her voice was strangely steady.

"By the time you got where?"

"Wherever he was taking me. I don't know," she said. I thought hard about that. Had she told me where before? Did I remember mention of a white room? The narrative of June's coma sublife is a riddle whose every word and every word's position with and against every other word holds a clue, each one aching to be found, to mean something.

"What made you think of Zeek at all?" My pulse beat in my temples.

"That thing on the church reminded me of him," she said.

"Is that what he looked like?" I asked.

"I don't know," she said. "I have to go to the bathroom." With that, she grabbed my forearm and I helped her back to the chair. My heart hammered. I was anxious and shaky with rule-breaking fervor.

41. Niobium (Transition Metal; Primordial; Solid)

I was fifteen. It had been four years since her accident. She spent almost a year in a coma and over three years in hospitals. I had spent those years expressing my pain in little explosions—stealing from stores and from other people, getting into fights, starting fires at school (this turned into an ordeal with police detectives searching lockers to find the arsonist, so mysterious and famous by then that the really bad kids in school, the ones who made a career of bad, turned themselves in to claim the credit), bullying girls I had crushes on, sneaking beers from the refrigerator, sneaking bourbon from the bottle—I never found relief. June had been home from the hospital only a matter of months, going to high school again part-time in a wheelchair. Mom usually stayed home with her but in the summer had to go back to work.

She propositioned me: instead of getting a summer job, would I stay home with June? It would keep me out of trouble and someone needed to watch her because she was crazy: delusional, paranoid, severely depressed, even homicidal. The brain injury caused chemical imbalances. That's what they told us, but which chemicals and at what level of deficiency or excess, they did not know. They had to experiment with different patches, pills, and potions in hopes of eventually stumbling upon the right combination of medications to stabilize her.

I was to stay with her all summer, but in the end it lasted seven days. Seven days that felt like seven summers. The first day, she kept standing up from her wheelchair, dressed in a pink sweatshirt that read: *I've been rotated* (from the rotating bed she had in step-down ICU that would stimulate her senses and facilitate circulation), balancing on unsteady legs, hips swaying and thrusting like a hula dancer, throwing her shaky arms straight up. Her mouth open, eyes closed, face upturned, she hummed and groaned.

I stood helplessly at her side, holding her steady, trying to pull down her arms, grabbing the wheelchair so it would not roll away, asking her to sit down, telling her how she could fall. Eventually she turned, glared at me, attempted to leap away, then fell and hissed "owww." She fought me when I tried to help her. "Devil! Bitch! Whore! Devil!" she shrieked, grabbing me, pulling my hair, clawing my face, my arms, punching me. Her brain damage had somehow granted her surprising power in her arms, something we had noticed in the hospital when she bent the first steel neck brace they put on her in half with one hand while in a coma, which was when they had to put her in the halo brace.

Her blows came down with such force, I had to curl up in the tornado pose until she wound down, giving her only my back and clasped hands behind my head to batter and scratch.

On the second day, there was more of the same, as well as some new behaviors, including pouring a glass of water on me so I would melt, refusing to eat what I would fix for her because it was poisoned, talking quietly as though conversing with someone secretively and it was just us in the house "June, who are you talking to?" I asked. She screwed up her face at me and answered: "I'm talking to Zeek, it's none of your business!" Her voice was a high, breathy monotone, her words slow and slurred.

"There's nobody here, June. We are the only ones here right now." She looked beside her on the couch and was shocked, then angry, then sad. She burst into her version of crying, a warped expression and a howl without any tears. Somehow the brain damage had caused her tear ducts not to work; she had not cried a drop since the accident.

"Why are you doing this to me?" she moaned, picking up whatever was in reach and hurling it. I ducked, dodged, and ran out of the room.

42. Molybdenum (Transition Metal; Primordial; Solid)

On days three, four, and five, she tried climbing out of her second-story bedroom window, the same bedroom we used to share, the same moonlit window. She yelled, whispered, and sang things to Zeek, her friend whom she had met while she was in a coma, who was going to come and take her away from the hellfire she was burning in at home. She really did feel her skin burning sometimes and would think she was on fire, and would crash to the floor and roll and roll. Zeek, she said, would save her. He was going to grant her special powers, like a god, and she was going to punish me with them.

The worst was when she lost control of her bowels without warning, the yellow-brown liquid seeping through her jeans, the stench, the agonizing minutes of wiping and washing that followed. The mere suggestion of an adult diaper back then made her face twist into the crying expression and brought on a long, deep depression.

Day six, I coaxed her outside with me. I thought the sunshine and the heat of the summer would help us both, and for a while it did. I fetched lawn chairs from the garage and set them up in the side yard. June lounged peacefully. I listened to my headphones and soaked in the sun, closed my eyes, relaxed. The physical and deep emotional exhaustion of the week had caught up with me. I slipped into a light sleep, just to rest my eyes. When I opened them, June was gone. I ran in the house and looked everywhere, calling then screaming her name. Her wheelchair sat where I had left it. Her walker had been with us outside and had vanished. I ran the streets of the neighborhood bare foot in my black Speedo bathing suit, my skinny, downy legs shaking, my frizzy hair puffed up and flying away, calling her name, indifferent to the strange looks I received, feeling my chest cave in from worry. I rounded the corner to the dirt road that led to the park and the field, saw the walker and June, her unsteady silhouette taking a few lopsided steps, falling, struggling back to her feet, and falling again. The sight made me weep. Aggravated, I wiped the tears away. She had scrapes on her hands and face and dark, moist, grass stains on her knees. I took the walker to her, pleaded with her to come home. She smiled warmly at me and for once, offered no resistance. Slowly and silently we made our way home together.

43. Technetium (Transition Metal; Natural Radio; Solid)

Each night I went to bed exhausted but could not sleep. I tried counting breaths, bottles of beer on the wall, sheep. Sometimes drinking a stolen can of beer or two was the only thing that worked. If I dared recall one of June's old bedtime stories, I would hiccup-sob or feel sick and empty. Mornings were the worst. Waking up, opening my eyes to those lovely June days, I would almost want to smile at the bright windows until the knowledge of facing the phantom of my sister again cast its shadow over the yellow summer sun.

On day seven, she had wild, panicked eyes because our mom was the devil, because aliens were coming to take June away in the night, because I was in on it. I was sitting on the couch in the living room and she was sitting on the floor. She looked up at me and narrowed her eyes. "What did you do with the babies?" she asked. My stomach hollowed, my skin shrunk, I started to sweat. Not again, I thought.

"June, there are no babies, what are you talking about?" I said weakly.

She narrowed her eyes at me. "You're with them," she said.

"June, I'm your sister, you know me, I'm not with anyone, I'm with you," I said. I felt weary. Very sad. Her eyes grew wide.

"You're with me!" she said, wide-eyed. "You're the one, the only other one," she said, in that ecstatic, wavering voice. I didn't respond. She made her way to the couch and climbed up next to me. She took one of my hands in hers and held it palm up. Her hands were shaking, always shaking. Her feral eyes danced, darting from one of my eyes to the other so rapidly it made me dizzy. I felt a sickening wave of bristled cold break out over my arms and back; my mouth was dry, my throat clenched. I couldn't swallow. I could hardly breathe. She pressed her index finger into my palm, leaned her head back and closed her eyes. I pulled away but she was very strong and she would not let me go.

"June, what are you doing?" My voice cracked, I might have been crying. She did not let go, did not move or open her eyes.

She said: "I am beaming the knowledge into you. I am beaming you all of my knowledge."

A soft static started quietly in my head along with her words and grew louder each second. I could feel her heartbeat in my palm and my whole body vibrated and twisted like my insides were in a blender on pulse, the rhythm in time with her incessantly beating heart. A balloon was inflating in my chest threatening to explode, the static getting louder and louder. I realized I was crazy, too, that slowly I had been going insane along with her, and now I was just as crazy as she was.

I tore my hand away and leapt up. I ran for the door without a word, almost tore the doorknob from the wood in my ferocity, burst through the screen door. I might have been screaming or maybe it was just the noise in my head, and I ran. I did not stop until it felt like my sides would rip open and all my ribs would crack and shatter and my lungs would explode.

Eventually, I made my way back but did not go home. I went to the neighbor's house. The woman who lived there had been one of June's nurses in the ICU when she first got to Highland Hospital. She answered the door, and deep lines of concern creased her face; a head of black, curly hair framed big, roomy eyes, welcoming. She let me in. I sat on her couch. She asked me to talk about it. I cried. No, sobbed. Gasped and rocked and shook. She held me until I was weak and empty. I don't think I ever said a thing. By the time I arrived home, hours had passed and June was gone. I looked around for a while and eventually found a note by the phone from my dad:

We are at the hospital. June tried to kill herself. She took a bottle of pills. Where were you?

I read the note and read it again. I lifted it from the counter and read it again. I buried it in my pocket and ran upstairs to my room where I had three cans of beer hidden in my closet. I guzzled all three of them down so fast that some dribbled over my chin onto the front of my shirt. When I finished one, I crushed it with my hand, threw it down, and opened the next. When all three were gone, I sat back and waited for an effect.

A wave of nausea hit me. I bolted for the bathroom. I vomited forcefully into the toilet, the water splashed up at me, and it went on and on, all of my insides were coming out with violence, my blood and my guts and my veins and my heart spilling out into the toilet, slopping and splashing red and brown onto the white seat and the collar of my white t-shirt. When I was finally empty, a rawness in my guts the only feeling left, I crawled to my bed, lay face down on the mattress, my head buried under the pillow, and pulled the covers tightly over me until there was nothing but blackness.

It was to be my first of two very brief, very failed marriages

44. **Ruthenium** (Transition Metal; Primordial; Solid)

I wooed her in high school with, I'll admit, June's help. I noticed her in choir—she was an alto and I, a soprano. I watched her on the opposite side of the risers every day in school and thought up ways to approach her, ways I might hook her interest. My interest in her was a phenomenon. She had black, curly hair, brown eyes, and white, white teeth—features shared by many whom I never noticed twice. It wasn't her appearance, yet I was inexplicably drawn to her. There was a poem I wrote. It was an amateur rhyme that put an optimistic spin on the tragedy of my sister's accident. I would give it to her. I would ask what she thought of it.

In the hall after choir let out, I caught up with her. I hadn't thought of an ice-breaker, so I uttered the first thought to arise: "Has anyone ever told you that you look like the Slim Fast girl?" It was a veiled compliment. The woman on the frequently broadcasted Slim Fast commercials was beautiful with long black curls and dark eyes with long eyelashes. She laughed and her head fell back. I was close enough to smell her shampoo and the feeling it produced was altogether new—a melting ache in my groin. I introduced myself. She told me her name, Cassiopeia, and that people called her Cassie. I decided not to conform to what people called her but to call her by her full name, which I thought was beautiful, and which I would repeat to myself silently or aloud hundreds of times for the remainder of that day.

I pulled a folded piece of paper from my back pocket and handed it to her. I hadn't planned a way to initiate it either, so I said, simply: "Here's a poem that I wrote." She received it graciously. She looked honored, even. We parted ways. She went to her advanced English class and I went to my average English class. I was a year behind her in school. She was a senior. I was a junior.

I sat in class unable to think about anything other than her. After class, I intercepted her again in the hall.

"How was your class?" I asked.

"It was interesting. We discussed the Western literary canon," she said. My pulse instantly turned rapid, boisterous. I felt light headed and shaky. I had read many of my grandfather's books, some of which were canonical. Already, we were connected.

"Speaking of great literature," she said. I stopped breathing and looked at the floor directly in front of my feet.

"That poem was beautiful and brave. You're an amazing writer," she said. I lifted my head and looked at her. Huge, brown eyes stared into me. Her mouth was only slightly open, its shape and the flash of white teeth commanded my gaze. I looked back up to her eyes. We were stopped in the hall, kids were bumping by us. I felt terrified and intoxicated.

"What's your number?" I asked. She uttered four digits that made themselves a home in my permanent memory bank instantly: 3223. Back then it was a small town, so the first three digits were the same for everyone. She walked into her next class just as the bell rang. I turned and walked to my class, but some real part of me stayed frozen there, staring after her, forever.

45. Rhodium (Transition metal; Primordial; Solid)

I called her that weekend and we went to a coffee shop together. Seven or eight years later, I sat at the same coffee shop, our coffee shop, the place it all started, waiting for her to arrive. In the beginning, we would go there and order steamed milk and sit for hours, long after our drinks were gone, long after we had anything left to talk about, as if staring at each other was a usual thing for teenage girls who are friends. It had been three or four years since I'd seen or spoken to her. I brought her a large box full of every letter she ever wrote me, and hardcover journals with ink illustrations of ornate roses, decorations and lettering that made them look like books, which she gave to me after adding her signature to the covers. For years, everywhere I had gone, every apartment I had inhabited held that box in its closet.

I was meeting her again to say goodbye before I moved to Chicago. I was giving her the box to punish her for marrying *him*. The nice Greek boy her parents liked. The one she left me for. The one she was never in love with. I had taken a brief note to her parent's dry cleaners where she used to work every day. It was the only place I knew to look for her. When I walked through the door of that place, I nearly fainted—the last time I smelled that air, I was in the back on that shabby couch in the dark, having my pants pulled off by the most perfect Greek girl ever born. I left the note. A bulge of the worst kind of emotional pain and fear lodged in my throat when a week later, she called. I asked her to meet me there. In disbelief, I listened to her tell me that she would.

And there I sat, still choking on that bulge. I had tried for years to forget her. I had tried to see it as finished, over, unchangeable and irrelevant to where I was going. I had tried not to carry it around with me, the box, but its contents were necessary. Without it, I felt I would not be real. Without it, I would have to lose hope that she was coming back someday. The hope that she would return to me kept its head low and stayed quiet, but stayed strong. Sometimes, I didn't even know it was there. When I heard from a friend that she had married him, it reeled up as though slammed by machine-gun fire and died a horrible, bullet-bludgeoned, bloody death. I was shocked at the pain, horrified both to have had the hope and to have lost it.

I should not have harbored that hope because, like her, I, too, was getting married. It was to be my first of two very brief, very failed marriages. I didn't know that at the time. At the time, I was filled with the confident assurance of a twenty-five-year-old about to get married. Even then, though, when I stepped back from that life and regarded it more objectively, I found doubt. She was the answer to every question involving that doubt.

She arrived and sat down across from me. She had stopped at the counter on the way in and ordered something hot to drink. The chair scraped with her shifting weight. It seemed to scrape the inside of my gut. She was wrapping the steaming mug with her familiar hands—hands with which I could not help but to associate my own salvation. She was even more beautiful than I had remembered. The black curls were pulled into a loose gathering at the back of her neck, the precise spot I once kissed with worshipful mettle. Her eyes and her mouth were symbols representing impossible promises we had made. They represented the inherent lies in those and in all promises. They were the death of those promises—intensely beautiful corpses.

46. **Palladium** (Transition Metal; Primordial; Solid)

"Thank you for coming," I said. She looked at me without smiling. She looked at the bag near my feet. The two stuffed bunnies she had made me, both girls, were poking their heads out the top of it. Her eyes had always been revealing of everything and that hadn't changed. I saw the ache. It pleased me.

"Why did you come?" I asked. She looked at me.

"You said you were leaving," she said. I smiled and she smiled.

"I am. I'm moving to Chicago," I said. The smiles subsided and we stared, expressionless at each other. When she graduated high school a year ahead of me, she went to the local state college (instead of the better, farther away school she's been accepted to) because she didn't want to leave me. When I graduated a year later, I went to the same local state school because I didn't want to leave her. (I had passed up a full scholarship to a university in Florida for swimming.) We both received sub-par undergraduate educations because we had loved each other too much. Sitting there then, across from her at that timeless coffee shop, it was clear that it was still too much. Also, not enough. It would never be enough.

"Why did you marry him?" I asked. She scowled and looked down at her mug. She touched her wedding ring. A long silence passed before she spoke. I thought about her husband. He was a chubby Greek boy with yellow teeth who sat next to us in our first-year Biology lecture. She had known him from church. He had had a crush on her. We had made fun of him.

"A few days before my wedding, I was trying on a dress in the basement of this wedding dress store. I stood in front of a mirror and saw myself in this dress with my sisters and my mom around me. They all looked so pleased, so proud. I just burst out crying. They all thought it was because I was happy." She kept her eyes on her mug, still absently touching and twirling the ring. Her eyes glistened.

I looked down at the open journal in front of me. I had written a poem about her, and the unintended searching I had done in the years since losing her. Searching for her. Everywhere and in everyone. I read it to her because I didn't know what else to do. Reading it felt like cutting myself.

"It's beautiful," she said. Her eyes were wet. I waited for more and when nothing more came I fished for what I wanted.

"Do you feel that way, too?" She blinked and looked at the table. She looked at me with something like resolve.

"I don't have an answer for you," she said. I stared at her.

"I don't know what you want me to say," she said.

"You started dating him and tried to pretend like we were just friends and had always only been friends. You didn't even acknowledge that we had been lovers for nearly three years," I said. Her face hardened. Defensiveness rose in her eyes.

"I've always been afraid of everything. You've never been afraid of anything," she said. It was true. I felt it breaking the bones of my hope's dead body. In that instant, I decided to let it all go. I had learned a valuable lesson, I thought. I had no way of knowing then, at twenty-five, that I would repeat this relationship with another woman six years later. She would be a married woman having an affair with me. She would not love her husband, she would love me, and she would not leave her husband for me. She would tell me how big her fear was.

I stood up from the table and pushed the bag of us toward her with my foot. She glanced at it again and frowned. She didn't ask what was in it; the bunnies poking out the top was evidence enough. She looked up at me and I wanted to walk away, but I wasn't satisfied.

"Did it even break your heart?" I asked. She winced and began crying immediately. She picked up the bag and stood up, saying, "You just want to hurt me." She walked out. I followed her, cursing myself. She was right. Was that what I wanted? I followed her to her car and asked her to wait. She put the bag I gave her in her back seat and turned to me, tears streaking her cheeks. I looked at her and said nothing, feeling the sad apology on my face. She softened, just to see it. I wanted to touch her but hesitated at its obvious inappropriateness. Then, I didn't care.

I hugged her hard, squeezed my arms around her waist. I felt her arms circle my shoulders, her hands on my back, trailing down like a garment sliding, draping my body closely, meldingly—a perfect garment that deciphers, spells the figure within. I worried I would cry. People walked by us in the parking lot and I imagined their perspective, the sight of us—two entities unrelated, mere, bare acquaintances, like a pair of subway riders jumbled together by chance, their accidental proximity, even intimacy, serving no greater purpose than to accentuate their separateness. This objectivity helped me to pull it together and move away from her, detached and unobligated, declaring in a single motion that I would never touch her again.

In the midst of this, as our faces passed closely, she turned her head and brushed her lips against my cheek, as gently as if touching it with a feather. If my cheek were a soap bubble, it would not have burst.

47. Silver (Transition Metal; Primordial; Solid)

In which I became a whale

I was just a shored whale, deflated and bleeding into driftwood and dead fish, suffocating above the surface. The tower appeared as a hallucination, a product of my delirium. It must have been. Its walls were dense and smoky, its windows covered with mirrors. At first I ignored it, expecting it to poof and disappear at any moment, focusing instead on the gulls crowding the shore and their buffet of dead fish. Their stiff-legged, archaic prancing, their bobbing heads. I watched their perverse pleasure as they filled themselves on soft flesh, its glistening decay caught like bits of murder on their beaks.

But the smoke tower loomed, and in its mirrors an image emerged. She watched me from behind a veil and I wondered about her while I lay there, crying whale tears. When the image floated down to me, the death buffet crept off, trailing shadows, away. The image was taking shape—her shape was familiar and unutterably beautiful. It was the shape of a girl from a fairytale, a tragedy, singing out sweet stories in the night.

The image came just in time. The bleeding stopped. I struggled to breathe again and at night, stole the image from her mirror and with her, slipped beneath the surface. Underwater, she was a bright shadow, a spray of light, flitting and converging around me like so many diamonds. I wanted her to be real again, so I swam her to other worlds, whale worlds, and she rode hard on my fins.

When light broke above the surface, the image grew nervous, anxious for her mirror. So I lifted her toward the thick sky and broke the surface, soared for a bit in the white foam rain, then dove, a quake of waves exploding around my immoderate size. "Keep quiet, we might be seen." So I kept quiet. The image returned by day to the mirrors and by night to me.

I tore currents through the sea, a physical sinew gaining in momentum, gaining in sovereignty. I floated together with the image, a sea drift, endlessly rocking in the light. There was no piece of her uninteresting to me, no single inch to go unexplored.

Now I'm on the beach at night, sipping alone the world below the brine, just to stay alive. Wearied, wavering, the image stays in her mirror, safe in her smoke tower, where she can be whatever everyone wants, a reflection of so many false faces. I long to smash the mirrors and let out the whale, dive down and swim hard, stay fin to fin in boundless depths.

But it's not for me to break. I have no fists. I have blood and size and whale tears. I have a belly full of fish and salt. I have scars from where I've been torn open and healed over.

I have the early moon to light my own reflection on the water.

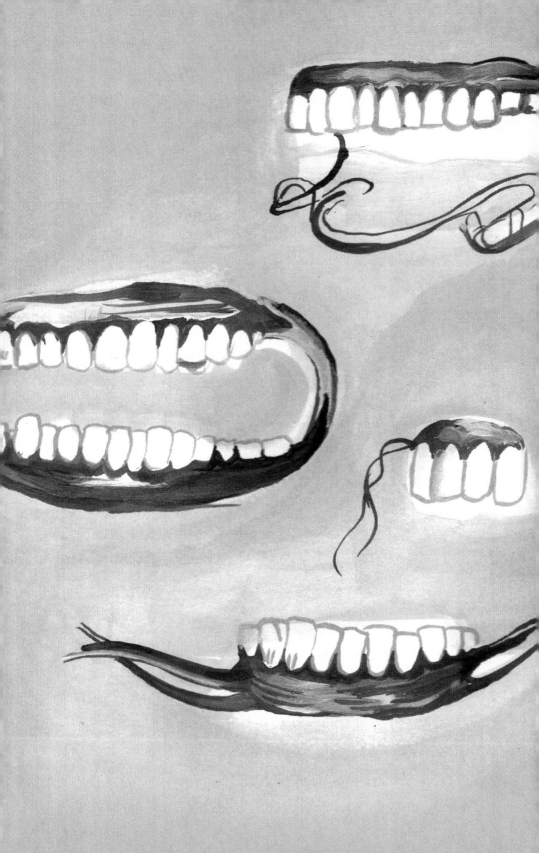

Conversations were like footnotes to
the footnotes of our existence

48. **Cadmium** (Transition Metal; Primordial; Solid)

Paris, day two

By the time we finished with the bathroom and waited in line for the elevator back down, the sun had sunk into its famously unfamiliar place leaving over dark, making way for those voracious clouds to go ahead and rain. The last task of the day was to take June on a Seine River boat tour. At the ticket stand, fat drops slapping our faces, we learned that the last tour of the day was pushing off in ten minutes from a dock that seemed too far away.

Feebly opening umbrellas, woefully unequipped, we set out at a trot toward the dock. The rain, of course, picked up and turned torrential. The clouds had found their prey and we were it; soaked along with the wood and stone, we were shuttled across in the sudden dead weight of our clothes and non-waterproof shoes.

Running with an umbrella valiantly poised against the sideways driving rain, positioned over June and our hunched heads (Lee and I were pushing the chair together for greater speed), a crosswind picked it up and turned it inside out, which would have made me officially grumpy had there not been a huge grin on June's face. What would make this worth it more than that alone? To not miss that boat. Alas, as we moved as quickly as we could but still too slowly, we watched the bridge to the boat retract. A noise characteristic of a huge ship breaking away from a dock began to roar up.

"No! Wait!" We all called, straight hauling ass by this point, barreling forward downhill with reckless disregard of the chair's faulty braking system. I'm not sure who started laughing first but it caught like hay under a magnifying glass in the sun and we were all limping and nearly falling from the bent doubled mirth by which we were suddenly possessed. They saw us, or perhaps heard us, and for some reason (it could have been the wheelchair, or our unmissable soaked selves hurtling toward them in hysterics), they reversed the retracting bridge and staff gave us a hand slowing down enough to maneuver up over it. The rough rain seemed to soften and turn almost tender the moment we took sodden steps on deck.

Once there though, we discovered that not only were we wet and cold, we didn't have towels or hot beverages. And the boat was packed, nary a seat to be found. All this was abruptly not funny and our collective good humor dissolved. Finally, after wheeling June up and down the rows of chairs, a few people took pity on us and moved to fill in single-seat gaps, opening up a couple of adjacent twos, one behind the other. We ditched June's wheelchair at the perimeter and Mom helped her struggle down her aisle to a seat, practically sitting on every lap as she went. Lee and I took the pair of seats behind. Seated, I felt the gooseflesh under my clothes and the aching in my feet as exquisite aliveness. We'd made it. June would have her river tour.

I pulled my camera out of my pocket, where it might as well have been wading in a shallow pool, and tried to prepare for the worst. To my amazement, it turned on without flinching, auto-flash enabled. I threw a soggy arm around Lee and reached out with the camera pointed back at us to click a self-portrait. We studied it immediately after on the viewfinder and as usual, I loved it and Lee thought there was some flaw in her appearance. Granted, we looked more like drowned, incompetent fisherwomen than clueless tourists ill-equipped for a rainstorm, but all the better. I tapped Mom and June on their respective shoulders and snapped a picture of them, too. The boat lurched forward and I put the camera away at the urging of Lee. Amazed, I listened to the tour guide give the introductory speech in at least seven different languages. The rest of the tour was like that, too, every piece of information delivered in French, Spanish, English, German, Romanian, Slavic, and indigenous pidgin Oklahoman. (Just kidding about that last one, but seriously, it was like the UN on that boat ride.)

Poor June sat, drenched and exhausted, looking from right to left with a glaze over her eyes like the sugary shine on a donut. No doubt she was utterly confused by the multilingual narration of the tour, probably as incapable as I to decipher when the English began and stopped, accented as it was and in the same voice. Eventually, people began to rise from their seats and move freely about the boat, further obstructing our view.

I went in search of photo opportunities along the banks. Exiting the central covered area through a Plexiglas door, I walked along the lip, watching the wake surge up the side. I leaned out and watched the bow pitch in and out of the black water. I walked forward, out along the bow line where I could feel the rising and falling of the deck at its apex, where I could ride its tumult. The night was especially dark and the rain had stopped. The biting chill in the air had softened into a pleasant coolness. I snapped photos of lit statues adorning bridges, which turned out blurry from the motion and thick darkness.

"What are you doing out here?" It was Lee, startling me from behind. I nearly ejected my camera from my hands into the water.

"Oh, hi, I'm just… taking pictures," I said.

"What are you really doing out here?" She asked.

"Oh, I guess I just didn't feel like being packed in. Needed some fresh air. How's June in there?" I stumbled, with a particularly sharp pitch of the bow, into her. She caught me and pushed me gently off. Her clothes were clammy and cold and she smelled like summer rain. She suggested we go closer to the stern or perhaps the middle to seek out the most stable standing point. The problem with that was the mass of people already occupying the space.

"June's having a great time, I think. Don't you think?" She asked, settling on a spot a couple average body widths from the next-nearest person.

"I hope so," I said. And then we started one of our long talks, recapping the events of the day and the events of the day before then reaching farther back to assess and analyze, through the gauze of time, our shared history or what we knew of it, pulling together strips and scraps and stitching them into something nearly animate, something hunched and solid with a shell, tracking a little stickiness behind it in its slime trail.

Our conversations were like footnotes to the footnotes of our existence, pursuing truth all the way back beyond the event of my birth.

Sometimes, even beyond her own. The only limiting factor to our talks was lack of time, never lack of things to talk about. This applies only to post sobriety, however.

There was a time when Lee never talked to me at all, except to tell me how disappointed she was in me, how she didn't know me anymore nor did she want to. Once, she even went so far as to tell me that I was no longer welcome in her home and that when I saw her at Mom's house, I should leave her alone. I can't remember what specific harm I'd inflicted to earn that final blow, but I have no doubt that I deserved it.

I was about two and a half years sober when I made amends, outlining the specific ways in which I had harmed her, admitting I was wrong, and asking what I could do to make it right. We were by the lake, just a few feet from the edge of the cliff across the street from her house. She listened to my litany and cried. She said she'd given up long before on hopes that we would ever be friends, but that I would always be her sister. It was less than I'd hoped for, but it was generous. I ended by thanking her for specific ways in which I was grateful for her, recounting all the times she'd been there for me that she probably assumed I'd ignored or forgotten. This, I could tell, broke through. The whole thing ended with a tearful hug to mark the beginning of that friendship she'd long before given up on.

Lost in conversation, we forgot about how cold we were and the fact that the boat tour was of a finite duration until Mom appeared to remind us. She poked her head out from the Plexiglas door and shivered at the wind.

"Girls, the tour's almost over and we should get the chair ready for June," she said. We followed her back to the now largely unoccupied seating area and fetched the chair to collect June for disembarking. The night was dark and chilly for the walk back to our hotel, which greeted us with warmth and a particularly stunning view from our room. There was the city sprawled out beneath, with the Eiffel Tower sparkling blue and silver like an enormous Christmas tree.

Dear June

49. **Indium** (Poor Metal; Primordial; Solid)

Dear June,

I was at Mom's house looking at the brick-patterned wallpaper, and I smiled because I thought of you laughing. That's what you would do if you had been sitting next to me and I had said: "June, look at the brick-patterned wallpaper. Doesn't it look just like real brick?" Then my eyes fell below the counter to the forest-green cupboards, which used to be brown. I noticed how the handles on the cupboards were smoothed from a lifetime of hands opening and closing them, rough kid skin gripping them like fine sand paper, wearing them down to the brass. You are like the cupboards, I think. One deep earth tone changing into another, always being gripped, handled so intimately by your family, always opening and closing.

Do you remember when we were kids and you were the one who Mom let stay home from school with me when I was sick? You made up the kitchen couch with blankets and pillows. The sick bed, you called it. I lay there with you pressed in beside me watching *The Price is Right* until I fell asleep. When I woke up, you were not there. It was the first thing I noticed. You were bent into the refrigerator, the top half of you disappearing into its guts, and I laughed at the funny sight of your small, bare legs coming out of those boy shorts. You must have heard because you popped up and looked at me and smiled. You grabbed something yellow up from the table and brought it to me. It was a menu you had written on a piece of manila construction paper folded in half. The cover read: "June's Kitchen," with a sketch of an old-fashioned grill. Inside the menu was a list of items: pancakes, grilled cheese, Pizza Rolls, fried zucchini. I was struck by the oddity of fried zucchini, so I ordered it.

"Would you like a glass of milk with that?" you asked, already walking to the refrigerator again to pull out the milk. Also in the refrigerator would have been a box keg of cheap wine. It would be refreshed every so often for the duration of our lives. Even then, when I was maybe nine years old, I was aware of that wine. When I was twenty-two years old, I was back on that kitchen couch sitting next to you when you asked me to take you shopping.

"Yes, we'll go to the mall," I said and looked at the refrige Suddenly and without warning, I was reminded of you taking care of me that day long ago, your voice and your small legs and the warmth of you flooded in so hard, I fell back against the couch. The time between the two experiences in that room collapsed and what remained was everything, the accumulation of what we chose combined with what we did not choose.

The wine, I thought. I would drink it and everything would be better again. It had been two weeks since I'd had a drink. I was trying to stop and failing. I had recently ended a two-year relationship. In the car on the way to the mall, you asked me: "Will it be a boy you date next time, or another girl?"

"A girl, June. There will be no more boys," I said, amused at your bluntness. If a thought comes to your mind it comes out of your mouth, which is endearing most of the time. You looked utterly confused then.

"But you're so pretty. You could have any guy you want. Why would you just waste that?" you said. I laughed and said, "That's sweet of you to say, June, thank you. But I think you're wasting your beauty on men. You could have any woman you want." You cracked up. Your laughing face so closely resembles your crying face that I always feel a moment of dread and uncertainty before being able to share in that joy.

I'm just going to be blunt here: I feel like providence (or whatever is to blame for the random events in our lives) got it all wrong: I should have been the one to become disabled and brain damaged, not you. You were the better one. You were smarter, had more potential, and were sweeter and more innocent. I cannot say the same for myself and yet I find myself unscathed after three decades in the world. I have had so many close calls, so many times when I should have died.

There was the time when I parked my car several blocks away and stole through the foggy night into the back yard of my girlfriend. We had walkie talkies and would converse over them almost every night, as her parents had banned her from talking with me on the phone, which was fine with us, because they had always listened in and our conversations were therefore heavily coded, stripped of heat. On the walkie talkies

119

though, words slid into and out of those little black boxes that still make my skin prick and flush to this day. I know I've never told you any of this and it might make you feel uncomfortable but oh June, to be that young again, falling in love with a girl for the first time, sinking into a hole of agony and exquisite relief.

I will never forget the time I crawled up that plastic, roll-up fire-escape ladder into her room, drunk enough to shed inhibitions but not too drunk that I would forget how I pulled off that little black dress she was wearing and watched her body reaching for me in the moonlight. I remember thinking somewhere in the midst of that whirlwind night how this was what all the fuss had been about. Here was what sex was supposed to feel like.

The night I am talking about, the foggy night, my drunkenness had the best of me and I mistook the banging on her window with a tree branch for a light tapping. The sound of glass shattering broke an incredible stillness that was all suburban nights and sent me fleeing to the shelter of the evergreen trees lining the yard, where I crawled under the canopy of branches and hid. I must have passed out there, because when I woke up, I heard the unmistakable crackle of police radios and saw numerous flashlight beams bouncing off the dewy grass of the back yard. I moved to see if there was a back way out of the trees by which I could escape, but the fuzz caught the movement and surrounded my evergreen tree with spotlights and guns pointed squarely at me.

One of them said something along the lines of: "Come out of there with your hands up." I crawled out as best I could with my hands up, asking them not to shoot, explaining that I was just a kid. I was lifted onto my unsteady feet and made to stagger along with them to the back of the police car, the smell of me filling the interior of the car quickly once the door closed, the smell of stale beer and cigarettes mixed with fear. I refused a breathalyzer. I was only seventeen so they took me home to Mom and Dad.

Dad got angry and threw a tantrum. Every other word was fuck. I was going to be either dead or in prison by the time I was eighteen, he said. Now I know he was just feeling guilty, angry and guilty that he had passed along his great doomed enterprise to me.

It was that same night that I took you shopping at the mall when I had my very last funny drunken episode. (All the ones after this one have no humor, just a sad, pathetic quality, like the sight and the smell of a street wino that has shit and pissed himself in public.)

I had purchased a hot little outfit on my credit cards, something that was sure to result in a hookup for me that night. Do you remember that? The black jeans and tight shirt and black leather jacket? I think you said that it made me look dangerous. I liked that.

I did not hook up. After the empty space in my memory that was the time spent inside the bar, I drove in the direction I thought was home, west, and that's where I blacked out. The next thing I remember is my car embedded in a mound of snow off the side of some country road I did not recognize. Only one house was in sight. I pounded on the front door. When there was no response, I pounded harder. Lights switched on, footsteps coming down stairs.

The door opened and an old man and an old woman glared out, he in his pajamas and she in her nightgown. The old man, after getting his boots, hat, and coat on and finding his keys, ended up pulling my car out of the snow and back onto the road with his truck and a tow cord. He pointed me in the direction of the highway. I took off.

The next thing I knew, I was on a narrow, black road winding uphill through the woods. At the top of the hill, I pulled into a circle driveway to turn around and drove my car off the driveway into the snow, where I was promptly stuck again, this time much worse, with the nose of the car buried and the back end sticking up, almost vertical. Once again, I climbed from my car and approached the door of this large, stately home and knocked. I knocked and knocked and nobody answered. I tried the handle and found it unlocked. Assuming nobody was home, I entered.

First, I used the bathroom. Next, I rummaged through the kitchen cupboards looking for a snack. I stood in the middle of the kitchen greedily shoving pretzel twists into my mouth, spilling most of the contents onto the floor in the process and then stepping on them with my wet, muddy shoes. It wasn't intentional, but I didn't care to fix

121

it. After that, I used the phone. I can remember calling our brother, John, and left a message on his answering machine, telling him in slurred words that I was lost somewhere, stuck in the snow.

I searched around for a clue to my whereabouts and found a piece of mail with the unfamiliar address: Little Mountain. I hung up and called 911. I told the operator that I was stuck in the snow and lost and could someone come help me. She told me she would send some help, and I proceeded to lie down on the couch where I swiftly passed out. Some time later, I woke up to the phone ringing.

As I sat up and struggled to remember where I was and what was going on, I noticed a sleepy looking man coming down some stairs in his robe. Skinny legs bushy with hair protruded from under the somehow feminine-looking garment. His face was young, 30's maybe, but tired, unshaven; pockets of coffee-tinted skin pouched below his eyes. He jumped when he saw me, sprawled out on his couch with my shirt riding up, my pants undone, and my dirty shoes on the carpet.

"Who are you and what are you doing here?" He asked, heading for the phone. I mumbled my name and sat up, also wondering what I was doing there. He answered the phone. He gave directions to his house and hung up.

"That was the cops, they were lost at the bottom of the mountain trying to find this place. Did you call the cops?"

I didn't know.

"Are you sober?"

I told him I hadn't been, but was now.

"You better be sober because the cops out here will throw the book at you," he said.

He pulled on his boots, coat, hat and went outside. He tried pulling my car out with his truck and tow cords, but my car would not budge and he broke two tow cords trying to get it out. The police arrived and began questioning him and me. He explained that he did not know me and had found me there. I told them I had been babysitting in the area and got lost driving home and ended up stuck in the snow. One cop was silent and the other fired questions at me, totally not buying my story.

Meanwhile, the nice man whose house I had broken into called for a tow truck. I rode down to the base of the mountain with the quiet cop and waited for the truck to arrive so we could escort it up to the house, which was hidden in the woods and apparently a complete puzzle to find. We watched the sun come up and he gave me a cigarette to smoke. I have this image of myself then: skinny and rumpled in black, long hair pulled back into a ponytail, smoky and surreal. I had to pee, so I got out of the car. The cop watched while I picked my way through the deep snow over to the trees where I found a place to pull down my pants and squat.

Between my white thighs was white, unbroken snow, its cold lifting to touch me in warm, hidden places. I let loose a stream of urine. I watched the snow drop away, collapsing in on itself in heavy yellow clumps and almost cried. This is the precise helplessness I feel with you, June.

You were untouchable, unmarred, crisp snow just radiating clean, bright cold. Why does my survival over you feel like going to the bathroom on it all?

There is another time I never told you about. I was twelve, maybe thirteen, standing there before those same painted cupboards in the kitchen. Mom was at the sink, framed by the brick-patterned wallpaper, washing dishes or her hands. I stood there looking up at her, searching among the limited collection of words I had in my mind for an assemblage that would articulate how I was feeling. Finally, I said simply: "I wish it would have been me in that accident."

Mom whirled on me, her face instantly red, dark red and growing redder as she leaned toward me, pointed her finger between my eyes in a rigid, angry way, and said: "You would never trade places with your sister. Do not ever say anything like that again." Tears welled in her eyes like they always do when she's angry and I felt some pooling in mine at the same time. I looked at the floor and tried to swallow it. She turned away from me again, back to the sink, resuming whatever washing she had been doing, as if it could ever come clean again.

What I felt then has only driven my guilt deeper and ground it sharper ever since. It is not something I have ever admitted, not even to myself. I will confess it to you now, June. I wished you had died in that accident. I just wished you had died, June. After I let that feeling rise to the surface and allowed myself to recognize it for what it was, I wanted to die myself. Right then, immediately and without a word. And part of me did die. The part that had held onto the way you were before and could not let go. The connection died. Its lifeline, filled with blood, severed and drained that part of me of its existence.

I went on for years with the dull pursuit of self-destruction. Don't feel that this has had anything to do with you, June. It had to do with the world and how unbearably beautiful it had been when you were unbroken. It had to do with the contrast of that world to its aftermath. It had to do with the unutterable need that filled me to brimming so that I walked around overfull, carefully avoiding spillage. Whatever it had to do with, the ultimate surrender of it was inevitable. And now I empty myself a little every day. Now I take you as best I can and you greedily receive me. Now we have our awkward, unbalanced dance. You are forever home from school sick. I have gone off to school anyway, without you.

Lovingly,

Your Sister

PS: I will never give you this letter. You will never receive it.

50. Tin (Poor Metal; Primordial; Solid)

In which I became a bird

I was born a baby bird with clipped wings, blue and gold flecked feathers, a string clutched in my beak. The string was attached to a kite — the most beautiful, rip-the-sky-wide-open kite. Her gliding, rigid structure, her curves and lines, her delicate balance of weight and air, light and shadow, lift and drag—they mesmerized me as I grew. The string from my beak was a nearly invisible line that reached high into blue air and attached to a bridle, which attached to an intricate frame. I could not be sure of what material it was constructed because it loomed high and far, but I fantasized that it was many things: delicate fish bones, toothpicks, stalks of willows, silver twine, or even my own feathers. The idea that my beautiful kite shared the raw materials of my body and used them for her aerodynamic forces riveted me, standing stiff on bird haunches, gaping at the sky. The sky was the open hand of God holding her, ever blue, mostly cloudless, lit from within by the sun. My bird eyes stared. My bird mind wondered, dreamed, expanded. The gold flecks in my feathers multiplied and divided into other colors to mirror all of hers. And there was no color she didn't have reflected in the graceful sway she made downward, a slender curve toward me, earthbound, tiny mirrors on her surface revealing translucent greens, rolling yellows of lemony waves, tufts of gray like billowed sails, frayed and flapping hard, ripping through wind. She carried me, flew me with her away from our sun into the purple-black galaxy with glittering, ringed planets and gaseous stars and chunks of dense space debris and all, to the corner of the universe and back again, following the trajectory of a boomerang, too long to return. Our journeys were often and varied, always very exciting, until the day a storm came to end them. Clouds descended, darkness came, wind funneled and stole my kite away from me, into a raging cyclone. It was not until the kite lay broken and helpless at my feet that I tried letting go of the string, unhooking it from my beak. Only the string disappeared down my throat and wove itself all through the inside, the dark chambers and beating organs of my bird body. I could not let go and I could not fly. Many healers attended my kite. Her frame was reconstructed out of balsa or bamboo or light-but-strong plastic tubing. Nothing magical, not fish bones or feathers. Not anything bird. They never got it right. She was grounded. She would never fly again. The sun became a torch and descended in a black, burnt path across the sky so full of stars that dark only peeked out from behind them. It made its light to shine only on my broken kite. I turned to wood and petrified in the shadows. The night lights lent themselves to me, filled in my notched wing tips, and lifted me into starry flight alone. I found my destruction in a dead black hole. I followed it to its depths, all the while being gagged by the string connecting me to my kite. I felt its weight in my bones, the energy of the carbons, the vanity of purity, and I missed someone I had never known. I went back to the kite lying there under torchlight. I looked at her closely and saw our own constellation inside, our tiny, muted and desperate destiny. I became earth blooded. My veins snaked out and rooted into the ground. My kite became my prison. I had to break free. Ragged and toughened, torn veins flapping in the wind below me, a broken piece of string lulling from my beak like a thin, worn tongue, I fly. I can be seen in any newly dark sky. A murderer. An orphan. A copout. A crime.

51. Antimony (Metalloid; Primordial; Solid)

You take June to the tanning salon where you work and give her a free tanning session. You will have to help her undress. Feel the tension that comes with regarding her scarred nakedness. It lifts your shoulders and hardens your abdomen. Help to maneuver her into the coffin-like bed of glass. Once she's secure, go to the front desk and offer to cover things while the other girl working there goes on a break. As soon as she walks out, find the pill bottle in the drawer. Take one of the red pills—it's the mildest of them. You have to drive June back home, after all. Sit on the stool while it settles into your stomach and disperses with the water you're drinking. Imagine it soaking in through the membranous lining of your stomach into the fine blood vessels and into the stream of blood, carried off to all your other organs and extremities until, fighting gravity, it rises to your head. Once this process completes and you feel the fuzz take hold—the exquisite relief—remember the money you need. Fumble through the keys on your ring until you find the small gold one that fits the locked drawer under the counter. Open it to discover only two hundred dollar bills. He always leaves you at least three, so this will make you angry. As though on cue, a dark-eyed, bearded man will walk in and drop off another envelope stuffed with cash. He simply walks in, produces it from the inside breast pocket of his suit, hands it to you, and walks out. You take an additional three bills off the top before locking it in the drawer. Now you have enough to pay the cell phone bill and the next couple of hotel room stays. Your boss told you never to take more than three hundred at a time, but he stiffed you this time on a whole hundred, and besides, he would never say anything.

(After the walkie-talkies became too restrictive, and because you could afford it, you purchased two cellular phones. It was 1995 and the technology was rather new, so they were boxy, antennaed contraptions that cost 25 cents per minute on both ends. Because you talked to her every day with them, the bills would amount to $400 or sometimes $500 each month. In addition, because you both still lived at home, you had to rent hotel rooms to get time alone with her. You would skip school and take her to a hotel where you would drink wine and make love and listen to music all day. This will occur so often during your senior year of high school—her freshman year of college——that you nearly won't graduate and she will fail every class that first semester. Her handwriting looks similar to your mom's, so you have her write notes to excuse you from school, accompanied by doctor's notes, which are also forged, taken from the small, pink pad you stole from your doctor's office. This will work flawlessly until you get caught when the school secretary calls your mom to ask why you are so frequently absent. Your mom will confront you and you will break down, citing your own ongoing mental anguish and your girlfriend's abusive situation at home as the reason for doing it. Your mom will want to fix it, and she will. She will go to the principal and plead with him, tell him a story, the contents of which will always be unknown to you, that will result in all of your absences being excused save the maximum number allowed. Similarly, when her parents find out about her grades, they will refuse to pay the tuition for her second semester. This will lead to her first and last rebellion: finally quitting the dry cleaner's and getting a part-time job at a retail clothing store. You will pay the second semester's tuition for her with the tanning salon money and her parents will beat her, then threaten to put her out on the street for daring to cross them. She will react by leaving home while they are away at the dry cleaner's, taking a garbage bag full of her clothes and moving in with you at your parents' house. There are positive and negative byproducts to your parents' inattentiveness, and this is one of the positives. Because they think she is just your best friend, they see nothing wrong with her staying and sharing your bed. This will last only a few days before her parents beg her forgiveness and she returns home to them. Meanwhile, though, you are concerned about the upcoming phone bill and hotel expenses, so you take the extra hundreds.)

Your boss will never say anything; he knows that you understand that he is doing something illegal and using the tanning salon as a front. Your part is simple: you receive and send faxes, all of them written in code. And sometimes, men would drop off envelopes of cash that you would lock up in the drawer. He compensates your participation and silent cooperation in this activity by inviting you to take cash from the drawer, but no more than three hundred at a time. You often exceed this limit, however, and he never complains. You are only seventeen, yet you have access to practically unlimited cash. What's more, there are multi-colored pills for the taking. You have no idea what they are, but they take the edge off and allow you to drink less, so you help yourself.

A few minutes before June's tanning bed is due to shut off, your co-worker returns from her break. You stand outside the door to June's room and knock. You might wobble a bit on your shoes and wonder if there's been a tremor in the earth. There hasn't been. You're just a little too high. You feel nervous that you won't be able to drive well. Slap your cheeks between your hands vigorously several times. If June hasn't responded yet, knock again. If she still doesn't respond, open the door with the master key. You will likely find it unlocked anyway. Walk in and find June asleep in the glass bed. Lift the top open and notice that her torso has pinked. You will worry that you left the bed on too long. You probably did, but it's okay, she won't be burned too much.

Wake her with a gentle nudge. Try not to react by whirling around when you see a bright object bolt across your periphery. You didn't actually see it, but you feel almost certain that you did. One side effect of the red pills is paranoia and, if you take too much, hallucinations. Start to panic because you can't remember if you took two or just one, or even three. Wonder whether you took one then took more subsequently. The light around the edges of your vision starts to burn and you are sure you smell smoke. Shake June roughly. She will stir and jerk up so that her head clunks into the glass. Mistake that sound for something else—something that's trapped under the glass and trying to get out. Help June to sit up and swing her legs out. Peer into the glass that was beneath her head. When you see another quick, bright thing, like light flitting under water, reel up and instinctively punch the glass. The glass will crack and June will yelp. Or was it you that yelped? Look around the room dartingly to see if it's actually burning. You don't see the fire but you feel the heat and smell the smoke.

Realize that nothing is burning but that you are hallucinating because you took too many red pills. You can't remember how many, but the smoke is stinging your eyes and you just broke a ten-thousand-dollar tanning bed. It occurs to you dully that this is the end of your illegal cash cow. When your boss finds out that you broke one of the beds, he will be very angry. He will want you to pay for it. You will have no way of doing that. Cover the crack in the bed with the thin head pillow and decide to pretend like nothing happened. Look at June's shaking hands struggling to clasp her bra behind her back. See the pinkish skin, the slight burn already looking irritated and inflamed under the tight, white straps. Look back at the cracked tanning bed. No one can come in here now. Realize this with a start. Serious injury can occur if someone tans in a cracked tanning bed. You remember from the orientation your boss made you take when he hired you that the glass serves as a filter for the lamps, and that cracked filters in beds can cause third degree burns and let out dangerous carcinogenic UVC rays. You can't have that on your hands. Try to remain calm while helping June get the rest of the way dressed. Ignore the flames licking the walls in your periphery. Ignore the smoke and the darting light. Ignore the sensation that your fingers are not solid, nor are any parts of you, but rather you are a loose, vibrating cloud of molecules like teeming gnats in the rough, wavering shape of you. Try to tie June's shoes for her many times and fail each time, unable to grasp the laces with your fingers reduced to a swarm of particles.

June's voice is sounding but you can't understand the words. Gently shush her, saying that you can't hear her right then; even though it sounds to you like your words are gibberish, hope that they're coming out coherently to her. But perhaps they hadn't come out at all, because June gives no indication of having heard a thing from you. She just goes on making noise. When she appears to be dressed and put together, walk out with June holding onto your arm. Passing the front desk, turn to your co-worker and attempt to say, "Thanks, see you later," in a normal voice. When she looks at you with a slightly horrified and vaguely amused expression, understand that whatever you attempted to say did not come out intact.

Walk through the door and out and try to remember where the car is. Look around for several minutes without seeing any differentiation at all among the cars in the parking lot until June makes additional noise and begins moving in the direction of one of the cars. Follow her lead and get in the car. Once you both have fastened seatbelts, start the car. Gasp because you remember the cracked tanning bed. You have to tell your co-worker that you broke it and that she should not let anyone else in there.

Tell June you will be right back and return to the tanning salon. Walk in and look at your co-worker. She will look up from her magazine. It's very likely that she will appear annoyed and confused when you try to speak. If this happens, don't repeat the attempt but rather approach the desk and take up a pen and a pad of yellow sticky notes from its surface. Write down, as carefully as possible, what you need to say: *The bed in room three is cracked. Don't let anyone burn to cancer in there. I broke it. Also, I quit.*

Lean back and look over the note for clarity. The handwriting is excessively neat and small, like newspaper print. Decide it's legible and push it across the desk to the girl. Smile at her and walk out. The smile will feel stiff and frozen on your face like hardened wax when you get outside. Walk, with the wax smile, to the car and invite June to walk to McDonald's and get a milkshake, which she will be sure to accept. You must do this to buy more time, as you can't drive her while you're tripping this hard. Walk slowly as though floating to the McDonald's with June on your arm. The flames will start to die down and a variety will begin to take shape among the cars in the parking lot. June's words will start to cohere and you will understand that she wants a strawberry shake.

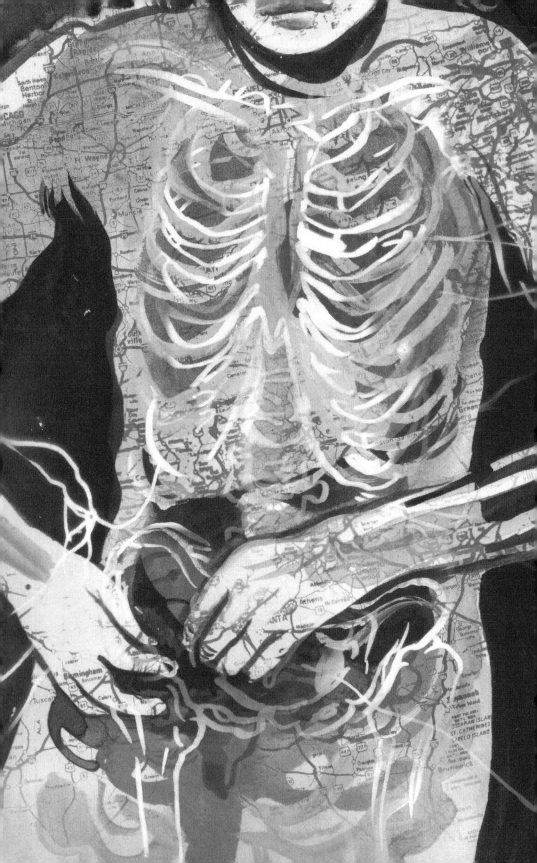

Whatever you do, don't think about
that time in the alley behind her church

52. **Tellurium** (Metalloid; Primordial; Solid)

Paris, day three

June wanted to take a train to Paris's famous western suburb, Versailles. It was on the itinerary for her class trip twenty years prior, as it holds the famous Château de Versailles, one of the largest palaces in the world. Throughout the trip to that point, we'd managed to avoid the Métro, the subway system in Paris, which is both inaccessible and fast paced. The smaller concern was accessibility, as we could get June up and down stairs when necessary. But the speed with which people must get on and off the train, however, was a frightening prospect with June—the main reason being the doors, which do not have a safety mechanism upon closing.

In fact, most Métro train doors feature a sticker with an anthropomorphized, bipedal rabbit dressed in yellow clothes (albeit barefoot) getting its three fingers smashed in the doors. Beneath this telling illustration, the sticker reads in French, English, German, and Spanish some variation of the warning: *Beware of trapping your hands in the doors*. I'd heard gruesome stories of lost digits and even limbs. The doors slide open, stay open for maybe ten seconds, then a buzzer sounds to indicate they are about to close. The buzzer is serious about this brief counsel, as the doors close unapologetically, with or without body part obstacles.

The train to Versailles was not the Métro, but the RER commuter train, which didn't have the rabbit sticker on its doors. It was a faster, above-ground train that traveled farther distances and ran on a more infrequent schedule. Still, they functioned much the same way, only with a precious few additional seconds of open time.

We arrived with plenty of time to spare and waited on the platform for close to an hour. Because these trains ran on schedule and ours happened to be a bit early, the train sat with its doors happily agape for plenty of time, allowing us to embark and find seats without incident. We sat strategically near the doors with June's chair collapsed and ready along the railing for quick and efficient deployment upon arrival. We planned ahead: I would hop off right away with the chair and have it open on the platform below while Mom and Lee helped June off the train, posthaste.

The train arrived at Versailles and we executed our plan like a military drill—boots on the ground in (had to be) under a minute. Only we paused in congratulating ourselves because, as this was the end of the line for the train, it sat there all easy like with its doors hanging wide open for the entire time it took us to walk down the platform, into the train station, and out the other side.

Wheeling June to the palace, we found it closed with gates chained and locked at the main entrance. June registered this as a very minor disappointment, bordering on indifference. Her delight at riding the train hadn't worn off, a value gaining in currency as Versailles continued to be a let down. We wandered around from there just looking at houses, June compulsively snapping pictures with the last unused disposable camera in her gallon-sized baggie, until it started raining again. Still traumatized from the soggy night before, we reacted to the drizzle as though it were nuclear fallout and trotted back to the drab strip of touristy shops directly across from the train station. We had at least an hour to kill before the next train back, so we sought first a bathroom.

There was a McDonald's in the strip, which offered the only public restroom for miles. It was therefore an unusually long line. As this was more of a proactive bathroom break for June and less of an emergency, we waited our turn. I worried when I saw face after disgusted face exiting the bathroom with a smell of sewage wafting after them. It wasn't what I'd feared—it was far worse. Every stall had feces in, on, and around the pot. By this time, June had to go, there wasn't any choice, but she understandably moaned in revulsion from start to finish. I had no choice but to clean one of the toilets enough to prepare it somewhat for her use. Wads of toilet paper and held breath were required for this foulest of chores, but after spots appeared before my eyes and I nearly passed out, I had to take a whopping gulp of that putrid air right in the middle of things. It was not pleasant. I continued though, as I couldn't allow my poor sister to sit in shit.

53. Iodine (Halogen; Primordial; Solid)

I didn't ask permission, I just took the car out, the blue Buick that my dad bought for $1500 after my orange Tercel (that I bought with my own $800 when I was sixteen) broke down for the last time. I was eighteen, officially an adult, and could do as I pleased. I thought about that and laughed as I backed down the driveway, finding it funny because I always had done as I pleased. Only then, I was suddenly allowed to. I turned left onto Lake Avenue and felt a sense of doom and foreboding. At first I didn't think much of it because it's how I almost always felt, but that time, I wondered if there was something a little more to it—a prophetic sense signaled with a visceral warning like the hot flash that precedes a fight, flight, or freeze scenario.

I drove to my boyfriend Joe's house and drank Natural Light with him and his friends.

When you're drunk enough to give in to sex, doubt whether you have the energy to attempt making it fun for him. Decide that you do not and consider doing it anyway. If you do, he'll humiliate you afterward by telling you in a nice way how boring a lay you are. He'll do this in one of two ways: 1. He'll roll off you and sigh loudly then say, "It doesn't even feel like you enjoy it, I mean, do you?" 2. He'll roll off you and sigh loudly.

To avoid this, tell him one of two things: 1. You have your period. 2. You feel sick and might vomit.

The former is preferable if used sparingly as it is fail-safe. The latter might not put him off, as he'll just encourage you to vomit then ask you to brush your teeth then want to have sex. In either case, he might leave you alone and be kind to you. If he does, pretend to be vulnerable. Just enough to allow him this. It won't be easy because it will make you think of the one place you can be vulnerable, with Cassiopeia, and to think about her is to yearn for her.

Joe will offer you something to eat when he notices how drunk you are. If he offers to thaw out some venison jerky, politely decline. If he goes further by explaining that it's delicious and that his dad cured it that week, impolitely decline. He may, alternatively, offer to go out to Taco Bell. If he does, accept, because when he's gone you can call her. You may waiver here, because if you do get her on the phone, she won't be happy to hear you drunk again. Yet, you can use this like you always do as license to say anything, like how she's beautiful in ways you've never seen before, and how you'll love her for the rest of your life. If you tell her you're hurting, she'll ask what's wrong. Her voice will be soft and warm, opening you like a bloom.

Whatever you do, don't think about the time in the alley behind her church, the Greek Orthodox temple, where you went with her after sneaking away from the Greek festival. You were drunk then, too. While making out with her against the wall, you touched a spot on her side just above her hip and she winced. You lifted her shirt and saw the bruise before she snatched it back down and told you not to look. "Again?" you said, feeling rage rise in you like lava. She told you how her dad kicked her there when he found her napping on the floor in the back of the dry cleaner's they owned, where she worked. You screamed and flailed, shouting about how she's a slave and he should be arrested. "Please stop," she'd said, "they'll hear you." You shut your mouth and instead, punched the brick wall with your bare knuckles until they were bleeding and raw and until she was crying and holding you back. You yielded to her because she cradled your bleeding, rough hands in her soft ones and kissed them and cried. She told you she loved you bigger than the ocean, older than water. You believed her. You took her to your car and made love in the back seat gently and slowly, so in synch that you breathed and moved and whimpered together until your satisfaction condensed on the windows, blinding your view. In it, she traced a heart shape with her finger and smiled. You traced your initial above it and hers below it, then opened the door and let it fade.

When Joe gets back from Taco Bell, you might feel angry that you passed out while he was gone and missed your chance to call her. Don't worry, your drunkenness spared you hurting her again.

Regard him looming double before you waving a bean burrito and decide to leave. Drop the keys on the floor of the car when trying to start it then tumble out sideways when you lean down to fetch them. Joe will appear and snatch them up so swiftly you'll think he's a ghost. He'll tell you that you're too drunk to drive. When you stand up to grab the keys back from him, you might get the spins. If you do, make your way to the back of the car, crouch down, and stick your finger down your throat. It will only take the slightest touch to your gullet to bring it all up. Hate the feeling of emptying out but let it happen. When it's over, feel clearer headed and rip the keys away from Joe with a growl. When he peevishly asks you if you're sure you can drive, tell him to get the fuck away.

In the car, light a cigarette to chase the terrible taste in your mouth. Turn on the radio to the country station and be certain not to wear your seatbelt. It's unlikely you'll think of it but if you do, decide to leave it off. Your blanket justification for this is to remember how June wasn't wearing her seatbelt and if she had worn it, she would have been crushed and potentially cut in half from the car closing in on top of her.

Drive too fast down the narrow, dark road. Turn on your brights, which will penetrate no more than a few extra inches of darkness ahead, and squint at the double yellow line. Attempt to keep your left wheels aligned with it. When a song you hate comes on the radio, take your eyes off the road to change the station. At the same time, drop your cigarette in your lap. Swerve and accidentally accelerate while thrusting up your hips and peering straight down to search for the fallen ember. In the midst of this, your car will fall off the side of the road, which has no shoulder but rather a sharp drop of about a foot, so that half on and half off, the blue Buick is barreling forward at roughly a 30 degree angle with no hope of maneuvering back onto the road. Later, you'll remember thinking that you wished you would have had time to change the station, because a song you hate is a terrible song to die to.

Mere seconds later, the car will collide with a driveway level to the road and go airborne, flip completely over, and nose-dive upside-down into a ditch. Upon impact, every window in the car shatters while you bang around in the front like a ping pong ball, hitting the ceiling with your head and slamming your face on the steering wheel a few times over from collision to flip to impact. The spray of glass shards cuts your face and arms and when the car settles to a rest, you're crumpled with your neck craned against the roof of the car, upside-down, watching blood fall from your arms onto your face. You won't be aware of yourself moaning in pain, but rather imagine the moans coming from out there, all around you, rising from the recesses of the mangled car. In your delirium, you think it's June moaning and you'll wonder what's wrong. Her moaning sounds awful and you begin to panic. Wish to help her so much that you're able to move. Roll over onto your hands and knees and crawl out through the passenger side window, ignoring the pain of the glass cutting into you.

Fall out into the muddy ditch and scramble up the side of it to fling yourself onto the lawn above, covered in mud and blood. Look up and stare in amazement at the figure emerging from the house across the lawn, advancing toward you at a frantic pace. Stand and walk toward the figure. Don't worry, it won't hurt, the adrenaline will temporarily both numb the pain and sober you up.

Accept the woman's invitation to come inside. See the shock on the man's face when he looks at you. Hear him declare that he is calling 911. Two facts will immediately occur to you: 1. Although you've sobered up, you're undoubtedly still legally drunk. 2. You can't allow your mom to get another call from the police telling her that one of her children has been in a car accident.

Insist on using their phone to call home before he calls 911. If he resists, explain quickly why you must. If your dad answers the phone, he'll be drunk. You can hear it in his oiled voice. Ask for your mom without giving him any information. Feel like you're going to cry at the sound of your mom's fear-tinged voice saying hello. Tell her what happened, emphasizing that you're okay and that the nice people will be calling you an ambulance. Hand the phone over when she insists on talking to the man to find out where you are.

Go outside and sit down in the folding chair that the woman has placed in the driveway. Time will pass. You will want to smoke a cigarette but you won't. The ambulance arrives at the same time as your mom and you hear her voice calling your name.

Pass out.

Come to in the hospital with Lee's boyfriend, Allen, standing beside you, roughly rubbing your arm. Lee is at the foot of your bed and she rushes around to your side when she sees you're awake. Notice that they don't look angry, but relieved.

In the car on the way home, realize with a start that she doesn't know you were driving drunk. Somehow, you made it through everything without being issued a DUI. This is when you will think of your story about how it happened: a big pick-up truck passed you on the too-narrow road, effectively running you off the side, which caused you to lose control and crash. Tell your mom the story. She believes you without question.

When you get home, your dad is pacing restlessly. Stop near the door and watch him with caution. When he sees you, he stops and his face softens. You can feel the cuts on your face and the ugly welt across your cheek from the steering wheel, which in that moment you feel grateful for. He strides up to you and bear hugs you. He says, "I love you, baby." Never in your life has he called you that. Mutter that you love him too. Don't try not to cry, just cry. Your mom's face will appear over his shoulder. Her hand is over her mouth and her eyes are shining with tears.

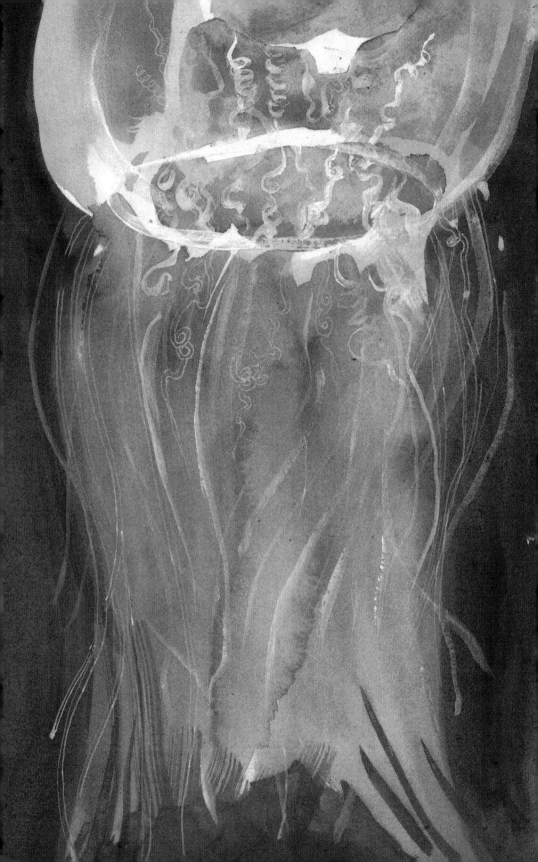

Fear...like a pyroclastic flow from a volcano

54. **Xenon** (Noble Gas; Primordial; Gas)

Paris, day three

With that harrowing bathroom errand behind us, none of us had an appetite (especially not for food produced in that establishment), so we proceeded to the adjacent souvenir shop and looked around at knick-knacks for the girls. The highlight of the visit to Versailles was Lee getting blatantly hit on by a dark and hairy French guy. He told her she was beautiful and asked for her phone number. She responded with a blush and an embarrassed laugh and the laconic explanation for why that wasn't an option: "I'm married."

Finally, after time was a glue-filled wade pool, stretched and slowed to an agonizing degree, we crossed over to the train station to await our transport back. After a few minutes, we discovered we were hungry and hadn't eaten lunch. Resorting to vending machine snacks was all we could do. June ate a bag of the French equivalent of Bugles and shared Lee's Red Vines. I got peanut M&M's, shared them with mom, and drank *une CocaCola light*. When our train arrived, it collected and carried away three puffed-up and proud-of-themselves ladies plus one exhausted, yet happy, June.

As the train approached the center of Paris where we wanted to get off, we noticed the brevity of door-openness at each stop. It wasn't good and seemed (although I'm sure this isn't right) to get shorter and shorter in duration each time. There were a couple of stairs for June to mount from her seat to even get to the exit, and then there was the matter of helping her over the gap and onto the platform.

Our stop came and I jumped off with the chair, but the second part of the drill was hindered by a steady flow of passengers, making it difficult for Mom and Lee to get June to the doors quickly enough. The dreaded warning buzzer sounded when June had just made it to the door. She was holding on to Lee's arm while Lee straddled the divide between the platform and the train. Mom was on the platform with me, but reached for Junes other hand when the buzzer sounded. The doors slid closed and Lee's leg instinctively escaped to the platform, leaving June as its only blockage.

The doors pinched closed on June and a louder alarm began to sound. People all about us were yelling, June's face looked pained, we were all struggling to pry open the doors. Strangers on the inside were trying to pull them open, I had one of them with both hands and all my weight behind my tug, Lee had the other one, and Mom was pulling on June, who was struggling against the brutish attackers like a cat in the jaws of a coyote.

The train hummed and started to move. Sheer panic took over and I was instantly sweaty.

"Open the doors!" I screamed over and over again. Others started to scream in French, but the train inched along threatening to pick up speed with June not budging and Mom, Lee, and me desperately yet unsuccessfully trying to wrench open the doors. In the midst of this melee, we all let the cuss words fly without regard for the usual unwritten respect Mom rule:

Lee: goddammit!

Mom: Shit!

Me: Fuck!

And with that chorus of swearing, the train halted once again and the doors released her, hissing open with a silencing of the alarm. She fell forward into us and we caught her, lowered her into her chair. The train spared no time resuming its takeoff and was pulling away within seconds. We waved at the anonymous helpers sliding off with smiles of relief. We checked June over for injuries. She seemed unharmed but looked understandably shaken.

We walked down the platform in silent shock, moving slowly. As the stun wore off, we looked at each other and smiled then laughed. We had to stop moving just to bend over and laugh. We staggered like drunkards, laughing so hard that each of us was silently shaking and gasping for air.

55. **Caesium** (Alkaline Metal; Primordial; Solid)

Having gotten so good at lies, with the utmost attention to detail (more intricate detail, in fact, than the truth could ever retain), I told the story to my dad as confidently as a nun telling Jesus that she will never stray from him.

"I was driving the speed limit, maybe a little over, and this big truck with its headlights level to my back windshield climbed right up on my ass and stayed there. I sped up because I was nervous the truck would hit me. Even when I hit 50 though, it still wasn't fast enough, and the speed limit was only 35." I leaned against the pillows that my mom had propped up for me on the kitchen couch and brought my hand to the welt on my face. It didn't hurt at all because they had given me pain killers in the emergency room and I was pleasantly high from my morning dose, but I kept touching it anyway as though it hurt terribly, both to evoke sympathy from my parents and to keep the pain killers coming. My dad expressed mild disapproval to my speeding confession, but he understood why I did it and I could tell that the admission of that lesser offense made my false story more credible. I continued delicately touching the welt across my face (adding the occasional, subtle wince) while I finished the story:

"When the truck moved to pass me, it was so close to the car, I swear it even tapped me. Reflexively, I just moved over to the right side of the lane to let it pass and that's when I fell off the shoulder. I couldn't get the car back on the road and I lost control then hit the driveway. It all happened so fast."

My dad asked me what color the truck was. I told him it was red. He called the police and told them an approximation of my fiction. While he was on the phone, I heard the back door open. My face turned hot: I hoped it was Cassiopeia coming to see if I was okay. I felt a plummeting disappointment when I saw that it was Joe. I mustered a smile for him as best I could when I saw that he was carrying flowers. When he kneeled on the floor next to me and tried to hug me, I pulled away, using my soreness as an excuse.

My dad came back in from the phone and told me that a police officer was on the way over to take a statement from me about the car accident. I reflected on the word accident and how inappropriate it almost always was.

When the officer arrived, I told him the story with the same nun-like poise. Joe hovered and listened and suggested a suspect—a girl he knew that drives a red pick-up truck. At first I tried to dismiss him because I didn't want to get any innocent people in trouble. But when the police officer asked Joe for the details and noted them down on his clipboard, I decided that it would be better if they do have a suspect. It would make my tale more structurally sound.

When the officer left, my dad offered to make chicken soup. I declined his offer and announced I was going to become a vegetarian. I felt like a terrible person, and hoped that being a vegetarian would help me to redeem myself somewhat. Joe asked why I would want to do that. I told him it was because I love animals. To emphasize this, I sat down on the kitchen couch next to my dog, Beans, and pet her head. When he convinced me that I don't, in fact, love all animals, because snakes are animals and I don't love them, I adjusted my reason to be that I respect all life. He argued that vegetables are alive, but that I will gladly kill and eat those. At that point, I just ignored him and decided to break up with him at the earliest possible opportunity.

When Cassiopeia walked in, I felt simultaneously elated and horrified. Here she was, in the same room with Joe for the first time, and neither of them knew about the true nature of the relationship I was having with the other. When Cassiopeia came to me and embraced me, I noticed a hurt expression on Joe's face. I closed my eyes and ignored him.

When he said, "Hi, I'm Joe," interrupting my hug to force his own introduction with Cassiopeia, I simply scowled at him and asked him to leave. I told him I needed to talk to my best friend alone. He slinked off and I was alone with her. I circled my arms around her waist and rested my forehead against hers. I whispered her name and told her that she was more beautiful than the five bright stars of her namesake on the clearest summer night. She kissed me on the mouth then pulled me close with a heave of a sigh.

"I'm so relieved that you're mostly alright," she said and I smiled. But then she scowled and swatted at me. "You're lucky you didn't get yourself killed."

I started to protest, but thought better of it and just nodded apologetically. She knew me too well to not know the truth and I couldn't find it in me to lie to her, too. At least not about that. I routinely lied to her about Joe and any other boys I had sex with, but that was only because I knew she would leave me sooner or later. And when that happened, I would need somebody to help fill the void.

I tried not to think about the fact that no one could fill the gaping abyss she would inevitably leave, but instead would only make it worse. All attempts at moving on with someone else would only call attention to the painful fact that no one else was her. Years later, when she was long gone and no longer willing to talk to me, I would be in Chicago, looking up at the same constellation that is her namesake. I would notice for the first time that its staggered points of light make up the rough shape of two joined chalices. Next to me would be seated the first worthy contender of hers that I'd met in all the years since. The two of us would be drinking coffee from cups between us, bumped up against one another, half full.

A week after the *accident*, I was sitting next to June when my dad brought me the newspaper to show me how they published a letter he'd written to the driver of the red pick-up truck. By this time, most of my superficial wounds were healed, which contrasted sickeningly with my brain-damaged sister. This, combined with the successful defrauding of my dad, was sufficient to avalanche whatever precarious ledge of self worth I had left, and helped me to plumb the depths of my continual self ruin.

I took the newspaper and held it in front of my face for several moments waiting for the letters to stop swarming. My cheeks felt hot and my throat was dry. I closed my eyes and counted to five. I then took a deep breath and opened my eyes, which first rested on these words:

The car was a total loss but my daughter, thank god, is, for the most part, okay. What kind of person causes an accident like that and just keeps driving? You should be ashamed of yourself.

56. Barium (Alkaline Earth Metal; Primordial; Solid)

In the fall of 1996, Jonas dropped out of medical school. I lived in the dorms at Winona State University and he moved back into his old room at Mom's house. When I went there to visit, he looked awful—a bloated, pale sphere for a head with a beard like moss stopping just shy of his Adam's apple. The skin that showed through the hair and stretched around his bloodshot eyes was impossibly pale, a kind of tissuey pink: the color of what it feels like to touch the tip of your tongue to the inside of your cheek. Coarse hairs from his top lip strayed into his mouth, stuck to his lip. He looked like he hadn't showered or brushed his teeth or changed his clothes in days.

We sat on the floor in that back bedroom he used to share with John. He'd only been there three days and the room was already a mess—clothes everywhere, food wrappers, dirty dishes, a dirty ashtray filled with butts. The smell was worse toward the floor, so I sat on the bed, looking down at him.

"What's going on with you?"

"I just can't do it, I had to get out of there."

"Why?"

"Because all I could think about was dying." My instinct was to frown or gasp, maybe climb on the floor and hug him. That's what he would have expected and probably what he wanted. But it wasn't what I felt. Instead, I felt curious. He tried to look aloof. I could tell that he cared because his eyes were wet and red. He looked so fragile, so on the edge, I was afraid to say anything. He was a dome of thin glass in my hands—any word, any move, and he would shatter. He lit a cigarette.

"I think about death everyday," I said.

I though I saw a slight furrowing of his brow but he went back to expressionless so quickly, I couldn't be sure. He sucked on his cigarette, took a big gulp of smoke and expelled it with a gasp. He brushed the hair from his lips.

"Cool," he said.

But I knew he hadn't understood. I didn't think about death with despair or even glumness, but rather with something more like appetite. Not appetite to die, but to explore the complex and multifarious passageways of thought and association attending the subject. That made me remember Andy and something he'd said about time. I remembered the hours I spent alone with him exploring completely unchartered thought landscapes. He had gone away when I found alcohol. I realized that I missed him.

"Being born is a sentence to death," Jonas said. I thought about that and frowned.

"It's more like a sentence to life. Death is just built into it."

Jonas smiled almost imperceptibly and said, "You're right. And life feels like a nightmare I can't wake up from. Maybe dying will be the waking up."

My frown deepened and I felt something dark and tidal start to rise in me. I sat up straight and stiffened to hold it down. But it was hot and fast and destructive and there was nothing I could do to stop it. Powerful fear instantly engulfed me, like a pyroclastic flow from a volcano. I was terrified because I agreed with him, somewhat. Life's nightmare was loud and harsh, like standing naked underneath a waterfall enclosed in a cavernous black cave, so that the waterfall's worth of sound was exponentially increased by layers of echo. It was so cold as to render the body unfeeling, so deafening and blinding as to remove any coherence of meaning. The only relief I'd found to that point was the same feeble mechanism Jonas was beginning to burn out on—drugs and alcohol. Chemical substance: it was a poncho and a volume dial. It buffered the weight and turned down the sound.

"It's not really as bad as all that," Jonas said. I looked down at him and realized I'd been close to tears and frowning hard. His face was pointed squarely at me and something like concern was evident in his eyes. I relaxed my face and tried to smile. He lit another cigarette and handed it to me. I took it and pulled in air through its tube of tobacco lit with fire. I squinted past the red ember to see Jonas gazing up at me, his face caught in a strange glow in my field of vision. He looked stricken, radiant in his struggle.

57. Lanthanum (Lanthanoid; Primordial; Solid)

In the years following June's accident, those stories about what we were doing during and in the weeks following the actual event that were told so often and with so much detail—they didn't continue. I had had so much interest in those stories, and in the lives of my siblings and my mom in general, that I would ask to hear about them repeatedly and would listen with reverence. As I got older and more dulled by alcoholism, I lost vivid access to their stories. Not because I lost interest, but because they stopped talking to me and me to them. It was simply the inevitable physical manifestation of the mental and emotional fragmentation set off upon the moment of impact. An approximation of that scattering, commencing about eight years after the accident, is as follows.

58. Cerium (Lanthanoid; Primordial; Solid)

Jonas continued to be a bum at home for about a month, emerging from his hellhole of a room only in darkness, right around the time my dad sat down to start his nightly drinking. Jonas would sit and have a few drinks with my dad then go out and not return until the morning. My dad was never a good-natured drunk; he only became progressively more miserable and mean with each drink. So one night, about a month in, when Jonas came down to drink some of my dad's beers, my dad blew up at him.

"You're a fucking bum and a failure, get out of my house!"

Jonas, I suspect, defended himself by pointing out the generously lacking quality of life my dad, himself, enjoyed. They fought, and though I wasn't there, I can imagine how it unfolded. Dad, red-faced and dome-bellied, dressed in stained sweatpants and a Browns T-shirt, the light and sound of the eleven o'clock news on the television flickering away in the background, swore and spit and raged at Jonas telling him exactly what a lowlife he was and exactly how unwelcome he was to stay even one more day at home. Jonas, either hungover or already high and primed for another night, thundered back at my dad, calling him John, pointing out how he wasn't his dad, and telling him what a waste of a husband and a father he'd always been.

Enter my mom, sleepy-faced and nightgown-clad from her bedroom, paperback novel still in her hand. "What's going on here?" She would have asked. My dad, directing his beam of rage now at her, because she was complicit, having birthed and welcomed back this loser of a son, shouted an ultimatum at her that would make her drop her book.

"He goes, or I go, what's it going to be?"

To this, my mom's expression and immediate resolve would have steeled and her shoulders would have squared before she said, without hesitation, "You go." And when my dad was momentarily baffled, she would have dealt him the uppercut: "Don't you ever make me choose between you and any of my children."

59. Praseodymium (Lanthanoid; Primordial; Solid)

About a month later, Lee sought out Jonas in his slum apartment after he failed to show up for work at the bar for three days in a row. Lee had been working as a waitress at the brewery and restaurant and had gotten Jonas a job there as a bartender after he left Mom's house. Jonas had rented an apartment very near the bar in the then-dingy Gates, a neighborhood in Rochester's near west side. Lee, newly engaged and optimistic about her future, spent a lot of time worrying about Jonas. It was a load of anger-tinged worry that she transferred back and forth between the twins, June and Jonas, for years.

Lee knocked on Jonas's door. He didn't stir, but she knew he was in there. She could smell him. She kicked and pounded on the door and rattled the door handle and yelled, "Jonas! I know you're in there, let me in!" There was no answer, no sound. Lee worried that maybe Jonas was dead. Panicked, she sought out the superintendent of the building, himself half dead, and threatened to report his intoxication on the job to his superiors if he didn't let her into Jonas's apartment. It worked. He let her in, and they both reeled back from the smell as the door swung open. Inside, there was a small mountain of unopened mail, a number of unidentifiable stains covering the carpet, and enough trash scattered about to fill a dumpster. On the walls, there was what looked like dried vomit. On the floor, deep in a shadow in the corner of the windowless room, was Jonas. Blood leaked out of his nose and mouth. He had soiled himself. He was unconscious.

What followed was retold to me in detail later on. Lee called an ambulance and followed Jonas to the hospital. Once roused with fluids and painkillers, Jonas was referred to the psych ward for an evaluation. Lee told the intake counselor everything she knew about Jonas's addiction. She also talked about his steady decline since his twin sister's life-threatening, life-altering car accident eight years prior. Jonas was a bit delusional, which helped Lee's cause, and they admitted him into the psych ward for three days. Lee visited him each day, bringing him things and trying to lift his spirits. Whatever she said to him during those three days convinced him to check himself into an inpatient treatment program upon leaving the psych ward. After 30 days, he transferred to outpatient, started attending daily AA meetings, and moved into an apartment with me.

60. Neodymium (Lanthanoid; Primordial; Solid)

John joined the U.S. Air Force after graduating from high school and spending the subsequent year delivering pizzas and smoking pot. I really have no idea what compelled him to do that and I was very worried about how he would fare, especially in boot camp. It turned out to suit him just fine. He later recounted stories about eating very little, exercising very much, pooping hard little pellets, and zoning out while being screamed at by drill sergeants. John was laid back enough to see that as the game it was and divorce himself from it. This was where years of experience playing and mastering video games served him well. Boot camp was just another video game for him to master—get to the next level, slay the dragon, save the princess. While other young men and women had their spirits broken and lay awake at nights crying into their pillows, John excelled at playing the game until he mastered it. His shoes were mirror surfaces, his pants perfectly creased, his face clean-shaven, and his hair military tidy. By the time he graduated boot camp he was earmarked for greatness.

He did his requisite four years, spending some of that time in the hot deserts of Saudi Arabia, and working mostly as an MP. We exchanged a few letters and when he came home on leave, we got rip-roaring drunk together. When drunk, John and I both had a penchant for emotional overflow. We had several long crying and hugging sessions during those drunks, but what the sadness was about, I can't recall. Viscerally, the memory feels like we were existentially distraught, simply crushed under the weight of the lead-like air we were forced to breathe everyday, every second. The intoxication took us by the hair and pressed our faces up against that naked truth so that we could do nothing but experience it in a raw, sensual way—its taste and smell and texture pressing into our eyes and noses and mouths.

When John finished with the military, his plan was to come and live with Jonas and me. But things don't often go as planned.

61. Promethium (Lanthanoid; Natural Radio; Solid)

June spent four years attending college at Wright State University. It was the only stretch of time during which I had little to no contact with her, save her infrequent visits home and one or two visits I made to her there. During my first visit to June at her college, I remember being horrified by her roommate, whose name I don't recall. The roommate was mean, mean looking, and literally walled off. She had built a wall dividing their small room, allotting more space for herself than for June.

"She locks me out sometimes," June said. We were sitting on her dorm room bed. The roommate was absent. I scowled over at her side of the room.

"She locks you out?"

June nodded. I had the urge to vandalize the roommate's bed and belongings.

"Have you asked her not to?"

"Yes! I knock and knock and she doesn't open up. So I go to the lounge. Once, I sat on the floor outside the room almost all night."

"June, what the fuck?" I realized I was yelling at her and I lowered my voice.

"Do you know why she does it?"

"She has a guy in here."

"Oh." Somehow, that made a difference. At least she had a reason. But still, I decided to wait for her and tell her never to do that again, or else. As if reading my mind, June said, "Don't say anything to her about it, okay?"

I vaguely remember the balance of that day. We went to an Italian chain restaurant for dinner, we walked around her campus. It was convenient because everything was accessible. Underground tunnels with elevators provided access to every building. The only thing I remember worrying about was the grocery store. It was across an athletic field that June had to cross with her walker, which wasn't that good at off-roading.

Some time later I heard a story about June falling in the field on the way back to her dorm with her basket filled with groceries. Instead of helping her, a group of kids apparently ran up and stole her groceries, then simply walked away with them. I imagined the scene with terrible, photographic clarity. June was wearing her Wright State sweat clothes and her chunky shoes with the brace underneath the left one (she had to always buy two pairs of shoes, one pair a size larger, to accommodate the hard, plastic brace on her left foot and ankle that prevented it from turning inward). It was probably the left foot that tripped her (she tends to drag it) and the wheels were stuck in some soft ground. She fell to the side, crashing with a holler and feebly reaching for her spilling groceries. A group of total assholes approached and June felt grateful to these kind strangers about to help her. Only they didn't. They ignored her protests and walked away, knowing that she would not be able to get up or move fast enough to ever catch up to them. June had to make her way back upright on her own. Get unstuck on her own. And the recurring grass or dirt stains that appeared on all of her clothes like emblems were there, highlighting her disgrace, underscoring her sadness as she made her way, emptied out, back to her cold, mean dorm.

62. Samarium (Lanthanoid; Primordial; Solid)

Mom left the night of Dad and Jonas's fight, as did Jonas. She checked into a hotel for a week and left my dad alone. We all thought maybe they would get a divorce. We called each other and talked about it. Jonas felt righteous in his being chosen. Eventually, Mom told my dad where she was and agreed to talk to him. He brought her flowers and apologized to her. She has always been too forgiving of that man. She went back home and forgot the whole thing. Jonas was out of the picture, so all was well. She passed the next several years in much the same way she always had, being neglected nightly by her husband in favor of booze and curling up with a mystery or a romance in paperback. She once talked about how she looked forward to the empty nest, because they would travel and see every city in the country. She envisioned the two of them in a camper trailer on a perpetual road trip, visiting all the places she never had a chance to go. Instead, she never stopped working, never stopped reading, never stopped taking care of June, and stopped wanting anything from my father. In bed, she would smoke, read her book, and try not to think about how she would have preferred her life to be.

63. **Europium** (Lanthanoid; Primordial; Solid)

I moved into an apartment with Jonas when he was released from inpatient treatment. My drinking was in full force while his sobriety was just beginning. I kept most of my alcohol in my bedroom closet just to be polite. Each day, I would transfer my daily ration to one of the bottom drawers in the refrigerator for chilling. Jonas and I quickly found a rhythm in living together. Walking down the long, narrow hallway to my bedroom, I would pass his bedroom. Often, the door would be open and I'd see him in there kneeling next to his bed with his head bowed. Every time I saw this, I felt a stab of pity in my gut. I was rarely home, which I know he preferred, and when I arrived home drunk and late at night, I sometimes got into his bed accidentally. Unlike when we were kids, he made me go to my own bed on such occasions. A few times he even carried me. I only know this because he would angrily tell me the next morning.

A few times, I accompanied him to meetings. I remembered liking his new friends. I found some of their stories and their enthusiasm inspiring. Their stories reminded me of cicada shells. Once, when I was a kid, the seventeen-year cicadas appeared—emerged from underground, scaled bushes and trees and molted, littering the ground everywhere with their papery and somewhat grisly shells. Our neighbor collected the delicate skins each day. At her kitchen table was a clear glass bowl filled with dozens of exoskeletons—their iridescent surfaces reflected off one another and made a colorful, metallic light. It was this same way with the stories of Jonas's new friends. Having sloughed off their old ways, they turned into something new while using their discarded pasts to make something beautiful together, something that never failed to feel powerful. But to never drink again? I watched it all with some wonder: a mixture of deep, plaintive admiration and the unspoken question of whether this might be going too far.

I watched Jonas transform. He cleaned up, lost weight, quit smoking, and dressed in clean, pressed clothes. He got two jobs, one as a third-shift security guard at a building and one during the day as a nurse's aid in the psych ward where he once resided. He went to one or two meetings every day. He made a grid on a piece of poster board and charted all of his creditors and all of his debt. He worked out what he was able to pay each month for each debt then contacted the creditors and explained that he was in recovery and doing his best to rebuild his life. Every one of them was willing to work with him.

It wasn't just his appearance that changed or even his behavior. There was something much more significant and dramatic than that. My brother became enveloped in a profound peace. The peace did not sit on the surface like it does with some people who are just inherently peaceful. Rather, it was filled up inside him like smoke. It leaked out through his increasingly clear eyes. I recognized it even while sliding further down my proverbial slippery slope. It was both unfathomable and immutable.

Things went on this way in our apartment for nearly a year until one night, everything changed. Again, I came home late and drunk but this night, in a black out, I ordered a pizza. I must have passed out after making the call because I vaguely remember being roused by an angry Jonas standing in front of a pizza delivery guy inside our apartment holding a box. I don't remember what happened next, but Jonas told me. Jonas went back to bed and I stood up from the couch, took the pizza from the guy, switched off the light in the living room, and walked back to my bedroom. Jonas said he saw me stagger past his bedroom with my head thrown back and that I was lowering the point of a slice of pizza into my mouth. I soon switched off my light and the apartment was totally dark. Then Jonas heard a male voice in the darkness call out, "Is someone going to pay me?"

Jonas got back out of bed and found the pizza guy still there, standing in front of the door in the dark, waiting for payment. I had even reached past the guy to lock the front door before going to bed. Jonas paid for my pizza and let the poor guy out. The next morning, he was up and dressed and sipping coffee when I came out.

"We have to talk," he said. I just stared at him and didn't say anything. I knew what was coming. I plopped down on the couch beside him.

"One of us has to move out," he said, "and I'd like it to be you. I can pay the rent here on my own now. You can find a place and John can move in with you. I need to live alone for a while."

I didn't argue. I knew he was right. John and I would drink together and it wasn't fair to keep torturing Jonas that way. Looking back, I wish I would have hugged him or thanked him for setting that boundary. But instead, even though I didn't feel it, I acted angry.

I moved out and before John could move in with me, I met Michelle at the bar and she moved in with me. John lived by himself, Jonas lived by himself, and I lived with Michelle. Jonas eventually went back to medical school and although he stayed sober during that time, he continued avoiding June. Instead, most likely to assuage his guilt, he volunteered through different nonprofits that help people with disabilities. I, too, avoided June, as well as everyone else in my family as much as possible for as long as possible. That decision was not as much about sorrow or fear as it was about the serious work of looking at and dealing with such enormity.

64. Gadolinium (Lanthanoid; Primordial; Solid)

Wake up to the sound of the garbage truck and say, "fuck me," because you forgot to take the cans to the curb. Sit up in bed and look around the room. Try to remember what day it is and why you're alone in bed. She must have taken your car to the methadone clinic again. She has to get her "dose" every morning between 7:00 a.m. and 9:00 a.m. and the clock on your bedside table reads 9:40 a.m. Lay down, slide to the edge, and reach under the bed for the box. Not finding it, pat around with your hand as far as you can reach in any direction. Take care that your knuckles don't bump the underside of the bed while doing this, but if they do, it will be useful as proof that you're actually awake. (The distinction between sleep and wakefulness has continued to blur to the point where most days, you feel as though you spend the clock around in a sort of shallow, fitful sleep.) If you still don't find it, roll out of the bed and onto all fours then place your face to the cold wood slats and peer under. The box is gone. Feel angry because she took it and hid it from you. You paid for all that weed and you should be able to smoke it whenever you want. Sit up and look around the room for a likely hiding place.

After turning the closet inside out and still not finding the box, growl in frustration and slam the closet door closed. Her shoetree hanging on the inside of the door will crash to the floor. Cringe at the sound of her shoes tumbling off with soft thumps. This will make her angry. Decide to fix it after you've had coffee and a little smoke.

Go to the kitchen and find the pills in the drawer. Take one of the big white ones with a little water and put the coffee on. Set about finding the box. Check the coat closet in the front room, the drawers in the dining room, and every concealed space in the kitchen. Failing that, get a cup of coffee and sit down to think. The narcotic in pill form has taken the edge off and will make it more difficult to concentrate. It might make you sleepy as well. Don't go back to bed because there is something you were supposed to do. Try to remember what it is while sipping hot, black coffee and looking around for the place she might have hid the box. Under the couch? Get up so suddenly that you bump the table and knock the coffee over, which makes a black puddle on the Formica and rivers off onto the floor. Proceed to step into the spilled coffee with your sock foot and utter an expletive.

Not wanting to forget where you were going, decide to clean up the spilled coffee after you check under the couch for the box. Move the coffee table out of the way and kneel down. Notice how dirty the floor is from your shoes and the dogs and whatever else and think about cleaning it one day. Reach under and feel around while bending and peering into the dark slice of space. It's a few moments of dirty nothing until you bump the box with the side of your thumb. Relief floods your mind. Pull the box out and sit down right where you are, pulling it onto your lap like a beloved cat. Open it slowly, reverently, taking in the smell that's released with the hinged lid's ascent. The baggie is nearly full as you just recently purchased an eighth. You got it on credit and you have to make it last until you have enough to pay your dealer for the front and the next bag, too.

Pick up the package of papers and remember that you can't roll a joint very well. Replace those and take the pipe instead. Reach into the baggie and pull out one stem with several fuzzy leaves on it. Bring it to your nose and take a deep inhale. You love the smell of the buds fresh out of the baggie. It calms you and makes you feel at home. With care, crush the stem and leaves into the bowl of the pipe. Pack them firm by pressing with your thumb. Bring the pipe to your lips, light the bowl, and suck hard. The first lungful feels the best. Hold it in and feel it penetrate into your veins, the soft tissues and organs around your gut, dulling away the sick feeling there that you wake up with every day. Feel it rise to your head and gather there. It sizzles behind your eyes and they water. Close them. Hold your breath a little longer until your body lurches for air. Exhale. Slow and controlled, let the smoke out of your lungs. Just as you lift the pipe to take another hit, you hear the car pulling into the driveway.

Hold still and strain your ears. Imagine them extending and bending from your head in the direction of the driveway. Wonder if you didn't hear the car after all but were paranoid. Resume your second hit just when you hear the unmistakable slam of the car door followed closely by the back door opening and footfalls ascending the stairs. Do a lazy calculation of what it would take to put out the pipe, re-hide the box, clean up the coffee, and fix the shoetree. There's no way, so sit back and brace yourself.

Close your eyes with pipe in hand and stretch out your legs. Listen as she comes through the door and walks to the dining room. Feel her eyes take in the toppled mug and spilled coffee. Then beyond, through the arched entryway to the living room, the coffee table askew and you, seated on the floor with the pot box on your lap, the pipe in your hand, and your eyes closed.

She will say: "What the fuck?" The last, hard syllable pitched high with emerging realization. Just sit still, don't react.

"What the fuck are you doing?" she will demand, walking toward you. The coffee table bursts away and your eyes snap open. She's standing over you, red faced, having kicked the coffee table.

Think of something righteous to say. Failing that, ask: "Why'd you hide it?"

Her answer will be: "Because I'm sick of you smoking it all when I'm not here." She says this with barely contained rage causing spit flecks to fly down from her mouth onto your outstretched legs. Numbed by the pill and the pot, you don't feel as afraid of her as usual. To reduce the fear even further and amplify the numb, take another hit.

"Bitch," she'll say, hissing it like a snake. Simultaneously, she will snatch the pipe and throw it against the wall where it will break and add another chip to the paint. She takes the box from your lap and retreats stormily, knocking books and picture frames off shelves in her wake. Listen for the closet door to open and cringe when you hear the grunt of rage she will emit upon discovering the devastated shoetree.

Sit and be as still as possible while she stomps back into the dining room, bends forward, and screams at you red-faced and trembling. Don't pay attention to what she screams, simply tense all your muscles and try to clamp shut your ears. Watch as she picks up the closest thing to her (a dining room chair) and smashes it against the hardwood floor like a wild animal killing its prey until she's left with nothing but splintered wood in her hands. Ragged chunks of chair surround her and you can see from where you sit that the floor has been gouged. She will stand there for a while trembling and looking dumbfounded at you, as though you just then materialized. After several moments, her expression turns to raw disgust, she drops the pieces of chair in her hands, turns, and walks out through the back door, down the stairs, and into the daylight.

When the car starts then squeals out of the driveway, only then will it be safe to move. Stand up and look out the window through the blinds. With dappled sun on your face, feel something caged and fierce behind your eyes. It's bound to break free. Stare at what is out there, free: Rooftops gleaming black, pavement glistening wet.

65. Terbium (Lanthanoid; Primordial; Solid)

Nobody ever thought they would have a baby. June went to Wright State University for four years, funded by The Bureau of Vocational Rehabilitation, or BVR. This after her honorary graduation from high school. While away at Wright State, she met a young man, also with a head injury, in the Office of Disability Services. They got together and in a matter of months were engaged. I will never forget them, hand in hand, staggering down the aisle after it was done, looking so happy and full of hope.

It seemed miraculous when June announced she was pregnant, and even more so when she carried the baby to term and gave birth, considering all the damage done to her insides, the pelvis bones having been broken in seven places and badly healed, with calluses like knotted pine over the mended parts.

June was on the table, her head strained up, face red, pushing. Far too many people were in the room: my brothers, my brothers-in-law, my oldest sister, my parents. Mom was standing on one side of June pulling back one leg while a nurse was positioned on the other side with her other leg so that they were spread wide, revealing her open, red center splayed apart and swollen for all to see. It was small, loose and pulpy, like a split filet, tender and seeping.

It wasn't right that so many eyes were on it, yet it was purely clinical and nobody looked embarrassed. It's as though we were all watching an instructional video, except that she was wearing fuzzy red slippers, which looked somehow vulgar there up in the air, framing such raw nakedness.

There was too much noise, people were screaming for her to push, she was grunting, something was beeping, people were breathing heavily, panting. All eyes were on my sister's vagina, a widening hole through which we anticipated the crowning of a small head any moment. Instead, just below that hole, from a dark, unnoticed spot emerged a snake-like rope of semi-soft excrement. It was pale green like the flesh of an avocado and coiled into a small lump on the edge of the table between her legs. A collective gasp escaped in the room. Hands shot up to cover noses and mouths.

I looked away reflexively, then back with concern to search out her face. She didn't seem to have noticed. This relieved me. The nurse standing by scraped the coil from the table in one quick, efficient motion with a metal instrument that resembled a spatula. She pushed it into a plastic, kidney shaped container where it remained nearly intact. She set the bowl on the counter next to the sink where it went on to sit for hours like a bowl of guacamole just missing some chips.

June couldn't push hard enough. Her muscles might have weakened or her brain was not sending the message to them like it should, damaged as it is. Because she couldn't push, the doctor had to take drastic measures. He leaned his face close to peer inside my sister's body with the help of a floodlight. The nurse handed him an instrument that resembled an oversized set of salad tongs, which he inserted and opened to widen the hole, then pushed deeper in. The nurse handed him another instrument that looked like a suction cup with a trigger, which disappeared along with his hand into the hole.

When he pulled out my niece with her head in the suction cup and tongs, there was too much blood to see anything. A moment of suspended silent dread hung like a windless afternoon until the baby cried, short little bursts of sound, and the wind resumed, curtains flapped and pages fanned once more.

But the blood. Panic made my mouth dry and my hands clammy almost instantly, worrying that the baby was hurt, or June was hurt, or both were hurt. Mother and daughter were cut apart. What had been held together for the better part of a year was suddenly snipped free in the most effortless way and the baby was passed along to a nurse, who walked out of the room with her. Everybody followed the baby and the nurse with furrowed brows and mumbled concerns. I joined my sister who lie abandoned and bleeding on the table, more exposed than I had ever known possible. The tongs tore the inner lining of her vagina, a nurse explained, and it would have to be stitched right away. I shuddered to think of it, but my sister's face was empty of fear or pain or anything like it.

66. Dysprosium (Lanthanoid; Primordial; Solid)

I made the decision while sitting in my cubicle at work. It was 2:00 a.m., my eyes were glazing over from proofreading legal and financial documents, and the bespectacled, tangly-haired woman sitting in the cubicle opposite mine was talking with the greasy woman next to her about building a fallout shelter in the garage of her rental. She had stocked up on canned goods, she said, and bottled water. Why then, I wondered, was she at work? If she truly believed that December 31, 1999, at 11:59 p.m. would be the last minute before the end of time, what was the purpose of showing up for her third-shift proofreading job? With only a couple of weeks left before the world collapsed in on itself like the demolition of a high rise, or like the final moments of a star—chunks of rock jetting from its surface, culminating in a blazing nebula before, blink, nothing—there was little reason to be at work.

Especially a job like that one, where weary backs bent over bright paper stacks and combed the bundles of black type for errors in spelling, punctuation, grammar, syntax. All night, when all a body wants is sleep, I fought to stay awake and focus on the hard little characters in a row, each letter harsh in its space, each sharp line stabbing my eyes, listening to the nearly unbearable sound of the middle-aged ladies' voices chattering on about everything in their nothing lives, like which roads on the way in were being repaved and how frequently they need to urinate while awake as opposed to asleep. It was there that I made the decision to leave her, the junkie I'd been living with for nearly two years.

I had written the question down, I had given it thought, I'd even talked to the sky about it, and when the longed-for, difficult answer came, I found myself feeling wounded. I should have been kinder to myself, I thought. Even if she hadn't been. My mom always said nothing's a waste, but those two years spent being loyal to her, loyal to pain, it was a waste of breath and life.

I met her two years prior while working in Rochester's only lesbian bar by way of my professionally altered driver's license. Although I was only nineteen years old, my illegal identification indicated that I was

165

two years older, so when I entered, ordered a beer, and flirted with the older woman who owned the bar, she hired me as the coat-check girl. The night that Michelle walked through the door, I was being sandwiched by two other women who were dancing with each other, using my body as a would-be pole. It was an activity that held all of my drunken attention until she walked in. The air shifted with her entrance. Mine was not the only head that turned. She stood up the collar of her jacket like a character in a detective novel. The smell of cold trailed her, the smell of snow about to fall. She glanced at me, then looked away, weary, gazing forward into the crowded sea of women.

The way she stood is what I noticed most, like she'd mastered herself. It was a trick; she hadn't. She was a dog wagging its tail, standing tall and bright eyed in a park, making another dog take notice, approach unwarily and do a play pounce, only to have its face viciously bit. When I was nineteen pretending to be twenty-one, even with all that I'd survived up to that point, I didn't know that things aren't always what they seem. She stood, I thought, in a way that meant she was a girl I could love. What it meant instead was: *I take everything new and good and make it tired and miserable. I take everything gentle and make it violent. I am a vampire and I will suck you dry.* But at the time, I mistook the darkness about her for a broken heart.

I approached her, all liquidly courageous. "You look like you have a broken heart," I said. She nodded but didn't speak, didn't open her mouth. For the longest time, she just stared at me. It was a look that made me feel larger than I was, more significant. And there was something in her eyes that held mine firmly in place so that I couldn't look away. Nor would her gaze ever back down. Her face was the landscape of bravery, from the plain of her forehead to the peak of her nose to the slopes of her mouth and chin.

I took her home with me that night. Two years later, after she almost ran me down with my car while tearing out the driveway to go score dope, after coming home with a black eye and not explaining anything, after smashing a wooden chair against the floor until all that was left were splintered chunks, after overdrawing my checking account, after grabbing me by the neck and slamming me against the wall, after all the anger and rage and tears and sadness spent me in ways I couldn't afford to begin with, I left. No, I didn't just leave. I disappeared.

It was that night, proofreading at 2:00 a.m., when I decided.

Proofreading legal and financial documents was my second full-time job. I also worked full time at a printing company during the day doing graphic design. Furthermore, I was finishing my bachelor's degree. Michelle didn't work. She just went to the methadone clinic, smoked pot, popped pills, and complained about feeling sick. After about six months of that, I had to take on a second job to pay the rent. She then decided to take custody of her troubled thirteen-year-old niece, who had been living in a violent house, and started collecting welfare checks and food stamps in exchange.

She might have been a terrible person but for her love of animals, children, and anyone with a disability. She loved June and Todd. This became evident the first time she met June. It was during one of June's crazy intervals, where her medications were once again in flux and not reliably normalizing her mood and her behavior. It meant she was on suicide watch and that she might get violent. Her eyes displayed the wild instability churning behind them. Her head twitched as though shorting out on its own volatility. She was liable to say anything at any moment. It caused us, the inner circle of her own immediate family, large amounts of anxiety even without other, non-family people in the room. It was as though, every time her mouth opened to speak, everyone would brace, grab hold of the counter or the arms of the chair, hold the breath and tighten the abdomen, prepare.

Bringing Michelle into this mix for the first time was a strained and highly anticipated event. She walked in through the back door and I followed, calling out an introduction to the room. Lee was on the couch next to Mom, and John was scanning the contents of the refrigerator. June was at the kitchen table, glaring at Michelle with a subtle scowl. Mom got up and hugged Michelle, greeting her. Michelle hugged back halfway, stiff and uncomfortable.

Without hesitation, Michelle crossed the room to sit beside June. I could tell she wasn't intimidated by June like most people seemed to be at first, nor was she looking at her with pity. Instead, she sat beside June as an equal, a fellow structure of bones with life inside.

"I'm Michelle," she said and stuck out her hand. June didn't move to shake it, just continued glowering at her, her head twitching. Michelle let her hand drop into her lap and sat back in the chair, looking around the room as blithely as the dog. Before anyone had a chance to talk and break the tension, June spoke.

"You fuck my sister with a dildo."

The words came out in her usual, high monotone, making them sound all the more severe. I might have gasped. Someone let out a short, awkward laugh. Everyone looked at Michelle for a reaction.

Michelle looked at June with the most loving concern and placed a hand on her arm as though comforting a friend in tears. She said nothing. It was the simplest gesture and somehow diffused the tension in the room. It seemed to confuse June, who looked down at Michelle's hand against her sleeve like it was a bird that had landed there.

Just in case the end of time was imminent, I quit my third-shift job. Then, I went to my first-shift job and, feeling like the walking dead, smoked a joint in my car during lunch. I stared out the window at a naked winter tree. I peered into its puzzle of bare branches as if it contained a reason for why I was the way I was. At Michelle's request, I hadn't drunk alcohol hardly at all in almost a year. Instead, I smoked marijuana and popped pills every day like her.

I was afraid to leave. Fear made me want to drink. Knowing that I would leave work early to go home and get some pot, my dog, and some clothes so that I could be gone by the time she returned from wherever she was, I knew I would soon be able to drink again. The thought alone was intoxicating.

I left. I went to my parents' house. My mom paid the delinquent amount on my overdrawn checking account and I promised to pay her back. I closed the account. I left no note, no explanation. I just took my dog, a garbage bag full of clothes, reclaimed my car (which she had dominated use of since I bought it), and left. She called my mom's house over and over again that night but I refused to talk to her. Finally, after maybe ten calls, I answered. She sounded terrible, said she'd cut herself and was bleeding on the floor. Said it was my fault. I hung up and called the neighbor, asked her to go check on her and call 911 if necessary. I stopped taking her calls.

That night, I drank. I drank from the boxed wine in the refrigerator, filling glass after glass. My dad sat at one end of the house drinking, and I sat drinking at the other end. I saw it then: I was just like him. But somewhere in that third or fourth glass of bitter wine staining my mouth cranberry red was a hallway. It was dark and warm and windowless. In it, finally, I thought I was free.

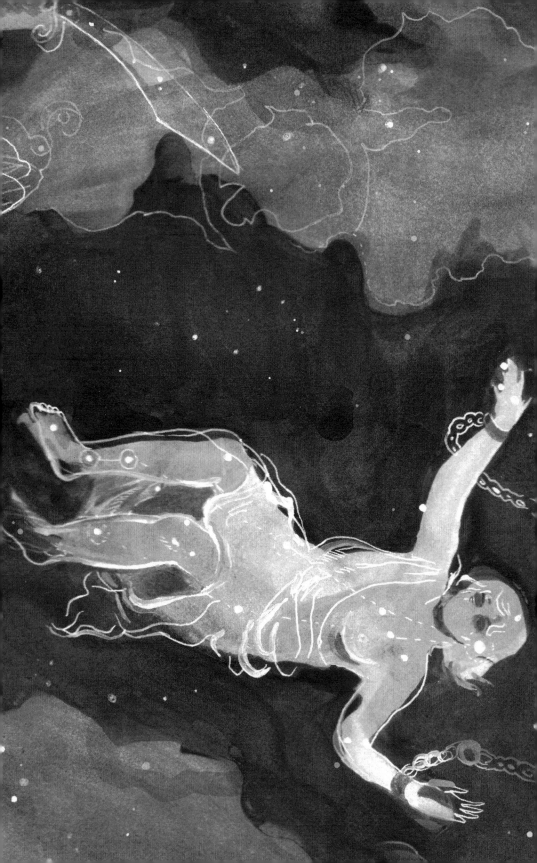

This will remind you of your life

67. **Holmium** (Lanthanoid; Primordial; Solid)

Paris, day four

On the fourth day of our Paris trip, we had Le Louvre in our crosshairs when a complication occurred. On the bus on the way there, a pad was used. This was not surprising because June had a decaf coffee prior to boarding, which I knew would consequently lead to at least two pee trips without a lot of lead time before the first. (As a side note, the decaf coffee symbolizes a whole additional area of challenge whereby both Lee and my mom took very seriously that this trip was for June, as well they should, yet that manifested in a scramble to immediately fulfill her every desire. If she wants a decaf coffee, we had better go find her one within five to ten minutes or the stress level skyrockets. This isn't to complain, but rather just to paint a full and accurate picture of what we were dealing with, in total.)

With the first pad down and one in her purse, and with us just getting started with a full day beginning with Le Louvre, the first order of business upon arriving there had to be finding the nearest restroom. Once found, there was a line out the door and strung down the hall, which is anxiety-producing in public places at home, but double that in a foreign country where the people I'm about to cut in front of may not speak English.

"Excuse us," I said, wedging her wheelchair through the door to the bathroom at the front of the line, "my sister has an emergency and needs to cut." Thankfully, most of the people in line were also tourists who for the most part seemed to understand me and they made way. June was smiling up at people and speaking French at them, which was a good sign.

Bathroom business out of the way, we then took care of the eating requirement before finally entering. The enormous halls of the museum were ornate, adorned and the walls we first encountered were mounted with paintings larger than small cars. The space was crowded with people, but still there was a hush uncharacteristic of crowds. I pushed June's wheelchair slowly along, staring at each painting we passed. The scenes were epic portrayals of women and children in gothic distress, sanguine men in the throes of battle, naked men and women in lustful embraces or buoyant flirtation, men fondling apprehensive women, women fondling themselves. Most of the women in the paintings had soft bellies and well-shaped breasts and the palest white skin, like a pool of milk lit from within.

June was barely looking at the paintings. She seemed bored or upset. I was about to ask her if she was okay when a particular canvas stopped me. The painting was so suddenly beautiful that it deadened my legs—I stopped feeling them entirely. It commanded my full attention. It was an image of a woman floating in water, bathed in light, surrounded by darkness. The way she was lit was like she was caught in a shaft of sunlight at dawn upon waking. But she wasn't waking. Nor was she sleeping, which is what I first thought. She was dead, but just. There was a halo over her face where she floated on her back. Her wrists were tied with leather straps and her legs disappeared under the water. Her face was glowing a pale pink. In the top left corner, there was a dark figure, which I thought at first was retreating, as though it were a shrouded evil creature that had just killed her. But when I looked closer, I could make out a face and a second figure tucked under an arm, as though it were a man with a child or a woman looking down on her body from afar, perhaps in fear. The darkness was disturbing, but that wasn't its power. Rather, it was time. The artist was somehow able to capture time breaking from moment to moment. It didn't just still time, as other paintings seemed to, but gave a succession of heightened moments all at once, hovered over them like frames of a film without the sense of motion. It was clear this woman had just been killed, or something terrible had just happened, and it was almost as if something could yet be done about it, but at the same time, too late. A tragic, sacrificial loss that is in one moment preventable and in the very next, irreversible.

68. Erbium (Lanthanoid; Primordial; Solid)

Christmas morning of 1999, I woke up hungover at my mom's house. I walked downstairs and brushed by June who was making her way to the bathroom. She tried to hug me and I didn't realize it until I got to the coffee pot. I felt bad but by that time she was in the bathroom. The coffee smelled strong and looked blacker than graphite. My reflection in the window showed me to myself: jumbled nest of hair, eye baggage, pallid cheeks, slouched carriage. I dropped my gaze to my mug and there, mirrored on the surface of coffee, my face, lunar and delicate, fractured into bands of light, eyes steaming like blown out fires. Seeking out cream in the refrigerator, I saw a bottle of Bailey's and used that instead. Pouring out half the coffee in the sink, I filled it back up with the liquor then added a splash of scotch. My gut burned in anticipation. I gulped down most of the first mugful before refilling it the same way.

Remembering June and her attempted hug, I sought her out. She was in the living room seated on the couch next to the Christmas tree and mound of wrapped packages. I fell heavily in beside her and laid my head on her shoulder, giving her a half hug. She leaned away from me and scowled.

"Have you been drinking?" she asked. A pleasant, familiar heat rose in my cheeks and I felt the softening of my senses from the alcohol.

"No, of course not," I said and moved away from her. "It's ten o' clock in the morning." She shrugged and diverted her attention back to the television, which was displaying (quite aptly) the bar scene from *It's a Wonderful Life*.

My brother, Jonas, had been sober in Alcoholics Anonymous for four years at that point. Since I'd moved out about three years prior, we hadn't spoken to each other except briefly and superficially at family gatherings. That morning, he asked me to come upstairs so he could show me something. When I got up there, he played a song for me. It was *Cool Change* by Little River Band. I felt awkward sitting there listening to a song with him. He looked at me with a pleasant, small smile on his face, like he was carefree all the way down. His eyes spilled that same deep peace, only now it was even more potent. I hadn't been listening to the lyrics, so I tuned in and heard this:

The albatross and the whales

They are my brothers

"This song just made me think of you," Jonas said. I stood up, walked out of the room, and back down the stairs trying hard not to cry.

That night, I went to an AA meeting. I listened, picking out and storing all the ways that I wasn't like those people. I'd never gotten a DUI, never been fired from a job (yet), never hurt anyone but myself (so I thought). It was clear, I decided. I didn't belong there. After the meeting, I approached the man who had been my brother's sponsor. He said it was nice to see me there and that a lot of people had been praying for me. Somehow, this softened me a bit. Without meaning to, I told him how I'd been drinking every night just like my dad, and how I didn't want to. I told him about the coffee and June and her observation that morning.

"You're sick," he said. "You're an alcoholic." His expression was soft and concerned. My breath grew labored. I felt a pounding like hooves in my chest. I couldn't accept such finality. I couldn't stop seeing my mouth opening for alcohol, swallowing chemical peace (the only kind available to me), a secret only I knew. It seemed to have a hand inside me, opening and closing with a flutter. I understood that as a gesture of panic, a gesture that meant how far I must reach and keep reaching to say come back, I need more.

69. Thulium (Lanthanoid; Primordial; Solid)

Take your sister out to dinner somewhere she will like, the Olive Garden or the Macaroni Grill. Sit across from her at your table for two and regard her oily face, her twitchy, thick hands, how they shake and jerk as she reaches to tear off another chunk of bread from the loaf. Push yourself back from the table, force a smile, and say: "Be right back, bathroom."

Sit in the stall and know that you failed her again. The feeling gums up your blood, slows your heart, its beefy beats slam hard in your hollow chest. Pray to a god you've never known to help you not to drink. Turn red in the face with the effort not to weep and with longing for everything that is to be another way.

After dinner, sit shifting on the couch next to her and think about her medication, her prescriptions in the kitchen. The television screen is a bright blur, the room a mess, reminding you on the whole of your life. Stand up from the couch without thinking or knowing where you are going to go. Probably, you will step on a magazine splayed open on the carpet. It will be a trashy tabloid magazine, the *Enquirer* or the *Star*. When she asks you where you are going, say you are getting a drink. You might ask her if she wants one too. If she says yes, you will have to make her hot tea. It is not likely that she will say yes.

In the kitchen, open the cabinet and scan the prescription labels. Select the one that reads: Lithium. Swallow six of them. This is important: be sure to have enough saliva in your mouth to lubricate the passage of all six of them down into your stomach. You might get one stuck at the back of your tongue if there is not enough saliva. If this occurs, take a can of Diet Coke from the refrigerator and wash the pills down with a burning gulp. You will see the rotten food, expired milk, and brown sticky matter within the refrigerator and you will instinctively want to fix it. To clean it would be too much. You would have to start over with a new one. This will remind you of your life. Stop thinking about it and close the refrigerator door.

Lay on the couch an hour later with the lights off, after your sister has gone to bed. Feel angry that you just blew three weeks of sobriety for a bunch of pills that had no effect. One worn-out indulgence will lead to the next and you will think about the time you never let yourself think about, when you were supposed to be watching her but you ran from the house instead. You found out later when you returned how she had tried to kill herself by taking a whole bottle of pills. You will remember that you were vomiting in the toilet while she was at the hospital having her stomach pumped. The damp, mildewed smell of the room combined with the thought will likely make you gag and cough.

Sit up, pull on your jeans, and force it all from your mind by thinking of the pierced, tattooed girl naked, the one you've been sleeping with. You will wonder whether or not to stay. Decide to leave. Grab the duffel bag you packed to spend the night and burst from the house how you do when you leave.

Before driving the three hours to the college-town bar where you know the pierced, tattooed girl will be, stop at the store and buy a half gallon of cheap vodka. Pour the bottle into the large, red thermos you keep in your car and be on your way. Drink from the thermos while you drive and do not stop for bathroom breaks. When you find you have to pee, reach for a big plastic cup that you might have gotten from a gas station soda fountain. You will find it rolling in the wheel well. Unbutton your jeans and shove them down to your knees along with your underwear. Try not to swerve while hurtling through the dark at eighty miles per hour. If you find that you can't lift your hips high enough off the seat to get the cup completely vertical beneath you, just pee anyway. Cringe when the warm liquid spills over your hand and onto the seat. Curse while the cup tumbles to the floor between your feet. There will be a sweater in your duffel to sit on for the rest of the ride.

Meet the pierced, tattooed girl at the bar and continue drinking. Go with her back to her small dorm room and watch her undress to loud, angry, heavy metal music under the flickering, dizzying light of a disco ball. Take off your clothes too. Cast them haphazardly onto the beanbag chair or the inflatable couch. Begin climbing the ladder to her lofted bed as she stands beneath and watches. It is very important that you do this

177

because having your bare ass so close to someone's upturned face is the perfect symbol for your failures. The merciless, naked vulnerability of this position will be similar to the way you feel whenever you are near your sister. While you climb, the short distance will seem very long and you will feel the pierced, tattooed girl's eyes on every part of you. This is fine and appropriate to the process. It will help you to climb faster, but be careful not to fall backward onto her as you scramble up and fling yourself onto the mattress.

When you wake up the next morning with a clamoring headache, you will feel angry that you blacked out for the best part. Try to piece together what happened during pillow talk. When she asks if you meant what you said last night, stutter for a while before responding: "What do you think?" If she scowls and says: "Sounded like it to me," then begin with a blanket apology to cover all bases. If she smiles and says: "Sounded like it to me," then respond with something like: "You know I did," and then quickly turn to face the wall because it will be easier to lie to than her face. You will feel so disgusted with yourself that you can barely stand it. Try not to be too hard on yourself. You will not always be so bad.

A day or two later when you're among a group of her college friends playing truth or dare, an activity you are just too old for, having graduated three years prior, say no without any hesitation when asked by the girl with the pink hair: "Have you ever sixty-nined with anybody?" When the pierced, tattooed girl points at you with an amused expression and says: "Um, yes, you did, liar," stare at her dumbfounded while everyone laughs, including her, then stand up and walk out, wanting to die.

Weeks later, though, you will laugh out loud to think of it. You will be with your sister at a chain Italian restaurant again and she will ask what's so funny. You will tell her nothing, knowing that nothing truly is funny. It's possible your laughter will threaten to dissolve into tears then because before you can stop it, the memory of her before the accident and how you used to tell her everything (believing that you always would, because there was no reason any of that would ever change between two sisters as close as you were) seeps in from the cracks in the wall you have erected in your brain to block out the unthinkable. Restrain the urge to cry in front of her. If you have to, excuse yourself and go to the bathroom. If not, smile at her and try to think of something to say. Failing that, fill your mouth with something other than words, a piece of bread or a cracker, and concentrate on the taste of this, how it isn't really as bland as it always seems.

It's important that you understand,
I wasn't trying to kill myself

70. **Ytterbium** (Lanthanoid; Primordial; Solid)

When the planet was young, volcanoes created everything. Their eruptions led to new land. Their elements mixed with air and water to form amino acids, which formed the first life. The chain reaction of creation perpetuated from there.

Destruction and creation are, like water and ice, the very same thing. One rises out of the other as readily and naturally as the tilt of the planet away from the sun brings winter. Rain is now snow, snow melts into rain, rain sinks into the earth or rises as vapor into the sky and the cycle repeats.

After volcanoes erupt and destroy, they cool and rest as new landscapes are formed. The calderas they leave fill with water and become lakes, serene and peaceful depths where people swim and drink, where new life is bred, where foliage proliferates.

71. **Lutetium** (Lanthanoid; Primordial; Solid)

To the Director of Outpatient Treatment for Juvenile Drug and Alcohol Abusers and Offenders of the Law:

I am writing to inform you of the faulty logic that exists in your psychological testing for the young people participating in your mandatory outpatient treatment program. The first and most obvious problem with this testing lies in the word, mandatory—that the participants are there not of their own will, nor even of their parents', but of the authorities and in lieu of some outrageous fine combined with a sentence to community service (whatever outlandish activity that entails), means essentially that they are guaranteed to be dishonest while answering your questions.

An additional problem exists in the test itself, the object, the piece of paper that is supposed to render some ultimate decision that will considerably affect this young person's future, but that lacks the level of individual, subjective interpretation that comes with a personal interview, perhaps conducted by a professional mental health worker, so that the potential addiction issues will be perceptible to persons other than the affected party.

Before I address this testing further, allow me to point out some key mistakes made during the time that I was in your program. I was seventeen years old. Eighteen, actually. It had been just two weeks before my eighteenth birthday when I broke my girlfriend's bedroom window while tapping on it with a tree branch, an attempt to get her attention, to get her to drop down the plastic roll-out fire escape ladder to me again, but I tapped too hard, and when the window broke, I ran, dove under the cover of a line of low hanging evergreen trees, and passed out there, being as heavily intoxicated as I was.

One of the high points of my life came next: The police surrounding the evergreen tree with guns drawn and pointed telling me to come out with my hands up. This incident landed me in your facilities, as you well know. What you do not know is that in the main hospital building, just across the parking lot from your small satellite building, on the sixth floor in the psych ward, my sister was sitting on a shabby couch in the community area surrounded by other insane people watching TV.

Whatever it was the group of insane people were watching over in the psych ward with my sister, they were probably paying about as much attention to it as I was to what we were watching in the chemical dependency ward, if you will, which was a video about what happens to one's brain when one smokes pot for too long, how the chemical THC builds up and clogs pathways, slowing or stopping synapses, tunneling vision. My sister in the psych ward, wearing a stained sweatshirt and her taped-together glasses with thick frames and big lenses, and her hair looking oily and unwashed, and her face breaking out with zits, and her eyes darting madly with unspeakable turbulence, was grappling with similar issues of slowed or stopped or misfired synapses in her brain that made her want to kill herself, or kill our mom, or kill me, or, a couple of years later after she had a baby, to kill her own infant

183

daughter, to want to smother her with a pillow because, who knows why? The baby was an alien or the agent of the devil or because Zeek told her to or some such insane reason.

But that was later, after the time that I am writing in reference to, which was when I was eighteen years old and sitting in your weekly outpatient treatment meetings that consisted of having candid discussions with the group about how much we really drank and what drugs we really used, which were not really candid discussions but a tyrannical barrage of poorly veiled questions posed by various members of your staff, all of them too old, none of them relatable, to which we responded with poorly veiled lies, dishonest answers that were sometimes more and sometimes less than the truth, but anything but the truth.

You should have known. You should have anticipated the dishonesty, taken it as granted even, due to the mandatory nature of our presence there, due to our ages, and due to the clear and plain fact that we were, each of us, nothing but scared, lonely kids wanting so much for someone to care enough to give us a reason to care, a reason to be honest about anything.

Your test, delivered at the end of the eight-week program, was wholly useless and worthy of ridicule from even yourselves. I remember hearing one of your own staff—the tall, dark-haired furry man with thick-lensed glasses—commenting on the futility of the exercise while handing it out. When handing me mine, he winked at me with one engorged eye, magnified to nearly double, orbed by the curved lenses like fun-house glasses that would soon pop out from the sockets on springs and dangle and bounce. I looked down quickly to the stained brown carpet, my white Converse upon it made almost black from ground-in dirt. In that moment, I was tempted to tell the truth. After all, looking at me revealed the truth just as plainly as the stains and the dirt on floor and foot. The mad hunger in my eyes, the shrill cries implied by my every move. Why not just state it outright, I'd thought.

But, alas. For the same reasons noted above, I lied with valiant effort on the test. A bit differently this time, though, because I was doing it with the goal of escaping the next phase of your program should I be deemed an alcoholic by my combination of answers to a group of arbitrary, irrelevant questions, which was that I would have to attend in-treatment for a minimum of thirty days.

My effort paid off. My answers drew a picture of me that clearly contradicted what was visible to the naked eye when looking at me (as noted above), that I was not an alcoholic, but that I did, perhaps, have a high-risk personality. With this information, you smiled and encouraged me to try healthy risk-taking activities, such as bungee jumping, skydiving, go-cart riding, etc.

Regardless of whether or not these alternatives to drinking and doing drugs are, as you said, actually healthy, what was wrong with your suggestions was that they would be impossible to follow, as I was, unquestionably, an alcoholic, and it would have been an easy fact to uncover if not for all your useless gestures, your by rote motions, your plastic, smiling words, your understanding, grave nods, your pats on the shoulder or the top of the head, and your patronizing videotapes.

In fact, perhaps all you needed to do to get at the heart of the matter was find out the easily discoverable fact of my sister's residence in the building across the parking lot and ask me about that. With a few probing questions, I would have told you that my drinking and my self destruction began and gathered momentum when I was eleven, when she had her accident, and when my parents had no energy or time to watch what I was doing or to discipline my actions. The connection could not have been hard to make. Not by you. Not by my parents. But alas, nobody made it, and I was set loose, released from your program back onto my path of destruction.

Not that I would have been saved or even helped by your inpatient program. Not that any of what followed in the next four or five years would have been much different. But then again, it just might have.

Sincerely and with warm regards.

72. **Hafnium** (Transition Metal; Primordial; Solid)

Paris, day four

"Let's go," June said after a while. I couldn't be sure how long I'd been standing there, staring. I looked around for Mom and Lee and spotted them up ahead. I began pushing June slowly.

Pointing at a sign with a familiar-looking icon and an arrow, June yelled, "the Mona Lisa!" Her voice echoed in the large corridor and turned several scowling heads in our direction. I leaned over her, shushing her, and she put her hand over her mouth, giggling. She was so excited. Here it was, the long awaited moment where she would lay bare eyes on the actual painting represented in those stickers adorning her old high school French class folders.

We made our way to the Mona Lisa room, mobbed with people hoping to get a look. The tiny, glass-encased canvas was underwhelming, at best. Not only was it the smallest painting we'd seen yet, but it appeared characterless, especially in contrast to the other works sharing its room, none of them with their own wall. There was an area roped off of about ten feet in front of the glass enclosure, so it wasn't even possible to get a very close look.

I pushed June up as close as I could, fighting the crowd, which sometimes but not always would part. She leaned forward and squinted and I waited for something miraculous to occur. She would burst from her chair and run circles around the room or stand up solemnly and gaze at the painting with increasingly clear eyes. Watching her, I saw the young, well version of her superimposed over this older, chair-bound version. Looking up, the framed Mona Lisa was the poster in her childhood bedroom, unframed and frayed at the corners. I looked again at June, sitting forward in her chair, and held my breath.

But now, no longer sixteen, no longer filled with passion, she didn't care. She dropped back in her seat with a huff and rolled her eyes.

"That's stupid," she said. People standing nearby looked almost offended, which reminded me of Graceland in Tennessee, where John and I visited with Mom and Dad when we were kids. We were in the gift store laughing over some of the ridiculous items for sale, like fragile figurines, coins with Elvis' head on them, and Jailhouse Rock snow globes. I picked up a small glass vial of dirt priced at ten bucks and read the tag to John, "dirt from Elvis' grave!" We both bent forward laughing and a couple of women looked at us like we'd shot them, really, with tears gleaming in their eyes. Apparently, Elvis isn't the only strange thing with devout groupies.

"I agree," I said, and turned her chair around.

"But look at that," I said, pointing to the gargantuan painting on the opposite wall. It was easily the largest canvas we'd seen yet, more than double the size of even the largest of the others. It depicted a crowd of people gathered in the courtyard of a palace for a celebration. The detail was baroque, including the texture of skin and the folds in the fabric of the clothing. Even the details on the building were sharper than life, with the asymmetrical, rose-gray swirls in the marble columns, the fluting in the stone columns, and the statues carved into the eves.

"There's Jesus," June said, pointing. At first I thought she was joking, but her expression was quite serious. And sure enough, right in the center of the forefront of the painting, nestled in among the crowd was a robed and bearded image of Jesus, complete with a halo. Suddenly, it jumped out like the red striped shirt and hat of Waldo in the *Where's Waldo* pictures.

Just as I pushed her into the next gallery, June announced that she had to go to the bathroom again, which was not good because we were on the second (and last) pad for the day. I turned her around and wheeled her back toward the elevator, signaling Mom and Lee (who were standing in the small crowd gathered in front of the Mona Lisa). They fell in behind us, catching up by the time the elevator doors slid open, revealing a packed car. I tried wedging June in but there was no way to make enough room for her wheel chair and the three of us. Everyone in there looked able bodied enough to take the stairs. Don't everybody offer all at once, I thought, to make room for the one person in this crowd who actually needs the damn elevator and isn't just lazy.

The doors slid closed. We would never make it. I pressed the button over and over again, as though that would bring it back up any faster. At least five minutes passed before the doors slid open again and still the thing was half full. There was not enough room, but I pushed in anyway. The doors just barely closed with the four of us and the chair pressed in, awkwardly facing several people standing at the back of the car. I looked down to avoid eye contact and noticed June smiling up at everyone unabashedly. She sucked air between her teeth and looked at me with a pained expression saying, "ooh, I really have to go."

73. Tantalum (Transition Metal; Primordial; Solid)

Dear Sophie,

Not long after I moved to San Francisco, I went walking in a Redwood forest. The trees were huge, some of them so wide, all of them with impossibly tall trunks rising so high that their tops couldn't be seen. They disappeared into the sky. Did you know that the reason why Redwoods grow so wide has to do with forest fires throughout history that burned their outer layers so the surviving trees regenerated, expanding and growing in the process? The trees were burned through living, through just being trees. Because of that, they had to regenerate and expand, deepen their roots, grow. This process gave them the sizeable beauty that draws people. The trees reminded me of you. You know what the trees know. You were raised in the fire.

It all started with blood. It was June 10, 1997. I was twenty years old and my only source of transportation was a motorcycle. So when I got the call that you were coming, I jumped on that thing and tore ass to the hospital. It was the first time I ever took the highway on two wheels and I must have hit 110 that day. I was wearing a small shirt that rode up my back and gathered around my shoulders and neck, flapping like the tip of a flame in the speed and the sunlit air. The hard wind might have torn it right from my body but I didn't care—I only wanted to get there.

The person we both know as the month when summer arrives is not the same person for me as for you. I would have you know my sister, the strange before and after of her. You would have me know your mother, only one way forever, a way I can never know her. In any case, she was your doorway into this existence.

There came a point in her laboring of you where she couldn't push anymore, as though her body wanted to keep you. Like a jellyfish, maybe. Did you know that jellyfish have two body forms, the first of which is one of the least known things about them? They start off as polyps that are not free swimming, but bound to something stationary on the ocean floor. Coincidentally, it's right as summer arrives that the polyp sheds off two parts of its body, each of which becomes a jellyfish. Actually, yes, this is a perfect analogy for us both, Sophie. June was the polyp, you were one body-part jellyfish and I was another. She shed me when I was eleven. She shed you when you were eleven. Jellyfish actually have a big hollow cavity right in the middle of their bodies. They are 95 percent water and can sometimes grow very large. The difference is that we don't live in the ocean and we don't have to stun our food with venomous tentacles to eat it. Well, maybe that's not the only difference.

So anyway, my point is, you were stuck halfway up the birth canal and that was a seriously dangerous place to be stuck. The doctor had to go in after you with a kind of suction device. It worked, he pulled you out, but in the process he cut your head, pulled it into a cone shape, and cut—no, tore—your mom's birth canal, too. It was a bloody mess and we all were terrified until you let out a cry.

Your mom didn't fare well with the hormones, post-partum. As you're now beginning to learn at age thirteen, hormones are powerful things. Imagine the havoc they wreak on a bruised brain, already precarious to begin with. It was this instability of June's that caused you to cling more to your father in the beginning.

You were a wide-eyed baby with a little sprig of hair on top of your head and a tiny, heart-shaped fruit for a mouth. We likened you to Tweetie Bird. You slept stretched out on your dad's chest, your arms dangling over his rib cage. You were a soothing little bundle of breath and pulse, lulling him, too, to sleep. The sight of the two of you sleeping that way reminded me of beached sea creatures, tumbled together while washed ashore—found, after a long parting. You brought out the best in your dad until the worst of him couldn't hide any longer. When he was at his best, you loved and trusted him, clung to him even. When he turned to his worst—his alcoholic, self-deprecating, self-destructing worst—you turned appropriately afraid of him. And while he was at his best, I was at my worst.

I'm relieved to say that you don't remember me drunk. The last time you saw me intoxicated, I was helping Lee give you, Mary, and baby Conlin a bath. You were just three years old, Mary was two, and Conlin was an infant, buoyed in the tub with tiny water wings on her pudgy arms. The sight of the three of you in that bath—shiny wet faces smiling, glistening pink, piled limbs—it claims a vividness in my memory incongruous to the blur of that general time.

I had been trying to get sober for months. For all everyone knew, I was. I'd been going to AA meetings and not drinking alcohol. But I was incapable of being present between my ears for longer than five-minute intervals, so I found other ways to be high. I starved myself, which produced a hallucinogenic state after a while, except that I was too weak and shaky to function. I deprived myself of sleep, which was a different flavor of hallucinogenic, a '*what-was-that-was-that-me?*' paranoid kind of high. To aid these, I consumed mass quantities of coffee supplemented with caffeine pills and abused diet pills, too. The pills alone had an effect, though mostly undesirable—jittery, twitchy, itchiness. I tried over-exercising, but the endorphine rush, although lovely and hearty in a seize-the-day kind of way, was short lived and disproportionate to the amount of work that went into it. As each of these failed in its turn, my desperation grew, bringing me to the Prozac-thieving place. I took four of the pills from my girlfriend's prescription bottle while she was in the bathroom, which sadly had no perceivable effect.

Then it happened. It had been three months since my last drink and none of the slapdash attempts at a sufficient substitute were working. I got a cold. A real, legitimate, coughing and hacking and raw-throat sickness. With the blessing of my sponsor (to whom I'd said nothing true prior to stating that I had a cold), I took some alcohol-free, narcotic-free cough syrup. As I did with everything, I took too much, more than the suggested dose, and I experienced what's often referred to as "medicine head." It was heaven-head. It was thank-whatever-god-is head. It was the closest thing to a real high that I'd felt in three long months and it was a relief of erotic magnitude. I found it like a long lost lover, too long to return. It took up the seat that alcohol had once adorned, filling the clatter in my head with empty space and numbness. I began planning my life around it, stashing it, even stealing it from stores.

It was being with you, Sophie, that day of the bath at Grandma's house, that woke me up. I had drunk maybe half a bottle in the car before going in and finding you three getting ready for your bath. My high seemed to amplify in pace with the tub filling up with water. A feature of the cough syrup high was its slowness of progression, making me more and more intoxicated over the course of an hour or so, lingering along a long plateau, then retreating just as slowly. It was as though it were a poisonous molasses stealthily coating the circuitous pathways of my brain, deadening things as it went. There goes my fine motor function. And now my vision is blurred. By the time my optical systems were breaking down, I was helping Lee to bathe you and your cousins. I held your small body up, my hands hooked under your armpits, and watched as all sharpness and contrast softened to blotches of pink and gray. Your solid body started buzzing in my hands like a slow electric current. It scared me—water being the conduit that it is, I didn't want to electrocute you.

It was in that moment, holding you up in the tub, unable to see, worrying that I might electrocute you and your cousins with my bare hands, that I realized I was very sick.

I went home that night and made a desperate phone call to a woman I'd seen in meetings but hadn't ever conversed with, who, at that point, had been sober unfathomably long—twenty years. Nevertheless, I'd always been inexplicably drawn to her. Judy. Her hair was curly big and her eyes were ice blue, as open and clear as water, as precisely searching as a microscope. She agreed to meet me at an AA meeting the next evening.

I went to bed, woke up the next day at noon, then sat on the floor in my one-room attic apartment and stared at the remainder of my stash: two bottles of cough syrup. I wanted to stop; I knew I wasn't sober. For seven months, I abused cough syrup instead of alcohol. Still, I went to meetings every day and lied, telling people I was sober, justifying it by telling myself I hadn't drunk alcohol in ten months. That day, I stopped being able to lie to myself. I had never been sober. It was something I needed to tell Judy. About an hour before it was time to leave for the meeting that night, I drank both bottles of cough syrup—the most I'd ever consumed at once.

Sophie, it's important that you understand, I wasn't trying to kill myself. Not consciously. Not by drinking two bottles of cough syrup. But after the bottles were empty, I realized, had I taken two bottles of aspirin, I might die. By the time I realized this, I was already somehow in my chair at the meeting and unable to move. The window of time during which a stomach pumping might be useful had expired. If I could have, I would have screamed out for help. But the poisonous molasses had shut down all of my cognitive functions. I no longer understood English; sounds were registered by my ears but indecipherable as language. Familiar features of the room, forms, faces—they all disintegrated into contorted pale shapes with light and shadow like an abstract watercolor.

I sat, helplessly cemented to my chair, paralyzed but for the ability to turn my head to my right, which I strove not to do lest I catch the eyes of the woman beside me and be caught with grossly dilated pupils. I struggled to pull myself back from the place toward which I was rapidly slipping. It was as though I were holding onto a greased rope in a hurricane. When I attempted to form a thought, I would watch it begin to shape, building tension as it did, then violently blow apart into a jumbled, jagged puzzle of disparate raw data.

At the end of the meeting, I stayed seated while everyone else got up and folded their chairs, carrying them off. The woman with icicle eyes approached, sat down before me, and gouged into me with her suspicious and knowing gaze. That look that speaks plainer than words: you're at a meeting, shitfaced.

I told her everything that night. And by everything, I mean every single thing. And do you know what? It was all true. The next day was my first day sober: February 7, 2001. I have been sober ever since. It's the hardest thing I've ever done, Sophie. Harder than falling in love with someone who couldn't stay. Harder than doing that again, then once again. Harder than surviving my sister. Harder than losing my mom's attention when I was eleven years old.

It was the same meeting, Soph, where I sat shitfaced for the last time, that I took you to later on. You sat beside me on a metal folding chair, your legs too short to even bend over the edge of the seat, content to color in a small notebook, patiently supporting me in your small-person way. At just three, you were already understanding of far more than any child should have to be, having begun to work on the problem of what it meant to have the parents you have. You recognized even then how different they were from you and from the rest of your family.

One day, I watched you watching your mom walking ahead of us with her walker, teetering on that stubborn left ankle that turned her foot in, scraping against the ground.

"My mom has bad balance," you said in your baby squeakface voice.

"That's right," I said. "Do you know why?"

You rolled your eyes up and to the side, listening, thinking hard.

"Because she had a car accident," you said.

"Yes, when she was sixteen years old, she had a very bad car accident," I said. "Now, she has a head injury." I waited for you to ask more questions, but none came.

I've often thought of it since—you must have understood your mother's condition far more with your three years clocked than I did with my twenty-three. For you, it was much more than an event, an accident. It was a precondition for your existence. More than that, prior to putting all your weight into her hands daily, you spent nine months growing inside her body. You know her insides. From the time you were an embryo, long before you ever met face-to-face, long before you met

193

—in fact, before you had limbs, even—you rode the world as a bouncing tadpole in my sister's womb.

Strangely, or sadly, I don't remember June being pregnant. I can see it only in snapshots, whether from life or photographs, I'll never know. But it doesn't matter. She went off all meds for nine months without incident, as far as I know. It wasn't until after you were torn from her raging body—her whole universe—that she lost touch again with reality. And you, gaining touch with reality by the brutal assault of life, the trauma of birth. And reality has kept on touching you ever since. Gripping you, even. Leaving bruises.

Sometimes, I look at you when you don't know I'm looking and I see the effects of the pressure on you. The pressure of having been with her. The pressure of having been of her. Thirteen years and you're almost as tall as me. Nine years before you were born, in my eleventh year, the quality of time changed. The years between then and now were a black hole, taking each of us as we were and eating us alive. Time is a cannibal that way. All consuming.

I want freedom for you, Sophie. I want for you to have known the carelessness of childhood like your cousins have, like I did for a time. But then again I have this feeling that your lack of such simple freedom, as much as it's been your prison, is also your way to a freedom greater than any of us will ever know. I want to see you get there.

One way or another, I will see you free. Just as you did me.

Lovingly,

Your Aunt.

The element of crime is unmistakable

74. **Tungsten** (Transition Metal; Primordial; Solid)

The day I showed up to take June's husband Todd away, there was a sloppy, dirty rain reflecting his pitiable state. It was the event that precipitated Sophie moving in with Lee's family. Although he'd stayed dry for most of Sophie's childhood, he had a particularly gruesome relapse when she was about eleven. After Sophie discovered him passed out on the kitchen floor, bleeding from a gash on the head, she called my mom and said her dad was dead. My mom came and rescued Sophie, June, and even the dog from the house, which allowed Todd to go on hijacking the place as his own alcoholic pit. My dad tried talking to him, but to no beneficial end. He was drinking so much by that point that every consequence just made him drink more. He was beyond reason.

I was home from Chicago for a visit and would be driving back the next day. In the car with my mom along with June and Sophie, we stopped at the public library. Sophie read voraciously and someone had recommended a new book to her, so she wanted to get it right away. Mom waited in the car with June while I went into the library with Sophie. When she got to the checkout counter, the librarian told her that she had many overdue items out already, including a couple of movies that were so late, she now had to purchase them outright. Sophie's face darkened with anxiety and she went mute, biting her lip. I explained to the woman that she was having a hard time at home and it wasn't possible at the moment to go there and search for the missing items.

The woman's face softened. She likely knew about Todd, as the library was close to their house and he was the neighborhood drunk. She offered to cut the fines in half, asking that Sophie find and return everything as soon as she was able. Sophie nodded. I paid the fines and we checked out her new book. Walking out, the shame and anxiety wore my niece like a hand puppet. As it happened with her in those days, she shut down under the weight of it and just stopped speaking.

Back in the car, my mom whispered to me that today was the annual block party for June's neighborhood, an event that Sophie loved because all the children came out to play with her. Only this year, it was certain that a drunken Todd would be there causing a ruckus and deeply embarrassing Sophie if she were to attend. The library was just at the end of their street, so we somehow had to sneak by without Sophie noticing, in hopes of sparing her the disappointment. But Sophie was staring out the window and caught sight of the festivities.

"Today's the block party?" She said, breaking her silence.

"Yes, honey, but you can't go this time. Your dad will be there and he isn't well. You don't want to be around him right now," Mom said. This was it—the final thing that put her over the edge. She started crying in the back seat, just weeping. Mom made compensatory offers like going to a movie or getting ice cream, but she was inconsolable. June sat beside her looking miserable, feebly patting her shoulder. Watching them like that, I felt a great hand squeezing and wringing my gut. They should not be driven away from their own home. Something had to be done.

75. Rhenium (Transition Metal; Primordial; Solid)

Having met the man on a few occasions but never conversing with him, I nevertheless decided to call Todd's father who lived two hours away in Toledo. I told him that Todd was a mess and had to go. Would it be okay if I brought him there should he refuse to go to treatment, which I suspected he would? At first, Todd's dad refused, said he couldn't deal with it, citing his poor health as an old man. I responded boldly that my parents, too, were old and they had been dealing with Todd for the past thirteen years—now it was his turn. Reluctantly, he agreed.

I called Todd next and told him to pack a bag, I would be coming in the morning to take him one of two places: treatment or Toledo.

"I'm not going to treatment," he said in his slow, deep voice that slurred even when he wasn't drunk.

"Then you're going to your dad's in Toledo," I said.

"I can't go there," he said, pleading. "You don't understand, I'll die if I go there."

"Why will you die?"

"I'll drink myself to death there, I know I will," he said.

"You'll drink yourself to death here, too. It's better you do that there away from your wife and child."

"Anne, please–"

"Todd, no. Do you realize that your child thought you were dead when she found you bleeding and passed out on the floor? Now she has to be kept away from you. It's not fair that you've driven your family out of their own home. I'm taking you away so they can come home and be in peace," I said, or yelled, rather. I listened to him breathing.

"Pack your things. I'll see you in the morning," I said.

"What time?" He asked. I was a little startled at this, half expecting him to tell me to fuck off.

"8 a.m.," I said.

"Okay," he said, defeated. I hung up the phone. I told Mom what I'd done and that she could take June and Sophie home the next day. She mumbled thanks. She shook her head at me, her mouth was hanging open and her eyes were wide.

76. **Osmium** (Transition Metal; Primordial; Solid)

The next morning, I pulled into June's driveway to find Todd outside in the pouring rain, trying in vain to light a cigarette. He was more disheveled than I'd ever seen him (and he was always disheveled), with one of those fake turtlenecks (I think they're called dickeys) hanging askew around his neck, complete with cigarette burn holes, an open flannel, and dirty jeans barely hanging on at the base of his hips, showing most of his underwear. As soon as he saw me, he grabbed a can of beer sitting beside him and guzzled it, spilling some down the front of his dickey.

Sick to my stomach, I slowly stepped from the car and approached him.

"Let's go," I said. He glowered at me, crunched the empty beer can in his thick paw and grabbed another, fumbling to pop it open. He drank it the same way as the first and I waited for him to finish.

"I had to finish that six pack," he said, wiping the back of his filthy hand over his mouth. A pack of cigarettes bulged in the front pocket of his flannel and he went for them.

"Todd, let's go, it's fucking raining," I snapped. He turned and walked in the house through the side door. I followed.

The house looked like a back-alley homeless ramshackle, with fast food wrappers, beer cans, bottles, and cigarette butts littering every surface. Drinking glasses lay on their side on the kitchen countertop, whatever spilled from them making a hardened path over the edge and down the side onto the cupboards and floor. I gagged at the stench of the place—some combination of piss, vomit, and rotten food.

Todd emerged in the doorway from the living room and stared at me. He held a plastic grocery bag with a few items of clothing in it.

"That's all you're bringing? You sure? You'll be gone a while," I said.

"How long?" He asked, so smashed he was cross-eyed, cocking his head trying to get a straight look at me.

"Long time. Maybe forever. You'll have to go to treatment first and get sober then stay that way for a while. From treatment, you can go into a halfway house, but that's if you even ever go to treatment," I said. He chewed on that for a while, gazing up at the ceiling above my head. There was something wrong with his mouth—I noticed it then—part of his bottom lip, red and raised. A cut? Another cigarette burn? He rubbed his eyes. His knuckles, too, were dark and cracked with dried blood. His thick fingers were stained brown, presumably permanently imbued from coffee. (Coffee was Todd's sole nonalcoholic beverage of choice. He was rarely seen without an oversized travel mug of black coffee in his meaty hand, stained down to the wrist with spillage. He didn't own a shirt without a coffee stain or three.)

"Maybe never?" He said with a mischievous smile, telling me he was either about to make a joke or try to bargain with me, which was amazing because I had no authority over him. But as long as he believed I did, I would let him. My only goal was to remove him from that house.

"Just get the rest of your shit and let's go," I said and walked to the door. He followed. I was about to tell him again to get more things but then I realized I didn't give a shit if he had what he needed or not.

77. Iridium (Transition Metal; Primordial; Solid)

As soon as the car doors closed, I had to open my window and let some of the stench of him out. I had about a quarter tank of gas and two hours to drive with him next to me, an hour and a half if I sped. The last thing I wanted to do was delay that timetable to stop for gas, so I didn't. I drove straight through and prayed the gas would stretch. Every second in the car with him was like rising water. Getting on the highway, it was already up to my neck. Mere minutes later, I was submerged and holding my breath. Every time he opened his mouth to say something, I couldn't hear it for all the water, but tiny fishes would hatch from his tongue and slither around my face. I didn't dare respond to his fish words lest I open my mouth and suck slime scales into my lungs and drown.

We arrived and I leapt from the car, gasping for fresh air. I turned to face a locked, empty house. His dad wasn't home.

"He's probably at church," Todd offered.

"Goddammit," I said, kicking the door. I couldn't stay around him one minute longer, but how could I leave him outside a locked house when it was cold and drizzly?

"When do you think he'll be back?" I asked, trying the door handle again just in case.

"I don't know, it could be hours," Todd said, "He can make a day of it."

"But he knew you were coming, I called and told him," I said, whining. I looked around and saw a building in the back yard—some kind of carriage house.

"Hey," I said, walking toward it. "What's this?"

"The guest house," Todd said, following me. I reached the door and tried the handle. It was unlocked. I stepped inside. It smelled musty and was cold, but dry.

"You can wait for him here," I said. Todd conceded and sat down on the wicker couch. I looked him over—this bedraggled disaster of a drunk. For the first time that day, I felt deep pity for him—enough to raise tears from the recesses of my cold chamber sentiment toward him to the back of my eyes where they burned at the dryness.

"It's cold it here," I said. "You'll be alright?"

He groaned assent.

"Okay," I said. "Bye."

There was relief when I got in my car and pulled away, but there was something else, too. Was it guilt? No, not exactly, not when I thought of my sister and my niece. Maybe it was my own hypocrisy. After all, wasn't I a drunk, too? But he's been given chance after chance to get sober. But what if he's not capable of being honest with himself? What if his brain injury prevents that crucial step? He wasn't a bad guy. He'd been so loving to Sophie when she was a baby. She had adored him, climbing all over him and kissing and hugging constantly. He sat with her and read to her for hours at a time, which turned her into the ravenous reader that she is. And he was a good caretaker for June. He made meals for her, made sure she took her medicine on time, helped her to get around. Sure, he was angry and grumpy and had a biting sarcasm that made him very difficult to be around, but he had the same problem that June had: awareness of his limitations. He wanted the simple things that he watched us all have so easily—a job, a car, a sense of a basic function in society, respect from other adults.

I stopped for gas and picked up a big bottle of water and a pack of cigarettes for him. When I got there, he was staggering around in the back yard, smoking. He looked up with a somewhat straighter gaze at me and I saw curiosity there, a softness.

"I brought you some water and more smokes," I said, handing him the bag. He thanked me enthusiastically.

"I'm sorry this is happening, Todd. I'm sorry life is so hard for you," I said. He nodded and rocked a little on his feet. He was like a wobble doll perpetually poked, always correcting and adjusting to balance upright.

"I love you," I said, which shocked me. I hadn't intended to say it, but in saying it, I realized I meant it. For the gentle caring he had given my sister and my niece, I did love him. I was just too disgusted by him to know it.

"I love you too, Anne," he said, offering it so easily and without hesitation. He stepped toward me to hug me but I moved away. I gave him a wave and left.

He ended up staying in Toledo for a month or two before agreeing to go to a thirty-day detox and treatment program at the VA hospital. From there, he went home, but only to June. However loving and well intentioned, June and Todd were not competent as parents. This had become apparent in many ways. Sophie would remain with Lee and her family indefinitely.

78. Platinum (Transition Metal; Primordial; Solid)

Paris, day four

"Ooh, I really have to go."

"I know, sis, we're almost there," I said. But just then the elevator was stopping at the floor right beneath and sliding open to several more people waiting to go down. Three guys managed to wedge themselves far enough inside to allow the doors to close again. One of them was standing perpendicular to Lee—her shoulder was in the middle of his chest. I watched her from the other side of June's wheel chair, amused to see how she would handle it. She dropped her gaze low and away at first and I saw her jaw clench. The elevator seemed to not be moving or moving so slowly it was almost imperceptible. I started to get hot under my jacket and felt sweat pasting my shirt to the small of my back. Lee stole a glance toward the guy, who was much taller than her so her eyes fell square on his chest. She did a double take and seemed to just be staring at his chest then (I could only see the back of her head). He looked down at her and she up at him.

"You're from Carpentaria?" she asked and nodded to his sweatshirt. He said he was, indeed.

The elevator stopped again and the doors slid open. A small crowd was revealed and I sighed. I wanted to shout, *why don't you lazy asses take the fucking stairs!*

"Oh wow, that's so funny," Lee said, "I lived there for four years, I worked at a bed and breakfast there. It's such a small town, what're the chances I'd bump into someone from Carpentaria in Paris of all places?" The guy laughed and so did Lee. Mom heard her laugh and looked over, curious crinkles in her forehead.

Two more rather large men squeezed into the elevator as the doors were closing, causing them to bounce back open and hold open.

"Mom, he's from Carpentaria," Lee said.

"Get. Out!" Mom shouted. The two guys who had just squeezed onto the elevator looked stung and stepped back, slipped back off just as the doors were closing. I laughed and grabbed Mom's hand.

"Mom, I think those guys got off because they thought you yelled at them to get out," I said. Mom slapped her hand over her mouth and a few people laughed.

"Oh no, really?" she said. I looked down at June to see if she'd caught it all, but she looked checked out, which meant she probably didn't make it. It's like her mind won't handle the humiliation of wetting her pants, so it just shuts down.

The elevator finally reached the bottom floor and we spilled out. I got June to the bathroom right away and let her go in by herself. She did and came out about ten minutes later. I told Mom that I thought she just did her last pad in, but I didn't say anything to June about it.

We wandered in the large atrium under the glass pyramid for a bit then strolled into another section of the museum that was filled with statues and sculpture. Large, intricate pale stone people frozen in dramatic poses as though suddenly turned to pillars of salt. There were many naked men statues along with a few topless women, including one of a woman holding one of her breasts in her hand.

"I bet a man carved that," Lee said and we laughed. I pushed June up to a display of two statues, one of which I wanted to see closer up to inspect the detail in the carved garment the woman was wearing, its folds and swells preserving the illusion of motion on the fabric, as though fluttering.

Something in my periphery made me turn my head and there was June, leaning forward in her chair and reaching toward the semi-erect penis of the unsuspecting neighboring statue, a naked man but for a crown on his head, looking heavenward. Instinctively, I slapped her hand away.

"June, what are you doing?" I couldn't stifle a laugh. June giggled like a little girl and didn't say anything. I looked to see if Mom or Lee had seen, but they were standing in the next room looking at the map.

"What's next?" June said.

79. Gold (Transition Metal; Primordial; Solid)

Witnessing her is like witnessing a crime. Only that would be easier because some justice might be had. Yet, the element of crime is unmistakable. It was there when the event occurred. (Calling it an accident seems wrong, so, *event*.) It was evident in her hospital rooms, the comatose months, her pallid face, the crust around her eyes, the milky muck collected in the corners of her mouth. It was evident in her slow emergence from the coma, like the real-life depiction of the evolution of man image, only to be arrested, finally, at this primitive, unbalanced stage.

It was evident in the violent, deep red bruise on her side, above her right hip. More than twenty years after the *event*, and this was the new evidence. She was standing in the open doorway of the dressing room at Sears when, having tried on a bathing suit, she lifted the draped top of the two piece to reveal it, a dark, palm-sized contusion like an angry shark bite without the teeth marks. I gasped and my hand sprung toward it. I hesitated then touched it.

"How did it happen?" I felt fresh outrage. She fell, of course. Still on her knee and thigh were the yellowing traces of an almost-healed injury from a previous fall, just a week or so prior. Just a few days earlier, her knee had been double its size. Before that, she bashed her face from a fall at the gym. She had lost her balance while dismounting a stationary bike and landed face first into the corner of a treadmill. The impact left a gash high on her cheekbone. Somehow, she came away with a welt on the side of her head as well. Gym personnel called an ambulance to rush her to the ER where they cleaned her up and did a brain scan. I remember thinking when I heard the story, how would they differentiate the old damage from something new?

I regarded her thick, wounded body and swallowed over that feeling of crime. I tallied up the evidence quickly, all of it. Someone had to be held responsible.

"That's not a good bathing suit, honey." It was my mom's voice, behind me. I winced at the blunt honesty. Would it hurt her feelings?

Miraculously, it didn't appear to, from the expression on her face, which always revealed everything she felt. Instead, she agreed without incident or emotion.

She was still showing me her new bruise. Her hand held up the striped blue fabric to allow my prolonged inspection. I looked up at her face. There was a reflection of my concern, but also something else. She was proud.

Her falls were usually bad, powered with all her weight against a hard object. These objects were terrorists—every single one in her path. Gravity, which seemed such a natural phenomenon to navigate in my own body, was much trickier for her. Her body lacked the dexterity required by time and space. These bruises and bashes were her body's continual persecution by the world, its natural laws. They kept the pain living. Pain was her identity. Her way of relating. Her food. Her home. Her everything. The cuts and bruises from the falls were badges of honor.

Finally, she lowered the fabric of the bathing suit and moved to step back inside, closed the door.

80. Mercury (Element; Primordial; Liquid)

I flew home from San Francisco on a red eye and landed in the morning. Mom picked me up from the airport and we went to meet my dad and June for breakfast at Denny's. In the car on the way there, Mom said, "I want to just warn you, I'm not sure how June will be this morning."

She was silent as though waiting for a response. After several moments, I said, "Why?"

"She had an evaluation done by BVR. An evaluator went to her house a few days ago and put her through a series of tests. It didn't go well; she was really nervous. Dad took her this morning to go hear the results and they're coming straight from there to meet us," she said.

BVR had been involved with June for years. They were responsible for sending her to four years of college, cost-free. "Why did she need to be evaluated?" I asked, staring out the window at the familiar storefronts sliding by.

"Because she went to them for help placing her in a job. She thinks she wants a job but she really doesn't. They told her she would have to work at least twenty hours each week, probably four hours a day each day and at first she agreed, but then she called and asked them if she could work just an hour or two a day or just on days she felt like it," Mom said and chuckled. I smiled at the dashboard. Mom's car smelled like cigarettes even though she had several air fresheners to mask it. There was a butt holder in the center console covered in black smudges and ash. I cracked the window.

"So if the results were this morning how'd you know it didn't go well?" I asked. Mom cracked her window, too, opening it twice as wide as mine.

"Because she called me after and told me that she blew it," she said, talking louder over the wind. "She said they did memory tests and she forgot everything because she was nervous. And, she had to do dexterity and agility tests, which she absolutely fumbled because of her ataxia," she said. My stomach burned. This wasn't going to be good.

We arrived at Denny's first and sat down in a booth. I sat across from Mom and ordered coffee. We reached for glasses of ice water at the same time. She laughed and held her glass up for a toast.

"To my beautiful daughter," she said and smiled. I smiled too and clinked her glass, then took a mouthful of water and ice and chomped on the ice. Mom winced.

"You're still doing that?" she said, sipping her water.

"Sometimes," I said. "It gets worse when I'm nervous." I said with my mouth still half full. I sucked more cubes from the glass and crunched.

"Oh honey, what are you nervous about?" she asked, leaning over the table a little. I regretted saying anything because the idea of telling her what I was nervous about made me more nervous. She looked toward the door. "There they are," she said. I felt relieved I didn't have to answer and turned to see June with her walker and my dad behind her. I searched her face. She was biting her lower lip, pinching up a frown. Her eyes watched the floor in front of her. She stopped and looked around. Both Mom and I waved. She forced the slightest, briefest smile then looked down at the floor and started toward us. Mom made a low moan.

81. Thallium (Poor Metal; Primordial; Solid)

June sat down next to me and I gave her a big hug. "Look who's here! It's your sister," Mom sang out as though to a child. I pulled away and June gave me a genuine smile that lasted a few moments until Mom asked the dreaded question, "So, how'd it go?"

"Terrible," she said and her features twisted into a dry sob. She struggled to pull it together enough to say more and we waited solemnly. I wanted more ice but I felt that I shouldn't move. In fact, I was holding my breath.

"They said I'm retarded and there's no job I can even do," she said. One eye squinted while the other drooped and her mouth contorted, pulling to the side of her face. It was how she looked when she cried and it was a heartbreaking sight. The coffee I'd been drinking felt like battery acid in my stomach and my heart picked up pace.

"Oh, honey, they couldn't have said that," Mom chided.

"They did! They want to refer me to MRDD," June said, snapping it at Mom like a whip. I didn't know what MRDD meant and as if she were reading my mind, Mom looked at me and said, "the center for mental retardation and developmental disabilities." She said it just loud enough for me to hear, but not June.

"What?" June said.

"Nothing, where's the report they gave you," Mom said.

"No, not nothing, I can't hear anything and that was another thing they said, that I'm not even deaf in this ear and I can hear out of it. I just think I can't," June whined, pointing to her right ear. Mom turned red with fury.

"That's ridiculous, they have no idea what they're talking about. That idiot probably just clapped his hands next to your ear to see if you reacted, right?" she asked. June nodded. "You have sound in that ear but no processing. Everything that comes in is just sound, the brain can't decipher what it means, so you're effectively deaf in that ear," she said. June just stared at her. I hadn't known that. All those years I thought she could no longer hear sound from that ear. I was fascinated. How could it be that one ear takes in words and registers the meaning while the other ear takes in the same words but only as indecipherable sounds? Did her right ear listen differently to music? If a dog barked, did that ear register that it was a dog producing the sound or was it merely an arbitrary noise?

82. Lead (Poor Metal; Primordial; Solid)

"They don't understand head injury," Mom said. I was out of ice so I reached over and grabbed her water glass, which was finished but for the ice.

"Where's the written report they gave you?" Mom asked June again. June dug in her purse, which was wedged between us on the bench seat. Past her, in the basket of her walker parked in the aisle, I saw a manila folder. Just as I was about to tap her, my dad reached over and grabbed it, asking, "Is this it?" He handed it to Mom. June didn't hear and was still digging in her purse. I touched her arm and she looked up.

"I have it here, honey," Mom said, opening the envelope.

"Oh, well. okay," June said and brought her convulsing hands to the table.

"Your sister's here," my dad shouted across the table, blowing me a kiss and sending me an air hug. June looked at me.

"I know," she said with a tinge of happiness. Sometimes, it was easy to take her mind off of what was hurting her. Her thoughts and moods could sometimes be directed as simply as a baby's, who, wailing one minute, might abruptly stop to break into a huge, wet smile once presented with a lollipop.

"What are you getting for breakfast?" I asked her, nodding down toward her menu. She opened it and leaned down, concentrating on her options. Relieved to have her occupied with a benign task, I reconsidered my own breakfast choice and leaned over to review her menu. She saw me and said, "What are you doing? This is my menu," in a playful and sarcastic way and leaned over to cover the menu with her arms. We all laughed.

Her sense of humor was witty and intact. Whenever she used it, we were all so delighted just to see that side of her that we usually belly laughed, feeling the joy all the way down. What it proved was that my sister was still in there somewhere. Her old, original characteristics could still shine through, even if slowly or occasionally. Those were not characteristics of a mentally retarded person. As though thinking the same thought, Mom said, "They just don't understand head injury." She folded the report and slid it back in its envelope, setting it aside. "You're very intelligent," she said. "You just can't always access it because of your injury."

"Hmph, well. Yeah," June said. She looked down at her menu, stared at it, then looked up and said, "That doesn't help me any!" She shot the words at Mom as though all of this were her fault. And, in both their minds, it was. Mom had been taking care of June and her feelings for so long that June saw her as wholly responsible for everything and anything that went wrong. Mom was the conciliator in all June's affairs and took her job seriously. Ascertaining June's needs and desires and finding ways to promptly meet them began at the time of June's accident. Mom was forced to advocate for her teenaged daughter in the healthcare system and that role has continued for more than twenty years. Naturally, then, Mom took full responsibility for any disappointment June experienced.

Mom bit her bottom lip and looked down at her lap. She took a deep breath through her nose, keeping her mouth clamped, trying to hold in whatever words would have come next. June was waiting, wanting a response.

"You're sister's here," my dad said again and June turned her accusatory look on me. I smiled and put my arm around her, rested my head on her shoulder. From across the table, Mom watched and softened. Her hands unfolded, her eyes lit.

83. **Bismuth** (Poor Metal; Primordial; Solid)

Paris, day four

"What's next?" June said.

"I don't know, there's more sculpture in the next room, it looks like," I said.

"No, I mean in the day. I'm ready to go whenever," June said, "I'm kind of hungry."

I looked at my watch, expecting it to be around an hour since we'd arrived, but it was actually closer to three hours. I patted her shoulder.

"You're a trooper," I said. "We've been here almost three hours already. Was it fun?"

She nodded and yawned. People passing by seemed to stare more at June than the art surrounding us. They must be Americans, I thought. In the streets and in stores and cafés, people didn't stare. It's something I noticed right away. People were more respectful and helpful in Paris than at home, at least toward June. Without June there, the same principle didn't hold and most people turned out to have a minute's patience with the fact that I didn't speak French. Even when I tried (albeit in vain), my attempts were met with scowls.

Mom appeared and asked June if she was hungry. Lee followed, covering a yawn. I was still jet lagged, too. At home, it was the middle of the night. We started back the way we came and soon became lost. The rooms kept appearing, corridors upon corridors of sculpture and then more paintings. Lee turned around and threw her hands up. "How do we get out?"

"*Sortie!*" June yelled and pointed. There was a small sign mounted high on one of the walls with an arrow in the opposite direction. We followed. June kept pointing and shouting "*sortie!*" every time we passed another one of those signs, which must have been at least five times. Finally, we emerged into the atrium under the glass pyramid, whereupon June nearly screamed.

"Oh my god, what?" I backed up from her and looked her over for an imbedded arrow or something similar that would produce a sound like that. Mom and Lee turned and seemed to do the same. June was digging in her purse. I wondered if she had to pee again and had just then noticed that she was out of pads.

"My passport! Where is it?" She said and started yanking everything out of the tightly packed purse.

"What do you mean, didn't you leave it in the hotel room?" Mom asked.

"No, I brought it," she said. Mom leaned in to help and I looked at Lee, who looked terrified. My stomach started to ache.

"Well shit, honey," Mom said, putting things back in her purse. "It's not here."

"Did you check all your pockets?" Lee asked. I scanned the ground but couldn't see much. A continuous stream of people separated around us and converged again once passed like shoals of fish. After a few more minutes of fumbling around in June's pockets, we came up with a plan: they would go and seek out information about what to do if you lose your passport in the museum and I would go back and retrace our steps to search for it. That exercise proved futile and frustrating, because the number of people seemed to have doubled, making it impossible to move quickly.

Empty handed, I rejoined my family who were engaged in a conversation with a uniformed security employee near the Information counter. Mom was writing down notes in the white space of the Louvre map.

"We have to go to the embassy," Lee said.

"Really? What about Lost and Found?" I looked at June, slumped forward in her chair, defeated.

"They said that the chances of recovering it aren't good and that she might have even lost it outside somewhere before we got here." I took a mental trip to all the places we'd been that day so far: a *boulangerie*, the park by the Eiffel Tower where we caught the bus, maybe a souvenir shop or two?

"Why didn't one of us hold her passport for her?" I asked. Lee shrugged and walked away to sit down. I leaned down and circled an arm around June, giving her shoulder a squeeze that I hoped was reassuring. Mom had thanked the security guard and was walking back to us with a dismal expression. Her hair was disheveled and she seemed to be limping a bit.

"We're going to sit and get June some food and see if it turns up within the next hour or so. If not, we can go to the US Embassy and apply for an emergency replacement passport, which could take up to two days to get," she said. We were leaving in two days, so we had to do it right away.

"Are you okay, Mom? Why are you limping?" I asked. She waved me off and said her hip was hurting a little but that she'd be fine. We moved toward the food court area slowly, as though we were now dragging a massive weight behind us.

84. **Polonium** (Metalloid; Natural Radio; Solid)

Sophie wanted to show me the high school and how much it had changed. She would be going there in just another year, which made me feel old. I hadn't been back to the high school since graduating fifteen years earlier and was both excited and scared to see it. We drove up the back way where I used to escape during lunch, leaving out the band door and hopping the fence. The fence was gone and there was more parking lot. The building had been extended, a new gymnasium added to replace the old, the old turned into a second auditorium. I nearly told Sophie about my school-skipping escapades, but thought better of it. I felt a sudden and certain call to stay quiet. She was a very different girl than I had been. She was more like June had been: very smart, a stringent rule-follower, afraid to take risks, trapped inside her own limitless mind—all its various possible untested, unsolidified meanings—and simultaneously set free by it.

It was Sophie's thirteenth birthday. We were to have a party at my mom's house later that afternoon. It had been two years since I removed Todd from their home, after which, upon seeing the condition of the house, Mom couldn't clean well enough to justify sending Sophie back there. Lee took her in to stay. Lee and her husband, Allen, and their three girls made space for Sophie, absorbing her into their family. They made a bedroom for her by transforming Lee's craft room. She'd been there for two years at that point. Todd and June didn't like it, especially Todd. Sophie had been a little daddy's girl when she was a baby, climbing him like a tree and always seeking shelter in his arms. But he conceded, at least most of the time, that it was in her best interest to live with Lee.

At thirteen, she was tall and slender, nearly my height. She walked me through the halls of the high school. Remembering them was like remembering a dream. I couldn't help but to see the kid I used to be among all the others, crowding those halls like threads of light treading endless afternoons in and out of doorways, in and out of lockers. There were details I couldn't remember, no matter how I strained, like where my locker had been. There were other details I couldn't ever forget—details that temporarily spelled me. We walked by what had once been the cafeteria, where I would find Cassiopeia studying every morning before school—her skirts and wool tights, her cups of coffee that I regarded as so adult. I remembered us from then, our rhythms and struggles and messes. And oh, how I loved them. They were real life happening: fiery, flecked, sparking life. Walking with Sophie then, fifteen years later, I saw that they were all shining hours, all-honeymoon: every wretched moment as well as every tender one.

A strange pre-unveiling, a promise
of what was to come

85. Astatine (Halogen; Natural Radio; Solid)

Sophie and I walked quietly. There was often a lot of silence between us. Neither of us talked much. I looked at her, watching her watching the halls and classrooms, likely thinking about when she would attend them. I noticed a change in her. A slight figure beginning to curve its way into her body, an eloquence to her movements.

"I can't believe it's been two years already that I've lived with Aunt Lee and Uncle Allen," she said, still walking, still looking around. I was surprised; this was an opening up from her. An invitation to talk about what happened. She had been going to a child psychiatrist that Lee had found for her. Maybe that had broken open some space around it; loosened its conspiratorial tight-lipped-ness.

"You know," I said, pausing to search for a way to say what I was about to say, "both of us had our lives irrevocably changed at the same age."

She looked at me and wrinkled her forehead.

"Age eleven. Both of us. And, really, because of the same person," I said. She made her thinking hard expression—rolling her eyes up and far off to the side while turning her head in the opposite direction— something she had done since she was a baby.

"I was eleven when your mom had her accident and you were eleven when you moved out of her house," I said.

"Oh," she said, "I was wondering what the connection was. Now, I get it," she said. And that was it. We continued walking close together, all through the halls until we got to the other end of the school before turning around and retracing our journey back out. Neither of us said another word until we rounded the final turn toward the double-doored exit: two shining beacons, like blown out whites in an overexposed photograph, sucking the colors all around them dry. Both of us squinted and looked at each other, shading our eyes from the daylight. Sophie smiled and giggled and my breath caught. There, fleetingly, was June. So long ago.

"Bright," she said.

86. **Radon** (Noble Gas; Natural Radio; Gas)

Sophie's thirteenth birthday party happened on a hot June day at Mom's house. Chairs and tables were arranged outside in the side yard. June sat in one of the folding chairs, under a portable shade provider—a tent-like structure erected in the middle of the sun-drenched grass. Balloons were attached to each of the tent's four corners, bobbing in the thick, humid air like bulbous plants on the ocean floor. All the colors surrounding June—the pink and powder blue and pastel green of the balloons, the orange and yellow stripes of the tent and its awning, the green of the grass, the salmon-pink of June's shirt, even the clear sheen glaze on the air— seemed to glow neon like a strange, glittering breed of open-air coral.

June stared at the ground and didn't look up when I approached. Her face was the tragedy mask iconic in stage theaters everywhere. Of course it was. There was never any ambiguity in June's facial expressions. I sat down in the folding chair next to her.

"Are you okay?" I asked, already knowing she wasn't. She looked at me, lifting her head as though it weighed twice as much and took all her effort. There were several moments of silence that passed between us and I wondered if my eyes were as magically blue as hers appeared just then. A plane passed in the sky above us, sounding like a slow-shoring wave punctuated by birdsong, the buzz of fat flies, and, farther off, the high-pitched voices of the little girls, our nieces, playing in the house.

"They think I'm retarded and can't do any job, I have no hope of any kind of future for myself, my daughter was taken from me, and you went to the mall without me yesterday." This last item in her list of grievances struck me as so funny that I had to engage my abdomen muscles to keep from laughing aloud. Not because it was trivial, not because it wasn't true, but because she stated it with the same weight and seriousness as the other items. Replacing the contained laughter was the old, well-worn guilt that had a habit of crashing every happy emotion to arise in relation to my sister, usually before it could fully form. The guilt walked in and sat down in my gut with such self-assuredness, like it knew it belonged there, like it had a reason and a right to be present, an inevitability that made it almost loving, as though it said, seated in a stuffed reclining chair, "It's okay, we're in this together, you and me."

87. Francium (Alkaline Metal; Natural Radio; Solid)

"June, first of all," I said, pausing, not knowing, in fact, what was fist and what was all, "I didn't know that I would end up at the mall. I went with Jonas to take his car into the shop. We had to wait for it to be fixed and killed the time by walking over to the mall."

Her expression did not register that I'd said anything. The flies buzzing near our heads, trying in vain to escape the heat as much as we were by taking shelter under the man-made shade, seemed to hear me more than June did. Suddenly I was angry. Who are you not to listen to my excuse, I thought, who are you to be so entitled? I felt the flush behind my skin, sprouting beads of sweat along my forehead.

"And your daughter wasn't taken from you. She's right here, she's right inside that house," I said pointing, sitting forward in my chair, raising and hardening my voice. This spawned a reaction from June, who looked up at me and mumbled, "No, no, no–"

"Yes," I said, yelling it. Then, fueled by this new mutation of helplessness resembling rage, I went on. "In fact, Sophie could have been taken from you. Child Protective Services could have come and taken her and put her into foster care where you would have never gotten to see her," I said. June looked down again, shifted her weight in her seat so subtly I couldn't be sure it happened. Her face pinched and she began to nod.

"Your sister has her, she's here with our family where you can talk to her and see her whenever you want. Why don't you think about that? Why don't you ever think about what to be grateful for?" I shot the words at her so quickly and angrily that it felt like a burst of accidental machine gun fire. I'd been handling this powerful weapon and my fingers had tripped on the trigger and before I knew it, slam! Bullet spray.

June's face pinch deepened into the twisted crying expression. She was crying, but I knew it wasn't from what I was saying. It was from what she was thinking. It was her astoundingly persistent self-pity that clamped down on her like the locked jaws of a pit bull and would not let go. And in those jaws, my righteousness crumbled. My anger melted into guilt and pity. I touched her knee. The gesture was so aligned with the helplessness it represented, so feeble in its ability to change anything, so ineffective in comforting her—my hand was a limp dead thing against her bruised skin. She wore shorts that were too short on her; they pulled tight and cut into her thighs. Her knees were set apart at shoulder width and the green of the grass visible between them lost its luster. The coral-like vibrancy was gone, awash with gray.

The door slammed. Lee and John and the girls followed their laughter into the yard and began throwing a Frisbee to one another. I took my hand from June's knee and sat back in the chair. Sweat trickled down the small of my back. The hair on my neck and the underside of my bangs clung to my damp skin. I brushed them aside with my fingers, away from my eyes. I had kept my hair short for years and was only then beginning to grow it out again. The extra length felt deviant and oppressive. Sophie saw me sitting with June and squinted. She trotted over. June hadn't looked up and her face was still contorted with tears. Sophie stood behind June and pulled her hair back. She leaned down with her hands on June's shoulders and said, "You okay, mom?"

June lifted her head and turned her face toward her daughter as an infant might to its mother, quick and wobbly, instinctually. "Mm," she said, and forced a tight smile. Her face dropped to the ground again but she wasn't as unhappy. Sophie ran her fingers through June's hair, combing it. She looked around as though forgetting something until she saw June's purse by her feet and retrieved from it a small hairbrush. Sophie brushed her mother's hair slowly and rhythmically. June's expression changed little, but her body relaxed. Much of the tension had gone out of her posture. The shorts didn't cut into her legs as much.

Watching Sophie brush her hair reminded me of the times my mom would brush the dry shampoo powder through June's hair during her coma, long before Sophie was born, long before there was ever a chance that June would speak again, much less be able to get a job. The rhythmic brushing and the slackness of June's body made me think of it so clearly. I felt the texture of that padded chair, the temperature in that room. I could almost smell the chemical scent of the dry shampoo powder. But before I could dissolve completely into the memory, one of my other nieces yelped. This was followed by cheers and applause. She'd caught a particularly challenging Frisbee throw. I stood and walked out toward them to join the game. The sun drenched me in its bright warmth and I squinted at the ground. There was that coral green again. There, in the grass, was the bottom of the sea.

88. **Radium** (Alkaline Earth Metal; Natural Radio; Solid)

Paris, day 4

After June was fed again and we visited the bathroom again, there was still no sign of her passport. We left the Louvre by ascending toward the glass pyramid in a lift like a large basket for people. The basket had a mini control station in its center operated by a security guard who seemed only to let on people who really needed to use the basket (as opposed to the stairs or the escalator). He was tall and old with sprigs of hair shooting out from his ears and nostrils. He wore an officer's hat, askew, and he kept his eyes on his feet.

What was it like to be him? I wondered. Had he worked there forever and did he have a family to go home to? Or was he new, having taken a part time job after years of retirement to escape pure boredom. His face was slack and somehow sad. It was the kind of face that inspires curiosity attended by compassion.

We walked out of the pyramid's tip onto the cobbled courtyard, which was shiny with rain. Lee pulled out one of the ponchos she'd bought and an umbrella, covering June's lap with the former and holding the latter over both their heads while attempting to propel the chair forward over the terribly bumpy cobblestones. She was right; it was awkward and ridiculous. I laughed and trotted up to help her push, allowing her that 'told you so' look for a few seconds before slapping her on the shoulder. She laughed and whacked me back and we bumped June along in the direction of the Embassy, Mom snapping pictures along the way.

We found a building much smaller than what I'd expected. A line was formed in front at a guard station—a first point of entry manned by an armed officer with a clipboard and a list. Anxiety amassed while we stood in line, because what if June couldn't get another passport? Would France take her and, stripped of her identity, absorb her? Would they keep her here in a cell for undocumented people? A pounding in my temples spread to the back of my head. I watched as he collected ID from each person in line then crossed their name off of the list before allowing them through.

"Do we have to have an appointment?" I asked. Mom shrugged and said she didn't think so, but looked worried. When we got to the guard, Lee explained the whole situation and the guard asked to see another form of ID from June as well of each of our passports. None of us had brought ours out of the hotel room, so we showed our driver's licenses while June started the long process of getting hers out of its fortress in her wallet. Once checked, he let us through as a group, where we advanced only as far as a line marked on the walkway with a sign that read, "Stop here and wait for signal from guard."

Up ahead, through a window, I saw a screening area where people were removing jackets and belts and passing them through scanners. We were waved in just as the people before us passed out of that small building into another one beyond.

The guard asked June to empty her pockets and all the contents of her purse, which was a disaster. She upturned it, shook it, and out came tissue packages and tampons and a pillbox and medicine and wads of crinkled up paper and candy. All the sundry supplies she required in a day.

The guard recoiled from the contents as though it were a nest of spiders. He placed a plastic baggie beside the pile and told her in a thick accent to load everything in there as well as whatever was in her pockets.

The procedure was worse than it had been at the airports. By the time we were done, June was rolled through the scanner. She was stripped down to bare feet and an undershirt and all the barrettes out of her hair so that it stood up at the roots in a failing attempt to hold the shape.

Once inside, there was yet another gatekeeper, a woman who wanted to know why we were there and if we'd filled out the proper forms. We had no forms, of course, so she gave us blank ones. We had to go down in a holding area to complete the stack of forms and have June get her picture taken in a photo booth.

"Should I smile?" She asked me, sitting in the booth trying to be tall enough to get her face positioned in the placement oval on the screen. She seemed tense and I wondered if she sensed my nervousness.

"No, don't smile, look deadly serious," I said, which made her laugh. That would have been a great time for the shot but she hadn't pressed the button yet, so I reached over and pressed it for her, then fooled with her hair to try to make it look tame (they'd kept her barrettes at the security desk in the front building, perhaps in case she stabbed someone in the eye with one?). When the camera made a hard internal *clack*, the picture it took froze on the screen and was predictably terrible—June's eyes were closed and there was a slight scowl on her face while my fingers were prominently featured in her hair. Thankfully, we had the option to discard that shot and try again. That second time, I waited until we were ready to push the button and the camera clacked again, this time capturing an acceptable passport photo, although her smile was fake and forced. I'd wished that the candid, spontaneous smile from earlier would have been captured instead, the real her. Although, what is unreal about any aspect of her? So rather, I wished it had captured her spontaneous joy. Perhaps allowing her to pass that port more often.

89. **Actinium** (Actinoid; Natural Radio; Solid)

"That girl has a head on her shoulders," a friend said after meeting Ariadne, the woman I promptly met after Aubrey broke my heart the first time, the woman who would strategize into the role of my (second) wife. "Nice teeth, too," added the friend. I recognized the latter comment as a compliment and I agreed. But the former. Everybody—every mammal, for that matter—can attest to the presence of a head situated atop and between the shoulders. Perhaps, when people call attention to the presence of the head, it implies certain prescribed qualities like responsible, mature, intelligent. She did have such a head. She was fit, green-eyed, Buddhist, debt-free, a non-smoker, and had astonishingly white and straight teeth. She was feminine and soft in her unemployment when I met her.

When she went back to the corporate world, however, the dresses went away and the trousers came out. A hardness overtook her. I found out she watched football on television while whooping like a man. She was guarded, angry, suspicious, volatile, still green-eyed, turned Christian (she watched and sent money to a TV evangelist and started listening only to Christian music), and still had perfect, perfect teeth. I felt tricked. We both changed so much between the beginning and the end, though, I'm sure she felt tricked too.

In the beginning, I was a mess. I was in a lot of debt, making very little money, smoking, having a crisis with my hair, and sober for some months past two years. My teeth were passable. I used whitening strips. Perhaps that's why she was attracted to me. Or maybe it was the mess. Maybe she wanted to clean it up. I was a dilapidated building, an architectural wonder, in fact, but with peeling paint and broken windows. I'd spent two-plus years gutting the interior and hauling away dump truckloads of debris. Meeting Ariadne was my signal that it was time to start the serious renovations. She helped. She erected scaffolding along my façade and covered it all with a black veil to hide the ugly and hold in the dust.

90. Thorium (Actinoid; Primordial; Solid)

On our first date, I told Ariadne all about my checkered past and showed her a collage of tastefully shot nude pictures of myself. A self-love project, I called it. She was horrified. She barely allowed me to hug her goodbye at the end of it. I was certain I would never see her again. But she called the next day and the day after that. She wanted to see me again.

After two months, I took her to Ohio to meet my family. She interacted well with them, as she did with everybody. Jonas thought she was pretty. June said she had nice teeth and asked her if she had had braces when she was younger. I spent a lot of time having solemn talks with people from my past during that and subsequent trips home. I went to old employers first, and stores I had stolen from. It was part of a series of exercises I was assigned by my mentor—I was to amend harm done. There were many people and establishments from whom I had stolen money. It was money that many of them were not aware of being owed.

On one such visit, Ariadne waited in the car while I went inside a building in downtown Rochester with a check in my hand. It was to an old employer for $1500.00. He had lent me money when I worked for him and I had never repaid. In my bank account, I had a balance of $1603.00. I was a little afraid to give this man all of that money, but I saw it as his money, and I trusted, somehow, that there would be more where that came from.

I sat down in his large office across a cherry oak desk from him. He didn't look surprised to see me.

"I had a feeling you would show up one day," he said, smiling. He was dressed in a suit and tie with lacquered black hair that looked like filaments of fine blown glass. I was stiff in the leather chair with nerves overheating my skin. The room smelled like fresh paint and drywall dust.

"You did?" I asked after a silence. He did not break eye contact and his expression was a cross between amused and grave.

"I did." I waited for more but it was all he offered. I was disappointed to hear it. I wanted him to be floored that I would return these years later looking so put together and healthy, asking to make amends.

"I'm an alcoholic," I said, half expecting his mouth to drop open and release a gasp.

"I know you are," he said and gave a soft chuckle. I winced inside.

"I've been sober for about two years and I'm trying to clean up my past," I said.

"That's great, congratulations," he said. It was genuine. I had always known him to be kind. I held a prepared letter in my hand, which was folded around the check. I lifted and unfolded it, deciding to read it verbatim rather than try to remember what I had to say. The paper was damp and warped where my hot palm started melting it. I felt the red of my face and heard the waver in my voice as I started to read aloud.

"I'd like to make amends for the harms I have caused you. I have had a pattern of dishonesty. I have had a pattern of stealing--" I went on, listing my patterns that were involved, listing the particular ways in which I had wronged him, including the matter of the money, asking if there was anything I had left out, asking if there was anything more I could do to make it right, and finally, thanking him for the specific ways he had benefitted me. He answered my questions graciously, telling me I had not left anything out. He encouraged me to continue on the path I was on. I handed him the check. He held it with a pained expression.

"I feel like I don't want to accept this," he said. I got excited—I wouldn't have to part with all my money after all.

"It's important for my recovery process that you accept it. I owe it to you," I said, without willing the words. Still, I hoped he would insist on declining, but he didn't. He conceded and pocketed the money.

I joined Ariadne in the car after it was done and we drove to my next amend—the man who lived in the house on Little Mountain that I broke and entered a few years prior. I had a letter and a check for him too. $100 for eating his pretzels and causing him to break two of his tow cords in failed attempts to pull my car out of the snow with his truck. To find him again, I had called the local police department and asked them to fax me a copy of the police report from that night.

I was looking forward to this, wondering if the kind man who refused to press charges against me would remember. Then again, how could he forget? Finding a drunk stranger passed out on your living room couch in the wee hours of the morning isn't something you would soon forget.

The house was much more difficult to find with the help of the directions than I expected, and I expected it would be difficult. A gatehouse hid access to the road so that the road itself appeared to be the driveway of the house. Once found, the road narrowed as it ascended and forked off many times so that we took several wrong turns in succession. Turning around wasn't an easy task, either, as the woods were dense and thick on either side of the road. Finally, we reached the address that I found on the police report. It looked familiar, but not very—it was as though I had dreamed of the house before and was remembering the tenebrous image from that dream.

I knocked on the door. No answer. I knocked a little harder. Nothing. I tried the handle for old time's sake, but it was locked. (Not that I would have gone in this time if it was unlocked.) The guy learned his lesson. He probably started locking his door every day after that night. I looked around and didn't see any cars. Through the side window I saw the interior of the living room, the couch where I had passed out. The floor was strewn with toys. I knocked one more time. Disappointed, I left the letter with the check wedged in the mail slot, half in and half out.

Walking back, I saw the spot where my car had gotten stuck in the snow and the reason why it had been nearly vertical—it was off the edge of a cliff. My car had buried itself nose first in a snow bank, the presence of which saved it from going over and killing me in the process.

Over the next two years, I paid back every person, employer, store, and establishment that I had taken money or property from. The more I repaid, the more money I made, both in my primary job and with freelance work on the side. The freelance work got to be so lucrative that I eventually gave up my full-time job and started my own business, which more than quadrupled my income. Having finished paying back all of my theft victims, I proceeded to pay off all of my credit cards and the IRS.

When Ariadne went back to her corporate job, we had a healthy double income, and with my debt paid off, we were free to travel the world together. We went to Spain, England, France, Mexico, and all over the States. In Barcelona, we walked the streets, taking in the art and architecture—Gaudi, Dali, Picasso. One of the most anticipated buildings for me on our tour, Casa Batlló, was under renovation at the time. It was lined with scaffolding and covered over with a black veil, hiding its transitory state. But on the veil, large and lifelike, someone had painted a rendering of what the building would look like upon completion. It was a strange pre-unveiling, a promise of what was to come.

With Ariadne as my coach, my life continued to improve, my business thrived, and the money continued to flow in. This financial abundance was what enabled me to take June to Paris along with Mom and Lee.

These are the four hands,
the four directions,
the four elements

91. **Protactinium** (Alkanoid; Primordial; Solid)

Outside the window, the sky is the color of ash. The clouds rest their arms on the gray belly of the lake. Winter has overslept again in Northeast Ohio and is taking its time to get out while Spring beats down the door. I am opening presents on my thirtieth birthday, surrounded by my family and friends. It's a surprise birthday party thrown for me by my second wife, Ariadne, whose extravagance defines her. Uncomfortable as I am (my family doesn't overdo birthdays this way), I play along and unwrap gifts with a wide smile like a doll in a display case. Her gift is, of course, the biggest. It's a trip to Glacier National Park, announced by glossy prints of its breathtaking landscapes. Everyone oohs and ahhs, including me, as I flip through the prints and hold them up to face the audience.

But not June. She is slumped in a chair at a table toward the back with a scowl on her face, staring at the paper tablecloth where she'd recently spilled some food. I try to look away and focus on the eager smile of my second wife, but my return smile will not come with any less than the utmost force. For the zillionth time in that relationship, I feel bad. In the end, we won't take that trip to Glacier National Park. It will be cancelled after I leave that entire whole life to start an entire whole new one somewhere else very far away.

When all the gifts are opened and all the gifters hugged, I go to June and sit next to her. I study her face, its roundness. The acne like wild strawberry patches in miniature on her chin. The wind and the water in her eyes, the inextinguishable fire, the unshedable tears. I don't have to ask. I know what's wrong. Thinking of the beautiful sixteen-year-old she had been, about to go to Paris with her French class, limitless possibilities in her face like a child offering the world on a stick.

Now, the stress of impact from head-smashing-into-windshield then head-crushed-by-dashboard is her unfortunate and prominent feature. It covers her like a statistic. According to traumatic brain injury experts, only ten percent of traumatic brain injuries (TBI) are considered severe. Of those ten percent, one out of three injured people die. Of those left alive, forty percent must live with very significant disability.

The characteristics of the disability vary and depend on the length of the coma following the trauma. The injury increases metabolic demand while O_2 and glucose delivery to the brain is impaired. The longer this goes on without relief, the more brain-cell death occurs. Depending on the extent of brain cell death, a person with TBI can experience a lack of emotion, an uncontrollable flood of emotion, a sense of deep rejection, and severe depression all within the same five minutes. Knowing her previous strengths and comparing them to her present limitations heightens these.

I know what's wrong. I ask anyway.

"June, what's wrong?" An echo of her teenaged self, speaking fluent French, sounds in my mind and, liquefying some hard barrier in me, spills out through my eyes. I swipe at the tears.

"I didn't get a surprise party when I turned thirty," she says.

I say nothing.

"I just sit here and rot," she says.

I say, "Let's go to Paris."

She looks at me. Her face is deadpan. It hasn't registered.

"I'm taking you to Paris," I say.

"I don't have an identity," she says.

"You mean a passport?" I ask and she nods. I laugh and she cracks a smile.

"You'll get one," I say, feeling giddy at the prospect.

92. **Uranium** (Actinoid; Primordial; Solid)

Paris, day four

With pictures in hand and forms complete, we had what we needed. We took this collection back to the final gatekeeper. The gatekeeper checked to make sure everything was filled in completely and that it all was there, then handed it back to June along with an assigned number that would be called when someone was ready to help her. The gatekeeper shooed her away with her hands and June said: "Wait! Aren't you going to give me my passport?" Lee was trying to push her forward to make room for advancing people in line but she held the wheels still. The gatekeeper stared at June, silent.

"You get it from the next person, June," I said and lifted her hands off the wheels of the chair. She tried again to stop the chair, having either not heard me or not understood me.

"June," I said, getting in front of her, "you have to come in here and wait to see the next person to get your passport."

"Oh, okay," she said, comprehension alighting on her face. She ungripped the wheels and cooperated. The next room was waiting for us with twelve or fifteen faces staring straight in our direction. Americans, most likely. We made our way to an empty bank of seats and settled in. The area was much like the DMV in the states with people sitting behind windows around the perimeter and a cache of seats for waiting in the center. Digital readouts of the current number being served dinged periodically on a wall-mounted display. We waited for several minutes before June's number appeared, whereupon we all accompanied her to the designated window. The man behind the glass looked at the four of us with disapproval.

"Can I have just the person assigned this number and no more than one person for assistance approach the window please?"

I started to walk away but June grabbed my sleeve. Mom and Lee shrugged and walked away. A small flourish of pride beat in my solar plexus, silly as that was. It touched me when she picked me, something that usually only happened on my visits home where I'm favored strictly as a byproduct of my infrequent presence. I stepped up to the window beside her. The man sat and looked at June, waiting.

"I don't have an identity," she said, shouting and straining to get her face closer to the window from her seated position in the wheelchair. Both the man and me looked startled at her phrasing. There was an extended pause where nobody spoke and during which I felt afraid that there was terrible truth to what June said.

"She lost her passport," I offered.

"Tell me how that happened," he said, but she didn't hear him, just nodded and smiled. He looked at me, his eyes crisp and alert, his haircut short with a neat hairline at the back of his neck, about an inch above his blazing white collar.

"We don't know, she dropped it," I said and helped June stand up to move closer to the window. The man asked a series of questions— when did you last see it, where do you think you dropped it, have you ever lost your passport before, when was your passport issued, where were your parents born—and June answered each slowly and in her own rambling way. The man listened patiently, not hurrying her, not cutting her off, just listening and taking notes. At the end, he looked at his computer screen for a few minutes, presumably looking her up and verifying her information. I wondered what was in that screen about her. Some official file that served to validate her identity, her existence? Did they know the kind of accident she survived? Did they know she was twenty years late for this visit to Paris?

We were released to go pay at the cashier window for a new passport. We waited perhaps another forty-five minutes to be called to a final window where June was interviewed in a similar manner again then asked to swear on oath that what she was saying was the truth, the whole truth, and nothing but the truth. She gave a solemn "I do" in response, one hand across her heart and the other held aloft, shaking in the air. I barely spoke, barely did any assisting during the process. I watched each interaction June had with the fascination of a foreigner witnessing the rituals of a new culture. June was at her most vivid, which was unusual for a pressure situation, yet she was here, in Paris, where people were speaking to her with accents and speaking directly to her. Under the scrutiny of the re-identification process, under the ray of all the attention, all the validation, June bloomed.

Her application was approved. June appeared very proud when the stamp slammed down, a moment turning this otherwise failure of hers into a victory and a new story to tell. It was the original, crisp-eyed man who handed over her new, yet temporary passport. It would get her home and then could be mailed in with yet another form in exchange for a new permanent one. I thought it metaphysically potent that she had lost her identification here and been issued a new, temporary one, which, upon returning home, should be swapped again for a lasting one.

New identification acquired, June radiated a smile toward all the staring faces she passed on her way out, including the guards at the outpost who, returning her baggie of purse contents, couldn't resist smiling back.

93. **Neptunium** (Actinoid; Natural Radio; Solid)

The last time June was in the psych ward, I was aged an ancient twenty-two, living my own version of insanity at the time, being near to the end of my drinking career. June's particular brand of madness was dark—not dark, the absence of light, but dark, a felt force. In a way, we had this in common, our darkness, but mine was of the former variety. The gowns on the ward were lilac-pink, as though to lighten things up. People's eyes seemed to blaze above their pink gowns—a hot, charged thing between their ears. June was no exception.

I sat with her, each of us in adjacent chairs pointed toward the wall-mounted television in her room. I remember thinking that she'd spent too much of her life in hospital rooms facing wall-mounted television sets. She glared at me her hot, charged glare. She pulled up her pink gown to her thighs and laid her hands, palms up, just above her knees. The scars there were wide and deep. She stared down at her hands then abruptly (for as much as June's slow moving can be abrupt) reached out and pulled my hands to the corresponding spot on my lap. She placed her palms over mine. I felt so much heat there.

"These are the four hands, the four directions, the four elements," she said, her eyes widening, mouth dropping open. Normally, I would be uncomfortable with her crazy-speak, or afraid even, but this time, I was simply curious.

"The four legs of the angel, Zeek, the guardian of the four directions, the elements," she said. There was that name again, always accompanying her psychotic breaks. She clasped her fingers around my hands and squeezed hard.

"This is touch, the air, the air brings touch and sound, flapping wings," she said, speaking very slowly, heavy lidded now. I felt the urge to pull my hands away but I let her go on.

"Earth is smell, fire is vision, water is taste," she said. She looked at me for a long time then said, "You're a whale in the ocean, you're a bird in the air, you're roots in the ground of a tree on fire."

She grasped my hands so tight that she pinched my fingers together until they were stinging and fire hot. I wrenched them away and gave a little cry of pain. She smiled rather wickedly, then placed her hands palms up above her knees again. The nurse walked in.

"How're we doing?" She asked and I smiled.

"We're just discussing the elements," I said.

"Oh right, the ritual four, that's right, she's been talking about that a lot," she said and laughed. She patted June on the head and walked out. Suddenly, I was angry—how condescending, how haughty! I wanted to follow after her ask her why she felt it was helpful or appropriate to make fun of patients. Was it helping them get well?

"She's one of them," June said, hissing it.

"Doctor Keene is one of them," she said. He was the psychiatrist in charge of adjusting her chemical cocktail enough to get her leveled out again.

"Are you one of them?" She asked, narrowing her eyes at me, squeezing her hands into bloodless fists.

"June, there is no *them*. We're all just trying to help you," I said, which was the wrong thing to say. She swung one fist right for my face and I dodged, feeling the swish of air it left. I leapt from the chair and hopped out of her range, standing behind her now. The television volume turned way up—it was playing *The Price is Right* but it was like a parody of the show we once watched together as girls. It was a screeching evil, mocking our insanity, cheering it on with a studio audience.

94. Plutonium (Actinoid; Primordial; Solid)

In which I became a tree

The fire burned our bark. Us, flocks of wooden bones in formation, having rooted ourselves where we hoped to bear fruit and carry birdsong in our branches. The spines of dry riverbeds ignited, and poof, we were all up in flames. Forest fires are soundless for trees, and sightless, too. But we felt it all. We felt the bludgeoning flames, the canting curls of smoke. Your durable tree heart, buried against blackness deep in your center, woven of beats, it generates power. But I can't make anything pound like that inside me, and I linger in alcoves of thought where the forest is lush and penetrated by solitary shafts of sunlight. The heat blows black caves in us, turns our wooden skin to ash and shuttles it back and forth through the barren and destroyed brush. After what feel like a hundred years of burning, the fire subsides and what's left of us is hurled into a new epoch. As though pulled by the moon, the long, blackened body you are stretches, repairs. Your growth is contagious. But I can't make anything pound like that inside me, abusing even my own reconstruction. As though there all along, my bare branches shiver with the tickle of your new leaves, laden with dew. Thrusting yourself back to life, settling in among the resurrected, I am a dark mass of a ghost beside you. I come close to believing that I survived, and although I remain naked with death, I remain agonizingly vertical, recovering slowly in your shadow, bending to just graze the light vanishing behind you. There is a hollow in my trunk, a little moss-covered temple. It's peaceful and sturdy, a place to kneel and to not be seen. But even there, a faint echo of the angry foam-hiss of burning trees can be heard. There is an injured synapse that makes its absence impossible. Even as you grow, your long body is covered with scars that expand into clean, white scorches of proof that you survived. Where's my proof? It's layered over with responsibility. It's buried with our tangled roots. It's in the sky, facing south, upside down in the feathered breast of a bird pointed cloudward that just launched itself from my branches in to brightness, day, light. It's in not being able to fly like that. Not being able to float away. Not being able to make anything pound like a heart inside me. Not being able to go back before the fire. It's in the ceaseless expanding of your girth. It's in the new life filling, gradually, the empty spaces with green. The proof is flooding the arches of my branches, blackened and gorgeous in contrast, as if waiting to be photographed or waiting for words to give shape to the shapelessness of hush.

95. Americium (Actinoid; Synthetic; Solid)

On the day we left Paris, it rained again, and we watched it from the windows at the airport as though slick pavement could change anything. But to have it change, even as far back as twenty years prior, would rob us of many things. It would rob June of the chance to bloom there in a wheelchair, bathed in rain. Standing some distance from her, I felt a heavy, complicated joy.

The life to which I was returning was a new life in a new place. After living in Chicago for six years, four of those with Ariadne, I moved to Phoenix for a writing job. But it wasn't the job that brought me there, it was the girl. The one whom I now see, in retrospect, as the catalyst for major change in my life. She seemed to arrive only to break me free and then disappear. I'd first met Aubrey in Chicago right after I moved there with my first wife. I was twenty-five, about a year sober, and had just gotten married to an amazing girl whose centuries-old soul snuck under the fence and slithered up the fragile pipes of my body, filling my veins with a dark silk love that just wouldn't be enough. I knew it one night after we moved into our Chicago apartment, watching shadows fall across her tear-streaked face in the dim light of our bed. I wanted to leave her but I didn't know I could. Until I met Aubrey.

She was twenty-one years old and less than thirty days sober, living with her boyfriend and giving me eyes whose brown dressed me like an emperor in shiny new clothes. The impetuous pull I felt was no different from the moon's on the tide and I was as helpless as those waves. Its authority over me was a muscled torso, whisking everything under its coat. I left my new wife and Aubrey left her boyfriend, but then she relapsed and ignored what announced itself everyday when we woke, as loud and clear as a car bomb. That ignorance allowed her to move back to Phoenix where she was from, tearing herself away from my codependent clutches. She got sober again and I went to see her five months later, only to discover that nothing about that pull had changed. I remember watching her in her mother's kitchen making salsa. She was wearing an apron with white lace trim. She smiled up at me from a yellow bowl of light and I swore I wanted to spend every minute I had left on earth with her.

She refused me, said she wasn't ready, and I went back to Chicago with the kind of broken heart that doesn't fuck around. It takes charge when faced with insurmountable cleaning jobs, stuffs dead bodies under the bed so the blue air can make everything look sparkling. I destroyed all evidence of her, deleted her phone number, even changed my phone number. Then I met Ariadne and moved into places we called home. Two years into that, she asked me to marry her. We had a small, private ceremony during which I managed to make no promises. I would have stayed if I'd been someone different. But like my first brief marriage, my second toppled over when the weight shifted toward what I gave of myself versus what I could keep. Also, there was that bad smell coming from under the bed.

96. **Curium** (Actinoid; Synthetic; Solid)

Four years later, my skull was a thin tight wrapping and I had nowhere to turn. So I left, in the company of motives I didn't understand. Three weeks later, I saw Aubrey again, only to discover that nothing about that pull had changed. Three months later, I got a job in Phoenix and moved there, my dog and me. Most of my stuff was in a remote storage facility until I found a house, which I did three months after that, only to be laid off from my new job the day after closing on the loan. The day after being laid off was the day I left for Paris, leaving Aubrey to move into my new house without me and wait for me to come home.

When we reached New York from Paris, the flight was late and I risked not making my connection to Phoenix if I stayed among the herd. I hugged my family goodbye and made my way to the front of the cabin even before they opened the doors. I ran to customs, passed through without incident, and ran to my departure gate, which greeted me with time to spare. The delay would be short, about thirty minutes, but it was enough to call Aubrey for the first time since leaving the country a week earlier. Her voice drove the rapids in my wrists, giving no clue about the following year when she wouldn't mean to hurt me again.

Meanwhile, until that time, I got another, better job, paid away her debts, took her to a romantic village in Mexico, took her home to my family, included her in the family portrait, bought her a car, adopted two puppies (we were going to get one but when they brought two littermates out, she wanted them both), bought her many things, bought her whatever she wanted that I could afford. It would seem as though I was trying to buy her love but I wasn't. I thought I already had it. Anticipating and meeting her every need was a side effect of being madly in love with her. For a while, she loved me the same way. Until the point at which the scale tipped toward what she gave away of herself and what she got to keep. She left under the influence of motives she didn't understand. Looking back, I can see how my doting might have felt smothering, consuming her independence. But that's one of those mistakes that can be mended with communication and willingness to change. The force behind her leaving was much deeper and inexplicable than that. It had to do with her sore, unhealed wounds and her intrinsic need to keep secrets.

She'd served her divine purpose, unsticking my eyes from the crust that had been fusing them closed. The second time, my broken heart didn't have the same strength. My old dog, the one who'd been with me for twelve years (my longest relationship), died, and I had two new puppies to care for alone, the three of us abandoned as a lot. I was wrecked. I crawled around my bamboo floors too weak from fits of weeping to do much more than change the furniture around and move bedrooms. In the process, I dragged the rotting corpses from their hiding places into the light and did the equivalent of calling the coroner—I started writing about them.

97. Berkelium (Actinoid; Synthetic; Solid)

The airport in San Francisco seemed to writhe with lesbians. All shapes and sizes of women holding the hands of other women, hairless arms circled around curved hips. The affect was inspiring of hope. I called June on my cell phone to kill time while I waited. This was my third straight week calling her after I promised myself again to call once each week. It had been nearly eighteen months since the Paris trip and I had been a neglectful sister in the interim, distracted by heartswoon and heartbreak. She answered on the second ring.

"Hello?" Her voice was deep and slow. It swung up with the second syllable, making a question of every greeting.

"Hi June," I said.

"Oh! Hi!" She said in a high-pitched, genuine excitement. It was the reaction I got almost every time I called. Involuntarily, I smiled. I searched for my next words carefully. Asking how she was ceased to be an option because the answer was always the same—something about how dull and unchanging her stagnant existence was. The trip to Paris only changed that for the time we were in Paris. Upon her return home, she was back to feeling stuck. Our conversations were therefore land mines. One wrong step tapped into a depression so deep in her that she would inevitably fall over the edge, irretrievable by any feeble consoling words. She said the next thing: "I heard what happened."

I sat down and sighed. The relationship with Aubrey was over and this one had left me flat on the floor, sobbing so hard I'd left a puddle of snot and tears on the bamboo.

"Yeah, what can I say? I'm just not good at relationships, maybe," I said.

"Well. You know. You're so nice and friendly and everything. You're rich, you have a lot of money. You just draw the girls in. They just love you because you just draw them in. But then you're too much and they can't take it. They have to leave," she said. I laughed loud enough to turn a few heads.

"Is that what it is, June?" She was refreshingly blunt. Also, sometimes, startlingly accurate. She could be like a wise oracle at the most unexpected moments, during a lucid interval. But I wasn't rich. Still, I felt truth in her observation. Being too much. I wondered how, with our limited contact and distance over the years, June could have known that about me. I felt equal parts touched and ashamed. I started walking to the bathroom. It would be easier to talk to her in there.

"Oh. Um. Where are you?" she asked.

"I just landed in San Francisco," I said and winced. If she thought my life was too exciting, she would feel jealous and sorry for herself. With most people, those feelings would be fleeting. For June, they might easily lead to another tour of the psych ward.

"Really? Oh. Why?"

"Oh, nothing big. I'm just meeting Judy here to go visit some friends of hers, that's all," I said, sounding casual. It was true. Judy was my oldest and best friend from home. Oldest in both duration and age—she was twenty years my senior. I met her on my last high after drinking two bottles of cough syrup in one sitting. She was responsible for getting me sober. I was meeting her there and we were going up north to a meditation retreat she was hosting. Thinking of it, I realized that June would likely think the truth more boring than visiting friends.

"I never get to go anywhere," she said. There it was.

"I'll bring you out to visit me. For you birthday, how 'bout?" I walked into a stall and closed the door.

"Oh. Well. Um. okay," she said. Her excitement would be delayed, but it would come. I undid my pants and sat down on the toilet to pee. June was the only person with whom I could pee on the phone and not be found out.

"I just sit here and rot," she said, her voice tense with sadness. I winced.

"I'll bring you out here to visit me," I said.

"Oh. When?" She said.

"For your birthday."

Outside the stall, heels clacked against the floor. I flushed.

98. Californium (Actinoid; Synthetic; Solid)

Two months later, I fell in love with somebody else's wife. Her name was Sara. Her arms felt more like home than any pair since age about ten, when the only arms that mattered got pried off too soon. It was that reckless ,year-long affair that finally showed me to myself and woke me up to the unconscious motivation propelling me into bed with women who loved me not enough (or, perhaps too much) to stay forever.

Everything I did and failed to do before, I did it again with her. And even in the white-hot center of the pain from never having enough, I found bliss so unadulterated, so high and fast in its flight that it orbited its own sphere and touched the very starting place of sorrow.

Our blood, the spell it casts

99. Einsteinium (Actinoid; Synthetic; Solid)

You recognized her as beautiful when you met her. There was something more though—you knew it even before you talked to her. There was a force between you, as though an invisible rope would affix itself to your bellies whenever you were in a room together and become taut. Initially, you were in a relationship and so you stayed away, knowing what the implications of the connection would be. But then she approached you, in a meeting after you spoke in a small group with her. She thanked you for whatever it was that you said and told you an abridged version of her life story. You just stared, mesmerized by her mouth, the shapes it took with her speech. She seemed nervous, talked fast. You noticed. So did your girlfriend, who was mad later.

You avoided her after that. Saw her every week but barely looked at her even though you couldn't help but to feel her in the room. Later, she would tell you how she felt the same way, how she noticed whenever you weren't there, and how she sensed the silent territorial warning of your girlfriend. When your girlfriend left and you were devastated, she was there to offer consolation.

Everything after that is a blue-green glistening pool you will always think of and miss. You will miss it and long for it because although it will grow rapidly like a fire in a dry forest, it will disappear just as rapidly. It won't subside, but it will quietly remove itself from your life. Words will be involved. Careful, spare words. They will be her lubrication, letting her out quick with a slip, as if you wouldn't notice. It won't be without grace, but nothing she does ever is.

Like the time she danced slow and naked against you, like flame licking paper, setting you immediately ablaze, how you kissed her, how she received your hands and tongue, the curves of her and how they moved with her gait, her warm body in your bed, and the slickness of her soaped skin in your shower. When, night after forbidden night, you ushered her out your front door, kissed her mouth in the dark and held her, then watched her walk to her car, she would say, "find your phone," and you'd smile. When you went back inside, it would be ringing by the time you found it, and you would talk to her while she drove home. Sometimes, you had nothing left to say, so you'd sit on the phone and listen to her in her car, breathing, accelerating away from you, tires humming over pavement toward home, toward her husband. You never wanted her to go. You never wanted not to be her home.

You will leave the pool where you found it, and her, light flickering through water, underground magma, contained nuclear power. When you watched the pool from just the right angle, it appeared to stretch out far and wide to a horizon that implied forever. But in reality, it was a small, round, contained depth. You could submerge, you could go deeper and deeper, but you could never go wide. Except in your powerful imagination, whenever you sat above it, brought your eyes close to its surface, squinted, and saw it stretch into that horizon. Those impossible implications. But the light will move in the depths and you will leave the pool where you found it. And her.

You will worry about her there—what will happen when it all comes to the surface? It's not worry so much as it's regret. You wanted to be there to see that.

100. Fermium (Actinoid; Synthetic; Solid)

I moved from Phoenix to San Francisco for a writing job. But it wasn't the job that brought me there. Nor, this time, was it a girl. At least not one I was moving toward, but rather running from. I've historically believed in instinct—that terrible wind cutting a path in the midst of my searching. The problem being the path, which is often a straight shot to what I want. Too often, it's turned out that I don't know what I want, even when I think I do. After Sara and I returned to each other's mouths for the hundredth last time, a hundred of her tiltings into me finally proved that there was gravity between us only states worth of distance could break. An affair wasn't something I was cut out for. It required holding silence, of which I'm incapable. It required not wanting more, of which I'm incapable. So I started looking for a job outside of Phoenix, but change had already gathered itself and leapt all the way to northern California, where it set up a net for me to fall.

After moving, I went home with my secret brokenness to celebrate my thirty-third birthday, combining it with my brother John's thirty-fifth, just less than a month before mine. We celebrated birthdays so often in my family of twenty (two parents, two brothers, two sisters, their spouses, five nieces, and four nephews), that they'd become the stock reason for gatherings, nearly indistinguishable rituals leaving us each wishing the other a happy birthday, confused as we were about whose it was, or if it was Christmas.

I sat beside my brother on the couch while the small mob that is my family sang "Happy Birthday" and my mom carried in a blazing pair of cakes that lit her smiling face. When it was time to blow out the candles, I closed my eyes to make a wish but all I could do was try not to recall the way I spent my thirty-second birthday just the year before with Sara on my couch, in my bathtub, in my bed all day until she had to leave to pick up her kids. I had to open my eyes to close them on those entwined limbs whose rematerialization became my solemn birthday wish.

Presents came next. There were thoughtful doodads and tchotchkes from my mom as well as the usual gift cards from siblings. John and I alternated occupancy of the spotlight, opening one item each in turn. When it came time for us to open June's gifts to us, someone plopped a messily wrapped, crumpled little package in John's lap and handed me a card. June yelled, "No! John! That's for Anne!"

Startled, he apologetically handed it to me and I swapped him the card. We were both taken aback by her outburst—the excitement behind it was very uncharacteristic of her. I'd never seen her so eager to give a gift, in fact, and the size and shape of the package defied the chance that it was her usual sort—a gift card to someplace I would never go given a choice, like Red Lobster or Olive Garden.

Curiosity thus piqued, I removed the wrapping paper that she so obviously applied herself, charmed by its excessive tape and small tears, to reveal a square, gray, cardboard box. Aware that June was on the edge of her seat watching, I carefully, almost fearfully, lifted the lid.

It was a silver ring with scripted letters. I inspected it closely and saw that it was the word, "sisters," with tiny hearts and x's and o's surrounding it. I felt a pang of deep gratitude for this unprecedented feting so powerful that I had to fight the urge to cry. The ring was what most (and even I under another circumstance) would call tacky, but it was so authentically June that it was the most beautiful piece of jewelry I had ever received. The price tag (in perfect June style) was still attached, showing that it was from Kohl's and had cost $50. This put me right over the edge and a short sob escaped my mouth so that I had to trap the rest in with my hand. This was a lot of money for June, far exceeding the usual $10 value of her gift cards. I removed the price tag and slid the ring over my finger, mumbling tearful thanks, looking up at her, sniffling.

"Does it fit?" She asked, beaming.

"It fits perfectly," I said, holding up my hand.

"Oh, good. I was afraid it would be too small cause you have pretty big fingers," she said. We all laughed and I playfully scolded her for telling me my hands were chubby.

101. Mendelevium (Actinoid; Synthetic; Solid)

I wore that ring boldly and permanently, not removing it to shower or to sleep, not wanting to miss for a second feeling the weight of it like a small miracle on my hand.

Two weeks later, I went to Phoenix for an impromptu visit. Sara visited me in my hotel, where we entwined our limbs for the last time. Lying next to her, spent and naked, I lifted my hand to show her my ring. I told her the story, holding my hand aloft, both of us watching the ring amazed, as though unsure it could actually exist. When I finished with the story I looked at her profile against the hair-swept pillow, smiling, eyes wet with easy tears. (When everything is done, that flushed smile remains one of the few reasons I believe in God.) She snatched my hand from the air, brought it down to the grace of her mouth, kissed the tiny piece of silver, and smiled at me.

"Beautiful," she said.

I turned my body and wrapped her in it. I told her I could keep doing this, I could continue on with her, keeping it quiet, seeing her maybe once a month or every other month, even if it took ten years. However long it took, I told her (contradicting what I'd said so many times before, thinking not about her husband and children), if it meant we'd be together on the other side, I'd do it. She told me I could no more do it than she could let me. She said we both knew I wanted more and that I deserved more.

"Why don't you want more?" I said, taking her face in my hands, swiping my thumbs over her tears.

"It's not a matter of want."

The conversation that followed was a variation on the same conversation we'd had many times, where she tells me she can't do that to her kids. Where she tells me her reluctance is borne of unfathomable fear, not lack of feeling.

"Faith is a choice," I told her. And righteously, I added, "You've made yours."

"Maybe you're right," she conceded. Certainly, my face was clouded over with pain.

"I'm sorry," she added.

But in that hotel room bed, with a shaft of light from the window hitting that body lying beside me with her hands, I knew I wasn't right.

102. Nobelium (Actinoid; Synthetic; Solid)

The day June flew in to visit me in San Francisco was the day I got my California driver's license. I went to the DMV that morning, not realizing that I would need a valid ID to get through security and meet June at the gate. It wasn't until they punched a hole in my Arizona driver's license, gave me a paper permit valid for 90 days, and told me that my new ID would arrive in the mail that I realized I would have a problem. I was already running late, so stopping back at home to get my passport first wouldn't work. I had to get there and take my chances without proper identification.

I have no identity, I thought and smiled.

103. Lawrencium (Actinoid; Synthetic; Solid)

I approached the check-in counter with my hole-punched ID and temporary permit paper and laid them out on the counter before a guy that looked like a young Rasputin with black hair, black beard, prominent brow, and black eyes. His forced smile was a little frightening, but I forced one back, knowing how important it was to be on his good side. I gave him my most cheerful slash faux bashful hello and asked him to give me a gate pass for my sister's flight.

"You need a valid driver's license or state ID," he said, having barely glanced down at my documents.

"This was it," I said, holding up the hole-punched card and explaining how it came to be mutilated that morning. He cut me off toward the rambling end.

"Do you have a passport?" He asked, bored with my story.

"Not with me," I said. He shook his head.

"Then I can't help you," he said and looked at the next person in line, trying to dismiss me.

"We have to figure something out," I said, "because my sister will be looking for me when she gets off."

He squeezed his bushy black eyebrows together. "Is she a minor child?" He asked.

"No, she's disabled. She has a traumatic brain injury and she needs my help, otherwise she'll be wandering lost around the airport with her walker," I said. He asked me her name then looked at his computer screen, typed, pursed his bearded lips and nodded, somehow validating the information.

"She's scheduled for a wheelchair escort off the ramp," he said. "The escort will bring her out to you."

My stomach burned up to my face. I knew she would have to pee the minute she disembarked, but she wouldn't be aware of that until it was too late. She would have an accident by the time they wheeled her out to me, which would humiliate her. I didn't feel like explaining all that to Rasputin, though.

"That won't work. Trust me, I need to be there," I said.

"Look, I'm sorry. You need a valid ID to get a gate pass," he said and again, looked at the next person in line. My face was so hot I thought it might melt from panic. I heard my heart in my red ears.

"Can you get a manager or something? Make an exception? It's important, please," I said. He scowled at the line behind me then called a manager over. She looked small and mean like an angry little terrier. As soon as I saw her I knew I was as good as fucked. I explained the situation anyway, pleadingly, but I found myself talking to a shaking head with its eyes closed. She started repeating the word, no, so I stopped talking. I get this from my mom: I start crying when I'm very angry. I had to not speak to close my throat and choke it back.

The manager mumbled an insincere *sorry*, said, "next," and

walked away. Rasputin and I looked at each other. I felt the expression on my face: utter despondency. He looked at my paper permit again, picked it up and inspected it, put it down, fingered my hole-punched driver's license, and sighed. He turned to his computer and punched the keyboard. In the next moment, a gate pass with my name on it printed out beneath him and he handed it to me.

"Go," he said, glancing nervously back toward his manager, who was obliviously wrapped up in some other concern. Relief cooled my face like a sudden splash of water. I thanked him and took off at a trot, worried I'd be late.

104. Rutherfordium (Transition Metal; Synthetic; Unknown Phase)

Her plane had been delayed, which was perfect because I got to the gate right in time. A crowd had amassed outside the ramp—passengers waiting to board the outgoing flight, also delayed. (I've never understood people's eagerness to board a plane first when everyone has an assigned seat and no one is going anywhere until they all do, together.)

I pushed my way up to the front to wait for June, who was the last one out. I saw her come wheeling up the ramp holding her folded-up walker out in front of her, resting on her lap and I smiled. She emerged into the melee and I took the walker from her, then led the way to cut a path through the mob, bumping more than one shoulder or protruding bag along the way. It felt like we were on the red carpet and cameras should be flashing and notepads being thrust in our direction for autographs. When we cleared the bulk of it, I turned to hug June. She looked strangely contained, swollen and wedged between the armrests of the chair, her carry on in her lap. It was a tiny chair, as though for a child.

"Is this a normal-sized chair?" I asked the man in the blue uniform pushing her. He stared back at me confused and said,

257

"wheelchair," in a thick accent I didn't recognize.

I turned my attention back to June and asked her if she needed to use the restroom, which she was shocked to realize that yes, she did, badly. I took her carry-on over my shoulder and helped dislodge her from the seat, then brought her to the end of the line out the door from the women's bathroom.

"I don't think I can hold it," she said, clamping her legs together. I did the barge to the front of the line announcing a state of emergency routine and we waited inside the fragrantly foul room for a stall to empty out. Standing in the stench, I glanced at myself in the mirror. There, reflected in glass, framed by the restroom filled with strangers, I saw within my face all the versions of me from over the years that had stood in similar spaces with June. I was seventeen with June at twenty-two, waiting for her in a bathroom at Wright State. I was twenty with June at twenty-five, helping her into the bathroom in her hospital room after she gave birth to Sophie. I was twenty-three with June at twenty-eight, standing in the bathroom at Olive Garden holding her walker. There were more, many more, hundreds, even. The snapshot memories were so vivid, it was as though my reflection were in a window, the image floating in a dark pane superimposed over several others, each a stamped impression in time, in spatial fabric, caught as I was in that moment, mid-motion, a trail of ghosts left behind spot by spot, bathroom by bathroom to haunt, to remain.

What struck me then was the importance of each of them, each version of me and the choices she made that led to my presence there, in that bathroom just then, living in San Francisco with June visiting me. What would happen if any of them had made even one of those choices differently?

June stepped out of her stall and looked at me, expectant, wanting direction. I walked her to the sink to wash her hands. I saw it then, in our two mirrored faces, the answer to my question. *We're already here, I am already her, she is carved into my illusory path. It's all right here, right now.*

105. Dubnium (Transition Metal; Synthetic; Unknown Phase)

Getting her bag (which had her fit to move in) and getting her into the car, all the while accompanied by the child-sized wheelchair escort, without any mishaps, and with June wearing a giddy smile, this long weekend between sisters was off to a promising start. Still, I drove stiffly, filled with anxiety about the days ahead. It was the first time in many years that we would spend time together alone, outside the warm knot of our family. Our blood, the spell it casts.

Do all families wind up having a spell like that? A time when, in retrospect, everything seemed to have been rattling, near to coming loose? Like the house where we grew up, how it revealed the effects of holding all our weight. There were always new cracks appearing in the ceiling, wallpaper peeling in curls, water stains spreading their yellow territories ever wider. Footsteps always pounding the stairs like a crazed pulse. Doors banged hard enough to split moldings. When I see June at home, she is often weary like that house, weighted down with the dullness of routine, the past and its consequences, the corners of her mouth weighted, too. But coming across the country to visit me, she seemed blissfully released.

The truth is that I have always been terrified of her: the dependence, the abundance of things it takes for her to function in the world, like pills and sleep and equipment and gear and more pills. Back when I drank, I used to disappear on her. I couldn't handle spending time with her and I didn't know why. Now I know it's because I was afraid of all her needs and certain that I would not be dependable enough to meet them. I'm still afraid of all her needs but I'm now obliged to face the fear and I'm capable of being depended upon.

We drove in silence and as we passed the water, an expanse of glassy blue that is the Bay to the east, June's head turned toward it as though it were a face she was about to kiss.

106.Seaborgium (Transition Metal; Synthetic; Unknown Phase)

I kept it simple that first day: unpack, get settled, eat, oversee medication dispensing, and get to bed early to accommodate the jet lag. June was in love with my dogs (as with all animals she encountered), so I had to keep pulling her away from them and remind her of what she was doing. I had bought a plastic folding chair for the shower and a waterproof sheet for the futon bed. When she was successfully fed, medicated, and showered, I showed her to her room. The light switch was just inside the doorway, yet the futon was across the room, so it was necessary to get up, walk to where the switch was, and turn it off, then return to the bed in the dark. This caused me anxiety. What if she fell making her way back in the dark?

When she sat on the bed, I told her about the situation with the light.

"Do you want me to go ahead and turn it off for you now?" I asked.

"No, I'm going to do my exercises first," she said, lowering herself to the floor.

"Okay," I said. "Well, when you're ready, you just have to come over here and turn this switch off."

June looked up at me from the floor and said, "Uh, gee, thanks, sis. I didn't know how a light switch worked."

We both laughed and I relaxed a little. Her unexpected wit and humor was refreshing, reminding me that I routinely underestimate her. She managed to live alone, after all, when Todd was gone all that time. June was on all fours lifting her leg up and back, up and back, an unsteady rising limb with a turned-in foot, the white sock loose and adorned with clinging dog hair. I told her goodnight and closed the door on the image of that sock flashing under the light.

107. Bohrium (Transition Metal; Synthetic; Unknown Phase)

That night, I had a vivid dream that is still with me now. There was a boy. A child who was beautiful and ageless. As soon as I saw him, I grew quiet and thought carefully about what to say. I held him at first, but then he grew, quickly and right before my eyes. I recognized him as though he were a very old friend. It was Andy again, after all these years. I wanted to ask him and I wanted him to tell me everything in the whole world. It was the same boy I had seen so much of that first year after June's accident, only now he was a man. A grown man with things to do. We were in his house and he was suddenly busy. I had been telling him about my plan, the one I had been thinking through and building and scheming my whole life. I don't know and could not convey now, awake, what the plan is or was, but I knew it there with him and spoke it to him rapidly, out of breath with it.

He listened and moved around the house, like he had something to do and then something else—he was busying himself but with nothing. When he stopped and faced me, we looked at one another in silence. He asked me if I was finished. Yes, I said, and what do you think? He shook his head, no. But it's a perfect plan! Did you hear me correctly? Do you need me to repeat any part that you might not have understood? A fine plan it was but empty. Nothing. An act of making myself busy, moving, speaking, as if I were doing something, going somewhere, or saying something. There was nothing to do but unfold. Nothing would bring the outcome but time and patience. I didn't understand, so he demonstrated.

We went to a building with a closed, locked door—a garage or a shed. Within the building, I knew, was everywhere I wanted to be. Everything I wanted was behind that locked door. Where will we find the key? How will we get the key? Can we make a key? Do you have the key? Can we pick the lock?

Just open the door.

But we need a key!

Just open it.

But it's locked.

Just trust.

I reached out and grasped the handle to the door. I pulled. It opened. I stared at him, wide eyed.

There is nothing that you need to do but trust.

How do I do that?

Trust.

108. Hassium (Transition Metal; Synthetic; Unknown Phase)

With the hills and uneven terrain of San Francisco, I rented a wheelchair. June's vacation-inspired good mood allowed her usually stubborn insistence that she walk to yield. She let me push her in the chair while we took the dogs for a walk. When the first steep hill came, I marched head down like a football player shoving a training sled. She helped me with one festive push of the wheels forward after another, the rubber wheels burnishing her hands with each too slow release, leaving red streaks. When we reached the top she laughed because she was happy. I took her hands and asked, "Are you ok?" She looked at them and smiled, said they didn't hurt.

We proceeded around the outer perimeter of the park looking for a ramp. Most of the entrances were stairs. I found one, but it was steep and the curb was not cut. Without too much forethought, I charged toward it imagining speed would help to bump over the curb and leave some momentum for a head start up the hill. I forgot about her foot rests, which hit first and cut the momentum, bringing the front tires to a blunt stop and tipping the chair forward. She was still seated, but wanted to help the situation, so as I tilted the chair back again, she climbed out onto the paved path with her hands, moving away in an unsteady bear crawl. I called out to her, pleading for her to be careful. She turned over and sat on the path, still smiling, still light. She got back in the chair with gravel on her hands and pants, giggling.

The next push uphill was a repeat of the first hill. Then there was the lowering down, letting her pick up some speed but not too much. "Weeeee," she called out and I laughed. On the other side of the park, the sprinklers were on. Fat splats hammered the paved path ahead of us, raking up and down it but never away from it. There was no escaping. I warned her we were going through it and took off at a cautious jog. It was downhill and a bit slippery so I didn't want to get going out of control. But I did. And we skidded into the grass, then backtracked and fumbled at the same uncut curb when the footrests hit the street.

Again she got up, trying to help, but I coaxed her back down. All during this we were subjected to interval showers as the sprinkler moved away then back, away then back. When we made it free of the obstacle park and were back on the safe sidewalk, I asked her jokingly if she'd ever had such a rough and tumble trip to a park before. She laughed and shook the water from her hair and hands.

109. Meitnerium (Transition Metal; Synthetic; Unknown Phase)

In the car on the way to brunch, she got a little testy about the wheelchair.

"When we get to the restaurant, I'm just going to use my walker," she said, nodding, as though yes, she agreed with herself.

"June, there's hills here, it's not very safe to use your walker," I said, inwardly cringing. This was a heartbreaking argument to have with her.

"It's fine, I walk really well now," she said. "I almost don't even need the walker."

"We'll see," I said, avoiding the rest. Maybe I'd be lucky and find a close enough parking spot so that she could use the walker, after all.

"I don't understand why I'm not all better by now," she said. "I mean, it's been, like, twenty years." She looked at me expectantly.

"It's been twenty-two years," I said, immediately feeling stupid for saying it, because that just amplifies her point—that it's about time she be back to normal.

"I know! That's what I'm saying," she said, a little louder, the dip and soar of her voice traversing at least eight diatonic degrees of tonal range.

I didn't have a response right away—it was a tricky thing to balance her expectations with reality. Telling her she would never be back to normal risked pushing her into a thick depression, while encouraging her belief that she was continuing to get better was setting her up for disappointment and confusion. Too often, people who don't know her, well intentioned as they may be, tell her she's getting better and better. The problem is that she believes them, subsequently wondering why she hasn't improved, why she can't speak and move and think and walk normally by now.

"I know, June. It's been a long time since your accident and you're much better than you once were. But just remember that you have a brain injury, and that's always going to have some side effects to manage," I said. She calmly assented, nodding and taking it in without incident. Once again, I was assisted by her bright mood.

When June is stripped of the pessimism and grumpiness to which she's habituated at home, there is such innocence about her—a sweetness. She notices and acknowledges invisible things like the birds on the street and homeless people. After brunch, she stopped with her walker and her unsteady gait to say, "Hi birdie," with impossible enthusiasm to a pigeon on the sidewalk. She stopped and bent to read the cardboard sign in a filthy man's hands that asks for spare change and she declared, again with enthusiasm, "I can spare some change!" Then she dug with shaking hands into her purse in the basket of her walker and fumbled crushed bills and coins into his cup. She has unbelievable brand loyalty.

On the way back to my apartment, we stopped at a store to get more pads and some contact solution. We decided that she would wait in the car while I ran in so that she could get home and take her meds (she was a bit past due). She was careful to tell me precisely what brand of each to get and very concerned that I get it right. For the pads, she told me the brand and asked that I get the most absorbent variety of that brand. In the store, I didn't find the brand of contact solution that she used, but I found the generic version that was identical to it. For the pads, the most absorbent were the overnight pads—they were the thickest. Upon presenting her with these items back in the car, June was devastated.

"Is this good for a stigmatism?" She asked about the contact solution, the entirety of her face scrunched together in utter worry.

"Hm, I'm sure it's fine, it's the same as the brand you normally get," I said, to which she yelled, "No, it's not!"

"Okay, we'll go back in and ask the pharmacist, how about that," I said. She then opened the bag with the pads and gasped. "No, no," she said, shaking her head and slapping her hand on her cheek. "These are for the night, I need pads for the day," she said.

"June, you can use them during the day, too, they're just the most absorbent kind, they–"

"No!" She cut me off. "It says right here, Over. Night."

"Okay, let's go back in and exchange them, no problem," I said. (So much for running in to save time.)

We got out of the car and walked together, June grasping my arm, across the parking lot back toward the store.

110.Darmstadtium (Transition Metal; Synthetic; Unknown Phase)

Later at my apartment, June was tired and sore. I decided to give her Reiki, an energy healing (a skill I had acquired along the way), and she was excited to receive it. I had her sit up straight in a chair and close her eyes. I pressed my hands first on her shoulders and then, with some hesitation, moved my left hand to the back of her head. Her head felt warm, almost hot, as though she had a fever.

"Are you feeling okay?" I asked.

"Um, yeah," she said, "Why?"

"You're head is very warm."

"Oh, it's always like that. I'm always hot."

With my hand on her head, I envisioned the biological system that she was working very hard—red blood cells being produced by the thousands and rushing everywhere trying to heal permanent wounds, trying to navigate the heavy artillery medication flooding her system each day. I imagined her skull, only it, separated from skin and flesh and gray matter teeming with activity. The whole, white bone of her skull. I remembered the halo brace and the metal screws that held it in place, drilled into her scull, into the bone. Into the solid, silent, and still bone. Unmoving amid all the chaos that was her rushing blood and brain and body. Not chaos, rather, but a precise system with mysterious mechanisms that animate a person, make them alive. I put my hands where the screws would have been, around the crown of her head. Again, I thought of Andy, which made me think of Zeek, and in that moment I felt compelled to ask her about it.

"June, do you remember anything that happened or that you saw when you were in a coma?"

"Yes," she said. I pressed my hands a little harder against her head and willed them to keep her safe from the memories that tended to push her over the edge into psychosis.

"Tell me about that," I said. She spoke softly, in a voice much different from her usual forced and pained sounding monotone. She told me about Zeek and how he brought her to a white room with an image of her connected to many strings, which in turn connected to points of light like stars. She told me about the pain she sometimes felt and the dreams she believed were created by the pain, like giving birth to five babies and leaving them in the woods.

"I had a strange experience happen while you were in a coma," I said. My heart started pounding harder because I was about to tell June something I'd never told anybody. "I had a sort of imaginary friend. Only I don't think he was imaginary. I think he might have been real and just from some other place. Maybe Zeek was real, too."

"They're real," she said and laughed, as though I were silly to even question it.

"But who are they?" I moved both hands to her head.

"I don't know. But sometimes people get in trouble, you know? People get hurt like I did or have a lot to worry about like you did. And then there's just help, so quickly."

111. Roentgenium (Transition Metal; Synthetic; Unknown Phase)

The next morning, I saw June on her knees next to the futon reaching all across and feeling its surface. Here it was, I thought. I'd been waiting for her to ask for a new set of sheets, knowing that she never made it through a night of sleep without wetting the bed, pad or no.

"Do you need a change of sheets? Is it wet?" I asked.

She looked at me and sat back on her heels, throwing her hands up and grinning like a little kid. "No, it's not," she said. "I woke up when

I had to go to the bathroom so I got up and went. I was just checking to make sure I didn't dream that." She laughed and the dogs charged her, coming in from the other room to find her on their level. They nearly knocked her over licking her face and arms.

"No lick," I said sternly to the dogs, which June repeated in a high, wholly ineffective baby voice. I was too stunned by her news to further correct them though. I almost didn't believe it and I half consciously started feeling and patting the bed myself.

"June, that's great," I said, acknowledging her significant and unusual accomplishment.

"I know, well," she said struggling to move from sitting on her heels to sitting on her butt, as a result of which the dogs immediately attempted to crawl into her lap, unaware of there prohibitive size. "I prayed really hard about it," she said, completely sincerely. I was a little stunned—I didn't know she prayed at all, much less for help in not wetting the bed.

"Really? You prayed?" I asked.

"Yeah, I prayed A. Lot. I really didn't want to wet the bed here with you," she said.

"June, you don't have to worry about that. I got a water proof mattress cover and we can always wash the sheets," I said, patting the mattress beside me, really to check again, because how could that be?

"I know, but still," she said and mumbled sweetly to the dogs while they wiggled under the weight of her attention.

The bed was dry. She had prayed. Something came over me then—some caught, stuck thing suddenly clicked into place and a whir of clarity lit up my brain. I had always felt most heartbroken for June because she's aware of her limitations. I'd always wished that rather, she could have the kind of brain damage where she remains blissfully unaware, oblivious and happy. But without it—without the complexity of mind required to fathom your own margins, to know what you could and couldn't do, whether because you're disabled or simply because you're human—would you have the ability to comprehend this idea of something greater to which you might appeal for help? Suddenly, what had always been kaleidoscope-like fragments of some big, unknown picture converged into a semblance where here we were, two sisters, equally complex, equally broken, neither of us surviving this life any more or any less than the other, each of us reaching out toward something incomprehensibly more for help with our eternal not enough.

That June had not wet the bed (and that she believed it was owed to some higher power of her understanding) made me feverish with relief—my whole body flushed with heat and I felt sweat break out across my forehead. That combined with the sweet innocence possessing her in that moment conspired to give me hope that I could trust whatever it was that woke her up to pee. In fact, thinking of it, I realize I have an archive of proof that, despite fuckup upon fuckup, everything has worked out. I didn't have to understand how that went down to be able to trust it. Even June with her broken bones and torn skin—there are now new bone shapes and white, thick skin where she bled the most. She didn't will that, nor did she understand or even think about it—it just happened. And watching her there, with her unsteady hands on one of my dogs (she was cooing at my dog, sweetly mumbling, *no lick, sweet honey, no lick, cutie poo poo, no lick baby,* while my dog's tail wagged rhythmically and she happily continued licking June's face), she was as blameless, as innocent as moonlight.

All our lives are practice for this

112. Copernicium (Transition Metal; Synthetic; Unknown Phase)

Since the initial volcanic event that froze us all in a perpetual pang of grief, there has been a series of such freezings, like stop-motion photography, solidifying so many versions of myself and the people I've loved into a trail of beloved relics. All the people I have loved—and still love—remain. Sometimes, upon inspection, they drip like exit wounds. Sometimes, they exist in my daily life and remain isolated from their pyroclastic counterparts. Only time will unveil what gets preserved.

Separation isn't required for preservation, as I have all of my siblings, family members, and many active friends turned to timber and fingernails in the infiltrated recesses of my heart.

Each of my siblings, for example, has a gallery. A gallery thatcontains both perfectly preserved moments and a sort of distillation of everything into an archetypal form that reflects his or her properties, graces, conventions, habits, openings, celebrations, and all such fragments. These archetype-statues are not stone, but colored by dirty-gold. Or, better yet, star-colored against black night, like constellations.

113. Ununtrium (Unknown Chemical Properties; Synthetic; Unknown Phase)

Lee is something like Orion with arms wrapped around flocks of vulnerability while simultaneously hunting and slaying adversity in all its manifestations. Jonas is Perseus, winning the ultimate prize for all to see while at the same time floating with his existential pain in a wooden chest through the sea. June is, of course, Andromeda, weighted in chains, both perpetually rescued and impossible to rescue. John is easy: Lynx, a giant seagull flying toward possibility with a heart thirty times bigger than the sun.

There aren't yet as many constellations in the Pompeiian galleries of my heart as there are in the night sky (officially, about 88 throughout the northern and southern hemispheres), but the correlation is poignant. The great majority of named star patterns bear little, if any, resemblance to the figures they represent.

Just as the heart doesn't actually contain the mechanism for love—at least not exclusively. Also, just as our bodies (faces, hands, hair, teeth, limbs) don't bear much resemblance to whatever it is that they represent. The constellations and pyroclastics preserved in my "heart" point to something inarticulable and too big to fathom. As does this throbbing and tender skin bag I find myself in.

114. Ununquadium (Unknown Chemical Properties; Synthetic; Unknown Phase)

Lee married and had three girls who are now teenagers. She also adopted Sophie at age eleven (now sixteen). All her girls are beautiful and smart. Lee has devoted her life to raising them and loving them as well as helping my mom with June and June's husband.

115. Ununpentium (Unknown Chemical Properties; Synthetic; Unknown Phase)

Jonas quit recovery after seven years, having acquired much worldly success. He worked as a podiatrist, met and married his wife (also a doctor), purchased a big house in a suburb, and had two children (a girl and a boy). He never went back to heavy drinking, but he developed rheumatoid arthritis and suffers from chronic pain. He's had three spinal, fusion surgeries and the pain has only gotten worse. Still, he seems to enjoy his family and his worldly goods.

116. Ununhexium (Unknown Chemical Properties; Synthetic; Unknown Phase)

June lives with her husband, Todd, in the same house that my parents bought for them long ago. A social worker visits with them once each week to help them with life skills, such as cleaning and having relationships with people. Also, not hating each other. It seems to be successful, as they bicker far less than they used to and seem much happier. June still calls my mom ten times each day with one need or another.

117. Ununseptium (Unknown Chemical Properties; Synthetic; Unknown Phase)

John was recently promoted again in his job, which he has been at for thirteen years since coming home from the military. He went to college part-time and got a degree in engineering. He met and married his wife who had a pre-teen son and they grew their family with two more boys. John is in love with his children, is an excellent father, and we are wonderful friends.

118. Ununoctium (Unknown Chemical Properties; Synthetic; Unknown Phase)

Mom finally left my dad after thirty-seven years of marriage. The final straw was an affair that he had with an old college girlfriend, carried on in secret for about a year. Imagine that: At seventy-one, an affair. He moved into a senior-citizen trailer park and my mom remains kind and friendly to him. She has six-hour lunches with friends, travels to see her brother in Florida, travels to see me, delights in all of her grandchildren, attends to the needs of June and Todd, works part time, and just generally does as she pleases.

0. The Beginning

I live in Boston, where I moved from San Francisco with an ex-girlfriend. We lived together for six months before I left her, knowing that I wasn't in love with her. When I moved into my own apartment, I realized I was done running. I hadn't even known I had been running for so long until I decided that I was done. In the previous five years alone, I had lived in four different states, travelled to thirteen different countries, been in four different relationships, and had innumerable jobs. What I accomplished was a kind of freedom and a lot of life experience. What I lacked was a sense of home, roots, community, family. I decided that I wanted that. But it was deeper than want. It was something that was required and necessary—to be in the same place around the same group of people for a long time and have them know me well.

After a little while, I stumbled into a ready-made family of my own. I met and fell in love with a woman with a two-year-old little girl. A year later, Mei, my girlfriend, is friends with her ex-husband, who now has a boyfriend. Her daughter, Li, is equally co-parented by the four of us. Li is now three and she continues to both delight and baffle me. One delightful thing about her is her purity, or rather, rawness. Everything she does and everything she feels—whether anger, sadness, happiness, excitement, love— she does it so purely and simply. It is a marvel to watch. She has a lively spirit that doesn't yet know how hard human skin can sometimes be to live in, which frees her from all myriad fears except one: primal, practical fear. Then again, how do I know what her spirit knows? There's no telling the age of the immaterial essence of a person or whether it has age. Although there must be something like age or experience level for souls, because I'm convinced that Li's is quite seasoned. In some ways, it's clear that at three, she's already smarter than me.

The five of us (Li and her four parents) get together often to spend time as one big queer, happy family. We did this just the other night. Oliver (her father's boyfriend) was wearing a red T-shirt with the periodic table of elements printed on it in white. Li was fascinated with this t-shirt.

"What is it?" She asked.

"It's everything," he said and laughed.

"Everything?"

"It's a chart of the base ingredients making up everything that exists. Kind of like a map."

"A map of the world?"

Li has a map of the world on her bedroom wall, so she associated the world with the word, map.

"Sort of, yes, but not really. More like a map of everything."

When Oliver said that, everyone chuckled and smiled appreciatively at the inquisitive cuteness of our three-year-old. Then they went back to the topic they'd been discussing before and Li ran back to her bedroom. But I lingered there on his answer to Li, feeling almost offended at the idea that the periodic table of elements represents everything that exists. Everything emerges from infinite chemical reactions and evolves with constant change. But surely it doesn't account for everything. It doesn't account for seemingly random, sometimes tragic events that intervene in a life in linear time. It doesn't account for the invisible helpers of young sisters. It doesn't account for metal screws twisted into the skulls of sixteen-year-old girls.

The periodic table says that we humans are soulless—we are chemical reactions. But reverence is not a chemical reaction, nor is hope, which, unfettered by gravity, extends itself over the valleys of our lives.

"Kiddo, come here, I want to show you something," Li shouts from the hall. She calls me Kiddo, a name she assigned to me and then stuck with (her grandfather had been calling her that). I stand up and walk toward her room where I know what it is she'll show me, what she never grows tired of showing me, and what I display excitement for every time she shows me. The multicolored, tiny holiday lights on a string we have up on her wall along with the colorful decals of owls and moons and stars and a map of the world.

"It looks like cake sprinkles on the world," she says and giggles. Together, we shout, "Happy birthday, world!" I gasp and fall to the floor. She laughs and runs at me, diving into my lap and hugging me.

I have planted myself here and am growing roots. I will walk through the inevitable change of linear time and accept its gifts and its removal of gifts. I will be gentle and graceful with loss. All our lives are practice for this. I will walk through my days like I always have— sometimes through air that feels like molten lead and sometimes through air that feels always like spring: petal soft, laced with breeze.

53296227R00170

Made in the USA
Lexington, KY
30 September 2019